DEATH AND THE MAIDEN

DEATH AND THE MAIDEN

A Daniel Jacobus Novel

Gerald Elias

LEVEL
BEST BOOKS

This book was professionally typeset on Reedsy.
Find out more at reedsy.com

To Ed, king of the single entendre:
The one-liners are for you.

Contents

Praise for the Daniel Jacobus Mysteries

"This fast-paced and punchily written mystery will entertain most fans, even as it delivers a fluid understanding of classical music."—*Library Journal*

"The book's real heart is the detailed behind-the-scenes glimpse of the classical music scene provided by the author, a violinist and music professor himself."—*Publishers Weekly*

"Blind Jacobus, a curmudgeon to the nth degree, redeems himself when he steps in to take the lead in 'Death and the Maiden' and performs with such emotional commitment that you'll want to race right out and buy the CD." —*Kirkus Reviews*

"...this mystery was every bit as intriguing and well written as Elias' two previous mysteries. I am sold on this series by Gerald Elias, and have just ordered the newest one, *Death and Transfiguration*. It is a pleasure to read a well-contrived, knowledgeable murder mystery where we as readers can join in with our own conjectures (all wrong, probably!) as we read." —Jean Rodenbough, author

Author's Note

String quartets are widely regarded by classical musicians as representing the pinnacle of artistic achievement. Composers from Mozart, Beethoven, and Schubert through Bartók and Shostakovich saved and savored their most personal statements about life, death, and the hereafter through the format of the quartet.

Each instrument of the string quartet—two violins, viola, and cello—provides a significant yet distinct voice in the four-way conversation. In its most basic construction, the role of the first violin is to sing the melody. The second violin sometimes joins in an octave or third or sixth lower, but more often teams up with the viola to fill out the harmony, create secondary contrapuntal lines, and generate rhythmic drive. The cello's lower tones establish the harmonic and rhythmic foundation upon which the whole edifice is balanced and supported. Composers of great quartets, however, create endless variations on this template: giving the melodic line to the viola, or having the cello play in its highest register, way above even the first violin, or creating remarkable textures in which every instrument is on an equal and seemingly independent footing. Perhaps it is the intricate interaction among these voices, which need to be perfectly tuned, balanced, and rhythmically integrated with microscopic precision for every split second of the music, that raises the genre beyond the level of entertainment to one of philosophy.

Equal to the sublime beauty of the string quartet is the profound challenge it presents to the four musicians. It takes years of painstaking practice for the members of a quartet to fully mesh, to discover a unified voice. Often, that unity that is the mark of a great quartet is, in fact, never achieved. Because each musician of the ensemble feels the pull of the music so strongly, he or she inevitably has convictions as deeply rooted as a religious flagellant about the way the music should sound, from the sweep of an entire phrase down to the finest detail. When we realize that the tonal quality of every single note on a string instrument is affected by considerations such as bow pressure, bow speed, the distance of the bow from the bridge, the location on the bow where the note is played, the speed and width of the vibrato, and the relation of the pitch to the instrument's open strings, we can begin to understand the challenge of four musicians agreeing not only on these technical details but also on the musical intent of the composer.

Playing in a professional string quartet is, on the one hand, a quasi-religious rapturous experience, with moments of sublime, transcendent revelation when one feels directly connected to a higher power. On the other, the intensity of the experience is akin to an emotional pressure cooker, making the antics of a circus high-wire act seem like child's play. When the stars are aligned, the pressure release valve is the music itself, and the result can be a profound and life-altering. All too often, though, the release is volcanic, with emotional magma slowly seeking weaknesses in hairline cracks and fissures in the subsurface of the quartet's psyche, finally erupting in explosive fashion. Many ensembles burn out after a few years, often with long-standing bitter resentments, sometimes worse. Even the greatest string quartets rarely remain unscathed. There are famous stories of members engaging in fist fights over seemingly insignificant musical details, the result of pent-up stress and hostility. I was told by the violist of a renowned quartet (long after he left it, and with some amusement) that on one occasion he grabbed the first violinist's valuable French bow and threw it out the window of a Caribbean hotel where they were on tour. It landed on the beach somewhere and was buried in the sand and washed out to sea, never to be seen again.

Perhaps the saddest case of the inflamed passion erupting from the boiling cauldron of the string quartet is that of the former Audubon Quartet. For years a highly respected ensemble, over time it became so rife with musical and personal internal conflict that it almost completely self-destructed, and each musician paid a tragic price. In 2005, after three of the players, including founding celling Tom Shaw, fired the first violinist, David Ehrlich,

Ehrlich sued for a hefty sum and won a Pyrrhic victory. The other three lost homes and beloved instruments when the judge, for the most part, ruled against them. Ehrlich, however, reportedly spent a large part of his compensation to pay his astronomical legal fees.

There is a certain irony in this story of a personal nature. Tom Shaw and I met at the Sarasota Music Festival in 1973, played chamber music together, and became friends. I admired not only his fine cello playing but also his magnificent Russian wolfhound. In the late 1970s I actually auditioned for the Audubon Quartet position ultimately won by Ehrlich, whom I have never met. However, I was gratified to see that after the disaster of 2005, the Audubon managed to regroup, and all the musicians appear to have found a way forward with their art and their careers.

"Death and the Maiden," the greatest string quartet by Franz Schubert and one of the monumental works of the entire quartet repertoire, is the setting I've chosen for my story. The music depicts the primal struggle between life and death. It asks: Should one resist death or should one bow gracefully to the inevitable? There is a saying that "music soothes the savage breast," but ironically it is also true that music, especially the string quartet, has the power to provoke even the most passive soul.

Death and the Maiden

Der Tod und das Mädchen
(Poem by Matthias Claudius; Music by Franz Schubert)

Das Mädchen:

Vorüber! Ach, vorüber!
Geh, wilder Knochenmann!
Ich bin noch jung, geh Lieber!
Und rühre mich nicht an.

Der Tod:

Gib deine Hand, du schön und zart Gebild!
Bin Freund, und komme nicht, zu strafen.
Sei gutes Muts! Ich bin nicht wild,
Sollst sanft in meinen Armen schlafen!

The Maiden:

Away from here! Oh, away from here!
Go away, cruel figure of death!
I am still young, so leave!
And do not touch me.

Death:

Give me your hand, you beautiful and tender image!
I am a friend and do not come to harm you.
Be in good spirit! I am not evil,
You should sleep gently in my arms!

Prologue

Kortovsky gave himself a final once-over in the elevator mirror before he reached the hotel lobby. He tugged gently at his shirt cuffs until they extended one inch from the sleeves of his jacket, subtly exposing his gold cufflinks, adjusted the knot of his tie so that it was centered and fully concealed the top button of his shirt, and quickly ran a comb through his hair.

He had been in the shower when the call from the desk came that there was someone waiting to see him in the bar—no, there was no name—but fortunately the ring on the desk phone was loud enough to wake the dead. As he had dressed, he reflected on who the lucky individual might be that had issued the invitation. At the concert earlier that night, the quartet had returned to the stage eight times for bows, and on each occasion he had made direct eye contact with a different young lady from among the adoring throng, as was his customary practice. It was contestant number five, not the youngest but definitely the sexiest—short, dark hair; glasses, no less; a very nice figure from what he could tell from her suggestive royal blue dress—who had returned his gaze the most provocatively. Though it could have been any of the other seven, he guessed it was number five waiting for him at the bar. In fact, he had selected a tie to match her dress, just in case. Kortovsky brought his hands to his nose and inhaled, making sure he had adequately sanitized them. Not politic to raise the hackles of a new love interest by having the scent of another woman on his fingertips. He looked in the mirror one final time, trying not to be smug, but conceded himself a smile.

The elevator door slid open. The cavernous, pillared lobby was quiet and almost deserted. Kortovsky headed for the desk to hand the oversized pre-Columbian room key, which formed an unsightly bulge in every pocket he had tried hiding it, to the receptionist, in the midst of a phone call. While waiting for her to finish, he changed his mind. He wasn't planning on going out of the hotel, and if, as he suspected, he would soon be returning to his room with a guest, he didn't want to risk any delay or potential awkwardness of asking for the key while a young lady in a green dress waited expectantly on his arm.

So he removed the key from his jacket pocket and placed it in the back pocket of his slacks where, though it wouldn't be comfortable, at least it wouldn't be seen. He smiled at the receptionist—who might be attractive herself in something other than her unfortunate utilitarian rust-brown hotel uniform—and gave her a friendly hand signal indicating that he didn't require her assistance. He made sure her eyes met his before turning away. No harm in keeping one's options open. She smiled back and continued her phone conversation as he walked across the lobby.

Kortovsky peered into the dimly lit bar. There were still a couple of dozen customers, all engaged in quiet conversation, some huddled at the bar itself, others at small round tables scattered in a seemingly random pattern around the room. He adjusted his tie one more time. Two in one night, Kortovsky thought to himself, an appetizing prospect that involuntarily caused him raised his eyebrows in anticipation. He scolded himself—don't count your chickens. Pride before the fall, and all that. But! A few drinks, a little light conversation, and then…well, we'll see. He entered the bar and though at first he didn't see number five or any of the other seven in the dim light, he did see a vaguely familiar figure in the corner.

Chapter One

SATURDAY

Hearing the tepid applause as the maestro du jour sauntered onto the Tanglewood stage, Jacobus relegated the lawsuit to the back of his mind.

He was among the sparse, haggard crowd that braved the damp chill to hear the Boston Symphony's next-to-last outdoor concert of the summer season, a Saturday night performance of Beethoven Ninth Symphony, a piece of music that he often turned to for life-affirming reassurance in moments of personal despair. More than a work of uncompromising genius, it was the most compelling clarion call to universal brotherhood in all of music. But as he sat shivering under the relentless frozen mist that lashed through the open-sided Tanglewood Shed, the overwhelming restless energy of the first movement served only to make him feel insignificant by comparison. Insignificant and mortally fragile, like a leaf in autumn. Unlike the millions of tourists who came to New England, Jacobus, blind, was unable to revel in the stunning brilliance of the impending fall foliage. The mental visualization of red, orange, and yellow, long lost to his mind's eye, was replaced by the decaying odor of moldering leaves, thickening day by day in layers under his slowing footstep, a harbinger of an eternal winter. He was a leaf, one of the thousands of leaves on one maple among thousands of maples, his vitality slowly but inexorably sapping, tenuously fixed to its mooring until even the most inconsequential puff of air would separate him from his station and blow him, brown and lifeless, to the frozen ground, to be covered by the snow.

Jacobus put his hands in his pockets. The violinists' fingertips must be stinging like hell in this cold, he thought—as the driving intensity of the music built to the defiant recapitulation of the first movement—especially the ones who had developed deep grooves from years of pressing the strings too hard. Jacobus laughed as he recalled one cold August night, back when he was still in the orchestra: Sal Maggiolo, who was from the Amalfi coast, had played with gloves on, the fingertips of the left glove cut off so he could still feel the strings. It was the most obscenity-laced Haydn symphony Jacobus had ever played.

But it wasn't just the cold that was making this performance listless and unconvincing. The conductor was run-of-the-mill at best, adding to Jacobus's discomfort. Someone had mentioned to the blind Jacobus who it was—some young Englishman, the latest to claim the banner of the newest in-term: the "historically informed" performance, as if Toscanini didn't know his music history. Jacobus had heard of this guy, though he'd never listened to his recordings, so he had come to tonight's concert curious about what he was going to hear. It became increasingly clear, at least to his own discerning ears if not to the philistines in the audience, that the conductor was one of the sort that revels in browbeating the musicians over every detail—"Beethoven wrote a dot above the E-flat, you dolts!"—without having an overall conception of the music. He may have done some homework about the performance style of Beethoven's time—more likely he just listened to some CDs from his own crowd—but used that always debatable information to disguise the absence of true musical insight. The result was a mishmash of insipid, disconnected wisps of phrases with little sense of continuity or purpose. "Beethoven Lite," his friend Nathaniel called it. As the musicians circled the wagons to counteract the directionless conducting and tried to play as best they could, the conductor would no doubt engage in greater and greater histrionics in order to elicit the kind of response he thought he deserved. This would arouse the resentment, if not the ire, of the musicians who, believing the maestro was trying to show

2

them up, would then become yet more obdurate. And on and on it would go. Jacobus pitied all those in the audience who had the gift of sight, because they would shortly be bearing witness to what he easily predicted would be a musical revolt by the orchestra.

Jacobus had long ago come to the conclusion long ago that great conductors and lousy conductors had much more in common than great conductors and good conductors. A good conductor has enough sense to basically let the orchestra play on its own, guiding it along a path without imposing his will upon it. Both the great conductor and the lousy conductor try to control all the details. The difference is that the great conductor *knows* how to do it; the lousy one *thinks* he knows.

As the tide of Jacobus's interest in the music ebbed, it was replenished by the knotty issue of the lawsuit in which his former student, Yumi Shinagawa, was now enmeshed.

For five years now, Yumi had been the second violinist of the world-renowned New Magini String Quartet, a source of secret pride for Jacobus. What dismayed him was that even though the quartet still played magnificently, it had essentially become dysfunctional. None of the members spoke to each other outside rehearsals, and when they were at work there was constant tension.

And then there was the lawsuit. The former second violinist, Crispin Short, whom Yumi had replaced in the New Magini String Quartet, had ongoing litigation against them, claiming that he had been illegally fired, had been deprived of his livelihood, and had had his reputation publicly smeared, making it impossible for him to make a living.

The kind of public airing of dirty laundry that occurred between Short and the quartet was almost unprecedented in the classical music world, and while it might have made for juicy reading, it had forced colleagues and media throughout the profession to choose sides. Right now, they seemed to be lining up behind Short. Akin to *omertà*, the Mafia's fanatic dedication to the code of silence, in-house backbiting among musicians might be vicious, but that's how it almost always stayed, in-house. The beehive network of artistic and professional relationships, so complex, so constantly changing,

3

and so based on lofty but easily bruised egos was usually enough to keep even the worst musicians insulated from public attack by colleagues.

Maestro Swen Anskerbasker might be universally regarded among orchestral musicians as a conducting hack who can't count to four without looking at his fingers, but you never know if he'll invite you to play the Brahms Concerto with his orchestra. Reginald Biffin might be too old and senile to remember that he plays the violin even when he's holding it, but if he's a friend of the local recording contractor, then he's magically transformed into a revered colleague with a world of experience. Larry Martino, chair of the string department, might have sexually assaulted his student, but then next month, just before your tenure hearing, you might have to play string quartets with him.

And don't forget the great, the esteemed, the infamous Feodor Malinkovky! thought Jacobus. That most revered violin pedagogue of the twentieth century. Pedagogue? Pedophile! Everyone in musical circles knew it, but even after he was deported back to Russia and disappeared in the darkness of a Stalinist purge, still the circles wouldn't say it aloud. And for Jacobus, the memory lingered on, etched indelibly in his being. As a pre-adolescent contestant in the prestigious 1931 Grimsley International Violin Competition, Malinkovsky, the head judge, had privately offered him a prize in exchange for...

Like a passenger in a car about to hit a telephone pole, Jacobus gripped the arms of his seat as the orchestra almost fell apart during the always mischievous tempo change into the Scherzo, but he relaxed again, at least for the moment, when there was a brief rapprochement at the beginning of the third movement, Adagio molto e cantabile. Unpredictably flooded with memories of his brief tenure with the Boston Symphony long ago, cut short by the devastating onset of his sudden blindness on the very day he won the concertmaster audition, Jacobus momentarily forgot the cold. If not for that freak medical chance, he thought, if not for that I might still be playing there on stage instead of dying of pneumonia out here.

Yumi's situation seemed as precarious, her career balanced on the head of a pin. It had been Aaron Kortovsky, the first violinist of the New Magini

Quartet, who had spearheaded Short's dismissal six years earlier. Kortovsky had taken an intractable artistic situation and compounded the problem by making it politically ugly, thinking that firing the first shot across the bow by recruiting a *Times* correspondent for an interview about Short's termination would gain an advantage in the public arena. It backfired in a way he could have predicted had his ego not blinded him. Short not only went public himself, he sued all the members of the quartet, including Yumi, even though she had become a member only as Short's successor. In a counter-maneuver, Kortovsky officially changed the name of the quartet from the original Magini String Quartet to the *New* Magini String Quartet and reapplied for non-profit corporation status. He claimed that since there was only one member of the original all-Russian ensemble left, cellist Pravda Lenskaya, the name of the quartet should reflect its evolution. In reality, he was attempting an end-around Short's tenacious pursuit of legal vengeance, and in that he failed. The four musicians were now on the brink of seeing their bank accounts, homes, even instruments go up in smoke if Short was successful in his litigation. It would be almost impossible to explain to a non-musician what the loss of a beloved instrument means. To be forcibly compelled to part with such an instrument would not be far removed from giving up one's own child. Jacobus imagined the judge doing a Solomon act and sawing a violin in half in order to be fair. When asked if that was the kind of resolution he wanted, Short's response was that, tragic though it might be, they brought it on themselves. And now the expectation was that the judge would be making a ruling within weeks.

Jacobus found that he was shivering from the cold, damp fog that had condensed into droplets on his dark glasses.

As the orchestra made the miraculous transition, seamlessly changing meter, key, and tempo into the second theme of Beethoven's love song for humanity, someone elbowed him in his ribs.

"Hey, pal, you want a pair of these?" asked the voice next to him.

New York accent, Jacobus determined.

"What? A pair of what?" he asked.

"Shhhh!" said someone else. "Shut up."

5

More New Yorkers, thought Jacobus.

His neighbor whispered, "Ear muffs. I'm no fucking Eskimo."

"How the hell do you hear the music?" Jacobus asked.

"Doesn't matter. We hear the Ninth here every year. Besides, Beethoven was deaf. Wasn't he?"

Jacobus got up and moved to an empty seat. Cold, tired, wet, he should have just left and gone home but hoped that somehow the last movement, the greatest single movement of symphonic music ever composed, would somehow redeem the performance. In that, he was again disappointed. If the musicians were laid low by the inclement weather, the singers suffered even more. The vocal quartet caterwauled like alley cats in heat, and the crowning sixteen measures of fortissimo high A's in the soprano section of the chorus sounded like a synchronized swim team in a pool with a great white shark.

By the time the symphony came to its crashing conclusion, the antipathy between the orchestra and conductor was palpable. Jacobus heard the seats of the folding chairs around him snap up, but suspected the audience rose, not to give the performance a standing ovation, but to flee to the protective comfort of their Volvos and Mercedes-Benzes. Tomorrow's review would no doubt extol the conductor's heroic, historically informed efforts while tongue-lashing the musicians for their halfhearted response. Equally certain was that the musicians' artistic committee would demand that management never again engage the boy wonder. What happened after that, who knew, except that next year there would be someone standing on the podium.

Jacobus followed the exodus to the main gate, shuffling along the packed clay floor of the Shed that had become as slippery as ice from the moisture it had absorbed, guiding himself with his right hand on the row of seat backs. With his left hand, he slapped his rolled up program against his thigh to try to ward off stiffness in both appendages.

Within moments of arriving at the gate he felt a hand on his shoulder.

"Hi, Jake," said Yumi, "Am I late?"

"Only about three movements' worth."

"Hmm. That bad?" she asked.

"The 'Ode to Shit'? Nah, it wasn't that bad. It was worse."

Yumi had parked in the handicapped section for Jacobus's convenience, so they were inside the car and out of the soaking mist within moments, but Jacobus felt miserable.

"Did you have a chance to think about what we should do about the lawsuit?" Yumi asked.

"Yeah. No. I'll think about it. Maybe the judge'll come up with a reasonable solution. Mind if I smoke?"

"Not in the car, please. Yes. I think he will, too," she said, turning on the engine and the heat.

They spoke little during the fifteen-minute winding drive through the darkened Berkshire hillside. Jacobus tried to focus his mind on the quartet's dilemma, but his concentration quickly wandered as he pondered the irony of musicians engaged in mortal combat over music that celebrated the brotherhood of mankind. Rarely did a light penetrate the mist-enshrouded woods; of course for Jacobus, it didn't matter.

Chapter Two

SUNDAY

It's not rare for the chill of autumn to announce itself in August in the Berkshire Hills of western Massachusetts, but this year it arrived even earlier than usual. Labor Day was still more than a week off, yet during the night they had had their first frost, a heavy one, at that. When she woke up, Yumi was able to etch her initials with her fingernail into the frozen condensation that had crystallized on the inside of the drafty, time-worn single-pane windows in Jacobus's house. Outside, the mist had not yet risen above Monument Mountain, and what was left of the grass was silvery spiked with frost. It would melt during the course of the day, but the handwriting was on the wall for a long winter.

Jacobus was huddled in a blanket with his back close to the woodstove, trying to coax the obstinate chill out of his arthritic bones. He had no doubt that all the Millers' heirloom tomatoes would be shot to hell. Jacobus, himself, had a single tomato plant near the screen door in the back, keeled over in the same cramped plastic pot in which he had bought it two months earlier. This current frost caused him no concern for its welfare because for weeks it had been standing withered and dead in mute testament to his negligent care. In any event, he didn't like tomatoes.

"What'll it be Jake?" asked Nathaniel, leafing through the *Times*. "New turmoil in central Africa, intrigue in Peru, drastic cuts in funding to arts organizations..."

8

Jacobus didn't respond.

Friends and colleagues since their college days, the blind, irascible, and wizened violinist Daniel Jacobus and the corporeally extravagant, congenial African-American former cellist Nathaniel Williams made an unlikely pair. The tradition of Nathaniel reading Jacobus the Sunday *Times*, initiated as an afterthought at some point after Jacobus emerged from his blindness-induced seclusion so many years ago, had developed so innocuously over the years that neither could have recalled when it became routine. Today's news had left Jacobus with an unsavory taste in his mouth, like Tuesday's meat loaf: Why, of all people, had he been allowed to stay alive, he wondered, when the world was going to hell?

"I was in Peru recently," Yumi interjected. "With the quartet. Our South America tour. Read that one."

" 'An uneasy quiet reigns over Lima,' " read Nathaniel, " 'where a body, apparently the victim of torture, was discovered only two blocks from the presidential palace in the Plaza Mayor, reviving nightmares of drug wars and political killings in this strife-weary—' "

"That's enough!" said Jacobus. "I've had it. Throw it in the fire."

"All of it?" asked Nathaniel. "You don't want me to burn the crossword!"

"The whole damn thing."

If there wasn't going to be anything in the paper worth reading, at least it would keep him warm.

Nathaniel furtively extracted the crossword, and then the arts section, and then the book review, camouflaging the sound of his actions with idle humming. In the end, all he tossed into the wood stove were the classifieds and real estate sections before returning to his chair on the opposite side of the coffee table from Jacobus.

Yumi, visiting Jacobus for an infrequent violin lesson—Jacobus called it a "tune-up"—was seated between Jacobus and Nathaniel, and continued to ponder her opening Scrabble move. With partners for Scrabble or chess or checkers a rare commodity, the sightless Jacobus more often used the table to eat what he referred to in cynical self-deprecation as his AM-FM

9

dinners, since TV was no longer an option, and even if he could see, there was nothing good on anyway. Trotsky, Jacobus's gargantuan bulldog, snored peacefully under the flimsy folding table, his massive left flank nurtured by the stove's radiating heat, unconsciously licking drool from his muzzle and offering up deep, contented sighs.

"You and Trotsky seem to be hitting it off," said Yumi.

"*Uch*, they should've put him to sleep when they had the chance."

"Jake, that's not funny! Dogs understand vibes."

"Who's joking?"

Trotsky, having heard his name, awakened and licked Jacobus's hand, then went back to sleep.

"See?" he said. "He's slobbering all over me. He doesn't even understand commands, like 'Die.' How many dogs do you know of get expelled from Seeing Eye school?"

"Jake, Trotsky couldn't help it. After all, it wasn't his idea to be a Seeing Eye dog. And who enrolls a bulldog in a course like that? Why did the previous owner do it, anyway?"

"She told me the dog was so ugly, only a blind person could handle it. She forgot about the sense of smell."

Jacobus heard the clinking of Yumi's Scrabble tiles as she rearranged letters on her rack.

"Trotsky has a good sense of smell then?" she asked.

"Hell, no! I do!"

"Then why did you keep him if he's so much trouble?"

"He was given to me by a former student who was trying to get rid of him because he howled when she played. So she tried the Seeing Eye school and when that fiasco ended she asked me to take him for a week."

"Why is she a *former* student?"

"Because I howled when she played. Plus, at the end of the week she never came back and didn't leave a forwarding address. I think she knew something. Now, are you going to play Scrabble or cut bait?"

"I'm working on it."

Jacobus, still experiencing bouts of the shivers from exposure to the elements at Tanglewood the night before, felt like death warmed over, except he wasn't warmed over, and wasn't sure how he was going to be able to make it through a lesson with Yumi this morning. But she had returned from her month-long vacation at her mountain home in Kyushu, Japan's south island, bearing gifts from her family and from Jacobus's friend and colleague, Max Furukawa, so maybe he would just let her play, emit an occasional *harrumph*, and get it over with. Thank you very much. See you next week. That will be a hundred dollars.

"Lima didn't seem so dangerous," said Yumi, who was seated to Jacobus's right. "Maybe because we were in a nice part of town. The people there were so sweet."

A damp gust interrupted. It rattled the overgrown English ivy consuming the stony exterior of Jacobus's house, making a brittle fluttering noise, which, like the clattering of his own chilled bones, seemed to chide him for his growing geriatric fragility. Jacobus extracted a modestly used tissue from within his woolen wrappings, and in strident defiance, triumphantly trumpeted a snootful of mucus into it.

"And the food was so good!" Yumi continued. "Jake, did you know in Peru they eat—"

"Just make your word already," he muttered.

"Okay" said Yumi. "Here I go. ANT." And for Jacobus's benefit: "A-N-T, vertically, with the N on the star. One, two, three, double-word…six points."

"A half hour and all you can do is ANT?" asked Jacobus. "What kind of pissant word is that to open the game?"

"I really have bad letters."

"What?" he said. He didn't hear her.

"I said, 'I really have bad letters.' "

"And after all I've taught her," Jacobus mumbled to nobody.

"My turn," said Nathaniel.

"Speaking of which," Yumi said to Jacobus, "I wanted to ask you about one of my students."

"Not now," said Jacobus. "I want to see if it's humanly possible to top ANT."

Using his sensitive, musically trained fingertips, Jacobus read the grooves of his Scrabble tiles. M-O-O-O-R-X-Y. He made his decision. When Nathaniel finally got around to finishing his move, Jacobus would place the R atop ANT and make the words RANT going down and ROOMY going across. A triple letter score for an O. Sixteen points. Not bad for such shitty letters.

"Are you going to take all day?" Jacobus asked Nathaniel irritably. "Or are you going to wait until the fire's totally out."

"You have somewhere else important to go? Like last night?" asked Nathaniel. "I'm tellin' you, you go to one more concert, it'll kill you, not that that would be such a bad idea. You just about froze to death last night, and now, just to keep you warm, here Yumi and I are sweatin' up a storm."

"Yeah, I can smell that."

"Here you go!" said Nathaniel triumphantly. "S-A-V. I'm adding it to the beginning of ANT to make SAVANT."

"*Bravo*, Nathaniel!" said Yumi. She clapped her hands.

"Dammit!" said Jacobus. "You took my word."

"*Your* word! My, my. I didn't realize you owned it. And I've got a double-letter score on the S. Ten points."

Jacobus fumed. "Just put another log in the stove," he said, "and don't look at my letters." The same fingertips that had spent a lifetime understanding Bach and Brahms now fidgeted for a few extra Scrabble points.

He was having a hard time concentrating. Not just because the unoiled hinge on the door of the woodstove squealed like a pig at the abattoir. Not just because he felt miserable, that the concert last night left him deflated, and that Yumi was bugging him about some student. What was preoccupying him right now was that with this damned clogged sinus he was having trouble hearing, and he was frightened to death. It was bad enough being blind, though blindness wasn't as odious as deafness. He couldn't imagine there was any visual art produced in the past thirty years worth seeing and was just grateful that a day before he was stricken with what the medical establishment refers to as foveomacular dystrophy, and what humans call sudden blindness, he had taken a break from his concertmaster audition preparations for the Boston Symphony and went to see a Turner exhibit at the Fine Arts Museum for inspiration. He could still conjure up the memory of the image of those Turners, if not the images themselves, those breathtaking expanses of sky and water.

But he couldn't imagine being deaf and unable to hear music. How had Beethoven survived? Survived! Deafness had made him an even greater composer, a superhuman composer.

But blindness *and* deafness? How would he communicate? If he were unable to hear his own voice, would he sound like a raving idiot? Jacobus would kill himself first. But how would he go about doing that if he couldn't see or hear? He could find a knife. Or a rope. How would he do it with a rope? Wrap it around his neck? Then what?

Jacobus put his hands around his neck and squeezed a little. This is only a test. It's just a goddamn head cold, he told himself. It will go away. It *will* go away. I should have taken those goddamn earmuffs. The performance wasn't worth hearing anyway. I should have taken those earmuffs from that fucking—

"MORON!" shouted Jacobus.

"What did I do now?" asked Nathaniel.

"Not you, for a change. That's my word."

Yumi laughed.

"What's so funny?" asked Jacobus.

"Only that Nathaniel chose SAVANT and you chose MORON."

"Jealous."

He placed the first four letters in front of the N in SAVANT.

"Wait a minute!" he said. "I've got an O, an X, and a Y left. OXYMORON. All seven letters! Double-letter on the M, and triple-word, too! Best word I ever had."

"Don't get all hot and bothered," said Nathaniel. "The game ain't over yet."

"Like hell it ain't," he said, toting his points in his head, starting with the extra fifty for using all seven tiles. It was dizzying. Easily a hundred-point word. He was beginning to feel better already.

Trotsky, luxuriating in the warmth of the woodstove, was sufficiently roused from his stupor by the excited conversation to determine it was now time to roll over to toast his right side. At that moment Jacobus's phone rang, an old-fashioned black Bell Telephone rotary model with a ring like a fire drill alarm. As Jacobus didn't often get calls, Trotsky never had gotten used to its shocking shrillness, so just as the semiconscious dog was turning over, the ring made him jump in a panic. He whacked his sledgehammer head against the bottom of the lightweight coffee table, spewing the entire Scrabble game all over the floor.

"You were right, Jake!" laughed Nathaniel. "The game sure enough is over. All over!"

"Goddamn dog," snarled Jacobus, further infuriated when he heard Yumi trying to stifle a laugh.

Trotsky, finely attuned to the subtleties of his master's every mood, was already licking at Jacobus's corduroy pant leg, his slobber soaking in, the stub of his tail trembling with love.

"How do you spell 'euthanize'?" asked Jacobus.

"I'll get the phone," said Nathaniel, patting Trotsky on the head. "Good dog! Good dog!"

"Hello," he said into the phone. "It's Cy Rosenthal," he relayed.

Rosenthal, the lawyer who had been a last-minute substitute to defend the crossover violinist BTower in the notorious René Allard murder case four years earlier—a case that almost cost Jacobus his own life—was the last person Jacobus expected to hear from. "What's that shyster calling here for?"

"It's for Yumi. I'm gonna go make some tea."

Jacobus heard Yumi take the receiver from Nathaniel and into the kitchen, which she was able to do only because Nathaniel had bought an extended chord for the phone ten years earlier. Jacobus had drawn the line with the chord and was obdurate in his refusal to get another phone or an answering machine.

As Jacobus waited, trying unsuccessfully with clogged ears to decipher Yumi's quiet conversation from the living room, his Scrabble wrath was replaced by concern. Yumi Shinagawa, his former prize student who had

14

become as much of a daughter to him as if she had been his own, was the only person in the world he truly loved, and though he had never said that, nor ever would, Yumi knew that that was the case.

Jacobus had a good idea what Rosenthal's call was about, and all the reasons why he had fled the professional world of classical music many years earlier flooded back. He put his head in his hands as he listened to Trotsky gleefully crunching Scrabble tiles like Liv-A-Snaps between his powerful jaws faster than Nathaniel was able to sweep them up. Jacobus pulled the blanket more tightly around him, seeking to snuff out the downward spiral his thoughts were taking him.

"You still cold, Jake?" asked Nathaniel. "Here's your tea. I found a jar of honey. It was stuck to the shelf but I managed to pry it off and chisel some into your tea. For your throat." He heard Nathaniel right the overturned coffee table and place the teacup on it.

"Honey? What, do want me to puke?"

"No. I don't want you to puke. I poisoned it. I want you to die."

"Thank you, Mr. Rosenthal," Jacobus heard Yumi say, followed by her footsteps back into the living room where she hung up the phone.

"So?" asked Jacobus, sipping his tea.

"Mr. Rosenthal said that Crispin's attorney has made a proposal to settle out of court, 'to hopefully avoid the kind of harsh media spotlight that none of us want,' or something like that."

"What a politely worded threat. Lovely."

"Mr. Rosenthal would like the members of the quartet to meet at his office in Uniondale tomorrow after the morning rehearsal. That's all. Shall we finish our Scrabble game?"

"Sure. Just let me know when you finish pumping Trotsky's stomach to get the tiles he inhaled. In the meantime, you had a question about a student?"

"Oh, yes. I just started with her at the Rose Grimes Music School. Her name is Louisa. She's been studying for four or five years—she's twelve or thirteen—but her previous teacher didn't give her great instruction, and she has a single mom and has to take care of her little brother, so now she's behind and has a self-esteem problem."

"Sounds more like she has a violin-playing problem."

"Well, yes, that's what I think accounts for her low self-esteem."

"Can she play scales in tune?"

"Not really."

"Then she's absolutely correct to have low self-esteem."

"But playing scales well in tune is so hard. It takes hours and hours of practice."

"Exactly. And when she's done the hours and hours of practice and can play scales in tune, then she'll have high self-esteem."

"But what if she can never do that? What if she just doesn't have the talent?"

"Then she should either get accustomed to low self-esteem, or go do something else. Not everyone was born to be a violinist."

"But—"

"That's three 'buts' in a row, Yumi! Who are you trying to make excuses for? I can't help it she has a tough life. But she's the one who decided to play the violin, not me.

"You want to tell her how great she is when she can't play scales in tune? What's going to happen ten years from now after everyone's inflated her self-esteem and then she has to go looking for a job? She'll show up for an audition, play one note, and they'll say, 'Thank you very much. We'll call you.' You asked me my opinion, here it is. Kick her butt until she can play her scales in tune. If she can't, then at least she'll go down swinging, and then neither you nor she will ever have to worry about her self-esteem again."

"I suppose that's what you did to me when I was your student."

"And you're still coming back for more. Masochist! What is it you wanted to play for me?"

"Schubert. 'Death and the Maiden.' "

"Must we? Must we really?" he asked. Some days, thought Jacobus, everything was meant to put me in a foul mood. Maybe I'm being punished by a higher authority. Fuck it, there ain't no higher authority. I'm going to enjoy being in a foul mood.

"Just because it's Franz Schubert's two hundredth birthday," he said, "why does every singer, every quartet, every orchestra in the world have to try to outdo each other? You want to celebrate the music of the man who might have become the world's greatest composer if he had lived beyond his thirty-one years? Fine. You've got no argument from yours truly. But why wait two hundred years? By the time the year's over he'll be celebrated so much everyone'll be sick of his music for another hundred."

"Yes, but—"

"But what?"

"I told you we've been contracted—"

"Suckered! Not contracted. Suckered!"

"We've been contracted," Yumi continued with patience, "to perform 'Death and the Maiden' at Carnegie, set to dance and video enhancements by the famed choreographer—"

"Charlatan!"

"—Power Ramsey."

"He's a charlatan! 'Death and the Maiden' is Schubert's greatest string quartet, maybe his greatest instrumental masterpiece, period. What the hell does it need 'enhancements' for? I'll tell you what I think of enhancements!" Jacobus coughed up some readily available phlegm and spat on the floor.

"And haven't you already performed it a million times with the quartet?" asked Jacobus. "Why do you need to play a second-violin part for me?"

"I'm just not feeling comfortable with it. Tomorrow's our first rehearsal."

"Whatever."

"So you don't mind taking the time?" asked Yumi, searching in vain for a flat surface on which to place her case. She finally put it on the floor in the corner.

"Of course I do!" said Jacobus. "Who do you think I am, Albert Schweitzer? Let's get it over with before I change my mind. And don't forget, the meter's ticking."

"I'll take Trotsky for a walk," offered Nathaniel from the vicinity of the front door.

"There'll be a lot of Tanglewood traffic about now," Jacobus mused.

"I'll be careful."

"No, I want you to leave him in the middle of the road."

Jacobus heard Yumi undo the clasps of her violin case, rosin her bow, and tune her instrument. He didn't really understand why she felt the need to play for him. To keep an old man "active"? To keep me from thinking about death, maybe? A joke on him, then, to bring "Death and the Maiden."

"Second movement," he said. The movement for which Schubert had adapted his song by the same name.

Yumi began the fourteen-minute Andante con moto, exquisitely calibrating her dynamics with finely honed sensitivity and maintaining a rhythmic pulse that was paradoxically under total control yet sufficiently flexible for subtle nuance. Though Yumi's part—the second-violin part—was more often than not the secondary melodic voice, the music nevertheless spoke with character and purpose.

What is there to say to someone who now plays so much better than I do? Jacobus thought. Or maybe better than I ever did? She's at the top of her profession and I'm at the bottom. Maybe I should be taking lessons from her. Can anything I say make her playing any better, or will I just make it worse? Jacobus mulled. Would saying anything at all make me an impostor?

He noted with satisfaction Yumi's ability to play espressivo even within pianissimo. And yet...and yet...

"Nyet! Nyet! Nyet!" hollered Jacobus. "Why do you keep pushing the tempo? And why's your vibrato so fast? You think Schubert meant death by buzz saw? Your vibrato's got nothing to do with what your right hand's doing. Something bugging you? Start at the third variation. Keep your shoulders and left wrist relaxed."

It occurred to Jacobus, as Yumi started over, that something indeed might be troubling Yumi. Rosenthal's call. Even before that—opening a Scrabble game with ANT! Jesus! Hard enough to play music, as it is; harder still to block out the world, and here she was, her future in limbo, trying to keep her mind on Schubert.

What's been my purpose as a violin teacher? he asked himself, his mind

18

wandering. To show a pupil how to plop his—or these days more likely *her*—fingers up and down in the right place at the right time? Could've taught a chimp to do that, but was that music? Teaching must be more than that. What, for instance, do I know about how Schubert's music should sound, other than what my own teachers taught me or from the performers I've heard? That's my entire experience. And where did they obtain *their* knowledge? And so on, all the way back to...Schubert himself. Teaching's not instructing. Teaching's conveying. Conveying the DNA of each composer's soul from one generation to the next. My responsibility. And what if I don't do it right? What if I tell the next generation how Schubert should sound and I get it wrong? What happens to the generations after that? What would my life have been worth if I blow it?

The movement gradually wound down from the climax in the fifth variation into the final G-natural whole note that tapered into nothingness. Jacobus sat in silence for several minutes, eyes closed behind his dark glasses, saying nothing. He had felt his mortality in listening to the music. His head bobbed.

"Jake, are you awake?" Yumi finally asked.

Trotsky lifted his head.

"Who are you?" Jacobus asked.

"It's me, Yumi! Jake, are you okay?"

"No, I mean in the music. Who are you?"

"The second violinist? Is that what you mean?"

"No. You're not Yumi and you're not the second violinist. You are Death. You are Death. '*Gib deine Hand, du schön und zart Gebild!*' " Jacobus sang, every note from his tobacco-ravaged throat stupendously out of tune and raspy as coarse sandpaper. " 'Give me your hand, you beautiful and tender image! *Bin Freund, und komme nicht, zu strafen.* I am a friend and do not come to harm you. *Sei gues Muts! Ich bin nicht wild.* Be in good spirits! I am not evil. *Sollst sanft in meinen Armen schlafen!* You should sleep gently in my arms!' Those are the words of Schubert's song, the second stanza, that he transcribed for this movement. Now play the beginning again, not plain old pianissimo, not Yumi. Death."

Yumi started over. Jacobus detected a slight tremor in her innately confident bow strokes. He could hear her bow slide perilously far over the fingerboard in order to create a tenuous, unearthly sound; and her vibrato, usually so rich and focused, was now almost pallidly nonexistent so as to portray shadowy lifelessness. Music over technique. Chilling. If Death had a heartbeat, this was its pulse. Then Yumi stopped.

"What about the Maiden?" she asked.

"What about her?"

"Why are you talking so loudly?" asked Yumi.

"Loudly? What do you mean?"

"Just that it's not your usual raspy mutter," Yumi chided.

Jacobus hadn't realized he had been talking loudly. Again, he began to panic. It's only congestion, he reminded himself.

"Where are my cigarettes?"

"You want one now? Before we finish?"

"Yes. No. Forget it." He lowered his voice to a level he thought might match Yumi's, hoping to disguise his anxiety.

"So," he continued. "What about her?"

"Doesn't she plead with Death to leave her alone? Doesn't she say, 'Away from here! Oh, away from here! Go away, cruel figure of death! I am still young, so leave! And do not touch me'?"

"You've done a little homework."

"You taught me to do that."

"No, I taught you to do a *lot* of homework, but I guess I was unsuccessful. The text you're quoting is from the first stanza. Schubert doesn't use that music here in the quartet version. But for argument's sake, say you were the Maiden. What would you do?"

"One must accept one's fate. No one can predict when one's life will end."

That's easy to say when you're young, is what Jacobus thought. No one can predict. Some end too soon. His own? If he were to lose his hearing, then Death would have been too late, in his opinion. If Death reached out to him, what would he do? When is the right time?

What he said out loud was, "Brave words, but what about the Maiden in

20

the song?"

"Clearly, she struggles. She can't accept her fate."

"And Death? Is he sincere about being gentle and loving? Or is he conning her?"

"I'm not sure."

"What does Schubert think?"

"I never read what Schubert thought about this."

"You don't have to read. It's in the music. Play it again."

Jacobus joined in this time. Playing the first-violin part he had learned so thoroughly in what seemed a lifetime ago, the music was etched in the muscle memory of his fingers. Though now slowed by age and infirmity, his hands led him unhesitatingly, and as the two of them soared together through the movement's five variations, no violinist could have been more expressive. Finally, the music evaporated into the ether from which it had emerged. A life cycle.

"So?" he asked.

"Yes," Yumi said. "She offers him her hand. She resists at first, but then at the climax of the fifth variation, she gives him her hand, doesn't she? And then the movement ends so peacefully, in G Major. She accepts him and then there's no more struggle. Is that right, Jake? Do we embrace Death when it arrives, or do we struggle to live?"

"How the hell do I know?"

Chapter Three

MONDAY

Jacobus knew it was dawn, not from anything as poetic as the peach-colored glow of sunlight magically transforming forested steeples of maple, ash, and cherry from dormant gray to radiant green, but rather from the increased traffic noise up on Route 41 as workers, making their way between West Stockbridge and Great Barrington, shifted gears going up the hill, and from the three circling crows that engaged in heated debate every morning without fail over which one had discovered the tastiest road kill. Jacobus also knew it was dawn because Nathaniel hollered cheerfully from the living room downstairs, where he had slept on the couch, "Jake, wake up! It's dawn!"

Disgruntled though he was at being awakened, he heard Nathaniel's voice loud and clear, and was heartened that his hearing was beginning to return. He also knew that, though it was still chilly, the inclement weather had departed. How he knew this he could never figure out. Maybe it was just in his bones.

"We have to leave for New York so Yumi can get to her rehearsal," Nathaniel continued.

"What do you mean, 'we'?" Jacobus yelled back. Pleading illness from the Tanglewood concert, he didn't want any part of the excursion to the city, especially in Nathaniel's duct-taped Volkswagen Rabbit, and congratulated himself on giving what he thought was a rather convincing portrayal of

Mimi dying of consumption in *La Boheme*.

But Yumi pleaded harder. It wasn't so much the rehearsal that was on her mind but the meeting at Rosenthal's law office. She professed inexperience in legal dealings and wanted to be sure her interests would not be subverted to Kortovsky's or to those of any of the others in the quartet. Still Jacobus resisted, and it was only when Nathaniel threatened to drive him to the doctor instead of the city that he finally relented, admitting that yes, he might survive a day or two longer.

Before they departed, and over Jacobus's profanity-laced objections, Nathaniel, a highly sought-after consultant to insurance companies in the realm of art and musical instrument theft and fraud, installed the only home security device that Jacobus had ever agreed to, but which he had never used: a bunch of one-by-three lengths of pine, each cut to fit wedged in between the top of the lower sash and the underside of the top frame of his cracked, dust-coated, lockless downstairs windows.

"You never know, Jake," said Nathaniel. "If anyone ever broke in and stole your violins—"

"Violin. Singular."

"Whatever. Violin. And if you hadn't done anything to keep the house secure, your insurance company might not reimburse you for the loss."

"What insurance company?"

Once the four of them were in the car—with Nathaniel and Jacobus in front; Yumi, lithe and lovely, ensconced in the backseat beside Trotsky, his tongue-lolling, eye-rolling, gargoyle head craning out the back window—Nathaniel lamented that if only Trotsky could play the viola they'd make a fortune as the world's most bizarre string quartet.

Nathaniel dropped off Yumi, Jacobus, and Trotsky at the New Magini Quartet's rehearsal space on the Upper West Side early enough to give Yumi a chance to rattle off a few scales to get her fingers moving before things got underway at 9:30. Nathaniel excused himself in order to return to his spaciously unruly apartment on East Ninety-sixth Street to catch up on the work that had accumulated during his Berkshire weekend getaway.

Emerging from the elevator at the second floor, Jacobus heard a lot of "busy" noise, but it was only when Yumi opened the door of the rehearsal space that Jacobus could hear Annika Haagen, the quartet's violist, and Pravda Lenskaya, its cellist, already warming up in the acoustically engineered studio at the end of the hall.

"You must've spent a few bucks on soundproofing," said Jacobus, as they entered the room.

"Some of the tenants complained," said Yumi. "They're all businesses on this floor—an import/export place, a printing company, a law office, an accounting firm—so there's no one around at night. If we rehearsed at night, it wouldn't be a problem, but since we perform so much at night, we prefer rehearsing during the day."

"And I gather the businesses don't like classical music."

"They said it distracted their customers, so they got together with the law firm and sued us."

"Good neighbors."

"They didn't even ask us first. We would have been happy to help solve the problem. But when they sued us, Cy countersued, saying the noise their businesses were creating made it impossible for us to carry out our trade, which by our lease required a 'quiet and settled ambiance.' "

"I guess even Rosenthal is worth something," Jacobus said. "So who paid for the soundproofing?"

"We paid fifty percent and the other businesses combined for the rest. Walls, doors, even the windows. We would have paid for all of it if they had only asked."

They entered the room, and Jacobus noted to himself that even though Yumi's two colleagues had not seen her for about a month since the end of their last tour, their only acknowledgement of her arrival was a momentary pause in their practicing.

"I'll just make sure it's okay with them for you to sit in," Yumi said to Jacobus, still standing in the doorway.

Jacobus heard the receding diminuendo of Yumi's footsteps on the hardwood floor to the other end of the room, and the quiet conversation that ensued. She returned moments later.

24

"They say it's all right. But they asked me to ask you and Trotsky," and here Yumi hesitated, "to be very quiet."

"Well, that's just dandy," whispered Jacobus. "You go on ahead and play with your pals, and I'll just find me a copy of *American Canine*. We'll try to keep our woofs down to a low roar. Think you can do that, Trots?" Trotsky barked agreement. Yumi slapped his arm, and he smiled.

Instead of a magazine, Yumi found him an extra chair, and he listened as she took out her violin and began a few preliminary musical calisthenics. Though the three musicians were practicing entirely different scales, technical exercises, and excerpts, the quality of sound each produced created a not unpleasant birdlike cacophony. If only some of the music being composed today could be as melodious, Jacobus thought.

A few minutes before 9:30, Jacobus heard the three women take their seats in the center of the room, presumably where the music stands were located. He was eager to hear their interpretation of "Death and the Maiden." Maybe if Kortovsky was late he could play the first violin part with them until he arrived. That pipe dream vanished almost before it appeared. He, Jacobus, was over the hill, and anyway, he didn't have his violin with him.

His daydreaming was interrupted by one of the musicians playing an A on the piano. Like a conductor rapping the podium with his baton, this gesture signaled that it was time to tune. He hadn't realized there was a piano in the room, but of course, it made perfect sense since the quartet often played with pianists—he fondly recalled a performance of the Brahms F-Minor Quintet he had done a million years ago with a youthful Claudio Arrau at the peak of his career. Some memories are just indelible.

"Steinway? Eight-foot?" he shouted.

"Nine-foot," answered Yumi.

My ears must still be clogged, Jacobus thought, but not so clogged that he couldn't clearly hear a particular sort of repetitive thud with which he was familiar from his days playing trios with Nathaniel; namely, the cellist, like a two-hundred-pound woodpecker with an attitude, drilling a shallow hole in the wooden floor with and for the instrument's endpin, so that the cello doesn't slide while playing. One always knew which side of the stage the cello section of the orchestra sat by the warren of divots in the floor.

In unspoken agreement there was momentary quiet as Lenskaya played an A on her cello, taken from the piano. Before Haagen, and then Yumi, had a chance to tune their instruments by painstakingly fitting their A's into the cello's lower frequencies, Lenskaya stopped abruptly.

"What is with this endpin?" she asked in exasperation. "First it gets stuck, then it doesn't stay. Is piece of shit, I think."

"Maybe you need to tighten it more," said Yumi. "Is it a new one?"

"No. Same one. Ever since South America, it gets stuck or it slips."

"Maybe it's the change in climate."

"Maybe. Who knows? I tighten. Let's go."

Once they finished tuning, there was an uncomfortable silence as they waited for Aaron Kortovsky's arrival. After a few minutes, Jacobus heard one, then another, quietly resume practicing some of the quartet's difficult passages. To Jacobus it sounded more like fidgeting than practicing, intended to relieve the awkwardness of waiting, like the crescendo in conversation five minutes before the beginning of a funeral service.

A watch was of no use to Jacobus, but like many musicians, especially teachers, he had an uncannily hardwired sense of time. He recalled how his own teacher, Dr. Krovney, after putting a student through the paces on scales, technical exercises, études, and repertoire, knew exactly when the sixty minutes were up so that the next victim could start on time. "And so on and so on," Krovney would end his lessons. It seemed to Jacobus that about ten minutes had elapsed when Yumi tentatively asked the others, "So, has anyone heard from Aaron lately?" To Jacobus's ear she asked the question with the same intent as their practicing, to occupy a void rather than to obtain information. When the question was met with monosyllabic negatives, two things became apparent to him: One, no one had not heard from Kortovsky; and two, that was the answer that Yumi had fully anticipated.

After another interminable ten minutes, Haagen asked, "So, what should we do?" Yumi suggested going over their rehearsal and concert schedules, but Lenskaya said, "I didn't bring."

"How long should we wait?" asked Yumi.

"I call Sheila," said Lenskaya, in her still heavily Russian accent. "After all, she's manager. She will know."

Jacobus heard Lenskaya gently place her cello on its side on the floor, walk to the corner where she had previously been practicing, open her case, and punch in a number on her phone.

"Hello, Sheila?" she began the conversation. "Aaron, he's not here."

When she hung up moments later, she said to the others, "Sheila doesn't know. She'll call around and get back. She said wait."

"Anyone for coffee?" Haagen asked.

This time it was she who was the recipient of the monosyllabic replies. She said, "Well, I'm going down stairs to get some."

Her coffee cup had long been empty when the phone rang. Lenskaya answered, spoke briefly, and hung up.

"Aaron is nowhere," she said.

"Hmm," mulled Jacobus. " 'Death' postponed."

Chapter Four

"How the hell can I have any idea where he is?" said Jacobus, as strands of semi-masticated sauerkraut made a vinegary jailbreak from his mouth, finding asylum with the vestiges of former fugitives on his threadbare brown corduroy winter coat.

Jacobus, Yumi, and Trotsky had taken a cab to Penn Station, arriving with a half hour to spare before a 12:03 train to Uniondale and the meeting with Rosenthal. Though blustery, the weather was just balmy enough to permit Jacobus—still dogged by the lingering effects of his cold—and Yumi to grab a bite at Frank 'n' Stein's outdoor hotdog and beer kiosk, a block from the station.

Yumi, distressed by the canceled rehearsal, had no appetite and was only drinking a root beer. She snatched a napkin urgently proffered by the sausage maître d', whose name, it turned out, really was Frank N. Stein, and passed it to Jacobus to wipe the sauerkraut off his jacket. Jacobus used it to blow his nose instead, then shoved it into his back pocket.

"What do I look like, a babysitter?" he continued, unperturbed. He knew he shouldn't be such a hard-ass, especially with Yumi. After all, she was a big girl now; one of these days even the "former student of Daniel Jacobus" would fade from her résumé. She had been a professional long enough to learn how to come to grips with the seemingly endless challenges that her livelihood of choice lobbed in her path. Many of those lessons couldn't be taught in the studio, and today Jacobus just didn't feel like being an enabler. He mumbled something about not showing up for a rehearsal not being the end of the world. You miss a flight, you eat some bad oysters, there's always a reason. Life's like that.

"What else did what's her name say? Your manager at InHouseArtists?"

"Sheila Rathman?"

"Yeah, Rathman."

"She only got Aaron's answering machine. The same message as always: 'Maybe I'll call you back. Who knows, today might be your lucky day.' But no one's ever lucky. So Sheila's called everyone. We've got rehearsals scheduled with the all the dancers and technicians for this Schubert concert, so she's frantic. Apparently no one's seen or heard from him."

"When's the concert?"

"Thursday night."

"Thursday? Isn't that a strange day for a big concert?"

"Friday's Labor Day weekend. They're afraid they'll lose audience."

"Ah. The final fling in the Hamptons before the long, hard winter at Zabar's."

"I suppose something like that. Plus, I think it would cost them more to hire all the support technicians if we do it over the weekend."

"But how many people are going to go listen to a string quartet in a cavern like Carnegie on a week night, even with Ramsey's dog-and-pony show?"

"That a good question."

"How long's Kortovsky been out of the loop?"

"That's another good question. We don't know. After our last tour concert in July, we all went our separate ways. I went to Japan. I don't know where Annika or Pravda went. We don't know where Aaron went or who he spoke to. We just assumed he'd show up like everyone else."

"Why's Sheila the only one who's trying to find Kortovsky?"

"Because no one in the quartet has been talking to each other for months."

Jacobus uttered a grunt that he hope conveyed a sense of disbelief and disgust at the same time.

"But I thought Kortovsky and Haagen were married," he said.

"Well, yes, they are, but in name only. They don't live together and the only times they talk are at rehearsals or when they're meeting with their lawyers to discuss Prince Rupert."

"So they have a bulldog, too?" asked Jacobus, yanking on Trotsky's leash just to make sure he was still alive.

Yumi laughed. "No, that's their son. He's about seven and goes to a boarding school in Westchester."

"A boarding school? Seven?"

"I guess it's because they're so busy with the quartet. *None* of us has any time for a family, really."

"What about Lenskaya?" asked Jacobus. "She have a communication problem with Kortovsky too?"

"I don't know, Jake," said Yumi. "I guess you'd call her the elder statesman of the quartet and she still plays incredibly well, but she just doesn't seem to care anymore. Sometimes Aaron gets so critical of her intonation and sound, and I think he has no right to. She's probably the best musician in the group and has such a deep tone compared to his. If I were as good as her I'd probably fight back, but she just sits there and doesn't respond. I get the feeling it's killing her on the inside. It's almost like he's trying to provoke her. It's all so silly, Jake. I don't know how much longer I can take it."

"Let's just try to solve one problem at a time, shall we?" He bit into his hot dog, licked at the mustard dripping onto his fingers, and belched. He had a case of heartburn that could be extinguished only by aerial fire retardant, but some things were simply worth dying for.

"Sure you're not hungry? Pretzel? Knish?" he asked.

"No thanks, Jake. I'm just enjoying watching you eat."

He chewed, not having anything to say other than *mmm*.

"It's not surprising for Aaron to be late to a rehearsal," Yumi explained. "In fact, it would be a surprise if he wasn't."

"How's that?"

"It's his style to show up at the last minute or five or ten minutes late. Never quite enough to really put you over the edge and say something. But he never says 'I'm sorry I'm late' or explain why. He doesn't even hurry when he finally does show up."

"No remorse, huh?"

"And he has the nerve to get irritated when someone criticizes him for not being on time, even though it's everyone else who's inconvenienced. I think that's one reason he and Crispin fought, and one reason why Crispin was fired."

"And one reason Crispin sued," said Jacobus. "Yumi, you know Kortovsky. I don't. Why pull that kind of stuff when you're trying to work together?"

"I think part of it is that he needs to show his power."

"Yeah? And what's the other part?"

"Breath."

Jacobus laughed. "Maybe then you shouldn't complain when he shows up late."

"Not bad breath. Alcohol."

"Ah. Hangovers?"

"I think sometimes he drinks more than a Japanese businessman on a golfing weekend. Since he sits next to me, I can tell better than the others. When he's not drinking he can be very charming, even considerate. But then, when he is... Between that and the tapping, it was driving me crazy."

"Tapping?"

"Aaron has such strong fingers. When he plays I can hear his fingers banging against the fingerboard. I know the audience can't hear it—"

"Probably sounds clear as a bell to them."

"Probably, but with his sound right in my ear it makes it really difficult for me to concentrate on my own playing."

"You're getting to be like me," joked Jacobus, "hearing and smelling people."

Yumi tried to drop her register two octaves in imitation of her mentor's gravelly voice. "And not tolerating their bullshit." She laughed, sounding mildly embarrassed using the profanity that she was accustomed to hearing from Jacobus's mouth, not hers.

"But, seriously Jake, it's unlike Aaron not to show up at all."

"Maybe you should count your blessings," said Jacobus. "As I recall, you had up-close and personal experience with sonny boy's penchant for being the gigolo. I'm not sure you're not better off without him."

"I'd rather not get into that, but yes, it would be so easy to agree with that, except Aaron's still an amazing musician, and..."

"And what?"

"And I'm just worried," she said.

Jacobus grunted, and then he grunted again. The first was to acknowledge Aaron Kortovsky's confounding reputation as a virtuoso violinist and virtuoso manipulator. But Jacobus, rubbing his bewhiskered cheek for guidance, asked himself what purpose would it have served Kortovsky not to show up for the first rehearsal of the season? The second grunt was to express his opinion of the extravaganza the quartet had gotten itself involved in, which seemed to be the pirouetting pachyderm in the room.

Jacobus thought fleetingly about suggesting that Yumi temporarily take over Kortovsky's first-violin position, but immediately abandoned it. That would be like having a pitcher and catcher change positions in the eighth inning of a baseball game. They were just two totally different roles. The Emerson String Quartet was one of the few exceptions to the rule. Jacobus had cautioned the two violinists on the difficulties of the switch when they suggested the idea to him way back when, but over the years they had become comfortable with the distinct requirements of each position, and the other two members of the quartet had learned to take it in stride, so it was no big deal for them. But even if Yumi were to replace Kortovsky, they'd then need to find another second violinist, and so would end up with two fish out of the water.

"Fire Kortovsky!" Jacobus blurted, but he knew it was a lousy idea even before it passed his lips. What would the press say if the New Magini suddenly sported a new first violinist? They were already having a field day over the lawsuit, and the quartet was suffering from it. The PR issue aside, to try to shoehorn in a new member at the last minute—especially the first violinist, whose musical personality sets the tone for the whole ensemble—would be idiotic, like putting mayonnaise on a pastrami sandwich. Plus, what would happen if in the middle of the rehearsals Kortovsky finally showed up? The others would have hell to pay. "Sorry, we thought you were dead. Our bad."

"Forget I said that," he recanted, even before Yumi could reply. "What about changing the program? Do the 'Trout' Quintet. You could play the violin part, easy." The "Trout" was another of Schubert's masterpieces and, like "Death and the Maiden," was based upon one of his songs. As brooding and otherworldly as the latter was, the former was frothy and down-to-earth. Side by side, the pair of works represented the yin and yang of Schubert's all-encompassing musical vision. More to the point, the instrumentation for the "Trout" was for only a single violin, plus viola, cello, string bass, and piano.

"I guess we could get Virgil Lavender for the piano," said Yumi. "We performed the Brahms Quintet with him a couple years ago, and he's amazing at fitting in with hardly any rehearsal. And maybe Gary Karr would be available for the bass part. I suppose we could give him a call." Her voice trailed off.

"You don't like Plan B?" asked Jacobus. "You guys too good for Lavender or Karr?"

"Oh, no!" said Yumi. "They're great to work with. It's just that Power Ramsey has already done the choreography and the light show for—"

"Light show?" Jacobus hadn't heard about that one. "What do you need a fucking light show for? What do you need dance for? This is Schubert! This is one of the greatest quartets ever written! This is—"

"I know! I know, Jake. But it's in our contract. It's opening our season and we're getting a lot of positive media attention, which, with the lawsuit coming to a head, has been in short supply lately. We have to do it. Plus, Sheila managed to get us a very generous fee. Anyway, it's time to catch the train."

Jacobus felt Yumi entwine her arm in his, remove Trotsky's leash from his grasp, and hustle him toward the station. These days Jacobus walked with a cane, the result not so much of his blindness but of the arthritis that had encroached upon his left hip and, to his dismay, was starting to spread to his hands. Their plodding progress was a boon to Trotsky, who, unaccustomed to the olfactory allure of the big city, took advantage of the leisurely pace to drag Yumi to every signpost, fire hydrant, and sidewalk-encircled tree for a thoughtfully considered inhalation and unerringly aimed whiz.

The trio's serpentine path into the station resulted in some unsympathetic jostling from impatient commuters, exacerbating Jacobus's darkening mood.

He had hoped that he had taught Yumi not only how to play the violin but also to put musical considerations above all others, especially money. Her ability to navigate around her professional obstacles seemed as tortuous as the route they had just taken to the ticket counter, where she purchased two round-trip tickets to Uniondale.

About to lecture her in no uncertain terms, he heard a whimper at his feet. He took the cue and dropped the remainder of his hot dog to the floor, whereupon the whimpering instantly became a squeal, then a slurp as Trotsky swallowed it whole.

Jacobus decided to drop the money issue. Yumi was stuck in a difficult situation with her quartet being sued and Kortovsky AWOL. None of it was of her doing and besides, he thought charitably, if Short won his lawsuit she might desperately need the cash.

Yumi guided Jacobus down a short flight of concrete steps. He heard the change in acoustics and the idling of engines as they approached the tracks.

"Here we are at the track," Yumi said. Jacobus started to move but Yumi pulled him back. "The train's not loading yet.

"Sheila says not to tell anybody that we don't know where Aaron is. Just to say he's not available. We've done the Schubert so many times. We could rehearse, the three of us, until Aaron shows up, because with the dancers and technicians it's mainly logistics. They really don't need the whole music. Better yet, we could get a sub in the meantime. Just temporarily. Sheila said she'd try to find someone."

"Who's both available and good enough? Good luck."

The doors of the train opened, only five minutes late. Jacobus found the handrail into the car and began to drag Trotsky, who for some reason sensed the three steps up into the train were the entrance to doggy Inferno and began to pull Jacobus in the opposite direction. Even being choked to death by the collar tightening around his neck did not seem to be adequate incentive to persuade Trotsky to change his mind.

"That a pet you've got, sir?" came the authoritative voice of a female conductor.

"No, it's my Great Aunt Lola," said Jacobus. "We're going out to the Island

34

for her sister's funeral."

"No pets allowed on the LIRR, sir," said the conductor.

Jacobus heard Yumi grunt and suddenly felt Trotsky's center of gravity surge forward toward its barrel chest. She must have slid her arms under Trotsky's belly and with all her strength lifted his hind legs. Jacobus yanked and the two of them were able to haul him into the train.

"Seeing Eye," Yumi said to the conductor in as pitying a voice as she could muster.

"A bulldog?" asked the conductor in disbelief.

"They gave me a bulldog?" hollered Jacobus. He flailed aimlessly with his free hand. "Blind as a bat I am, ma'am."

"Well, welcome aboard, then," said the conductor, though Jacobus was fairly certain he heard a note of suspicion in her voice.

"I think Trotsky's cute," said Yumi once they had found a seat, "in a bizarre, surreal kind of way, maybe. Why was he named Trotsky? After the Russian revolutionary?"

"Nah," said Jacobus, who, like his dog, was still panting. "He was named Trotsky because he can't runsky."

The train pulled out of the station in fits and starts, as did Jacobus's heart. He would never admit to Yumi that their just concluded exertion came close to killing him. Echoes of "Death and the Maiden" from yesterday's lesson rekindled thoughts of mortality that he seemed less and less able to extinguish no matter how thoroughly he tried to douse them. He felt an increasingly urgent need to transfer his knowledge, his very identity, to the future, to Yumi, so that the past, everything from Schubert to life's most trivial details—his "legacy," he would call it if his existence had been of any significance—would not disappear. It was under the latter category, the trivial details, that the night before, after they had all retired, he had prepared a little "gift" for Yumi. .

"Got something for you," he said, removing a petite unwrapped white box, slightly larger than a jewel box for a ring, from his coat pocket.

"Jake!" exclaimed Yumi. "It's so unlike you to give me a present."

Jacobus grunted.

"I mean," she said, putting her connotation in a more positive light, as she had intended, "what have I done to deserve a gift?"

"Well, didn't you bring me the wind-up sushi toy from Japan, and the Suntory whiskey from Max Furukawa, and the irises from your grandmother? You Japanese, you've got a thing about exchanging gifts. So I got this from Dedubian for you." Amid the swaying and joggling of the train car, he cupped the box protectively in both hands as if sheltering a baby bird fallen from its nest. "He doesn't just sell violins, you know. He also trades in musical reliquaries, shall we say."

"Reliquaries?"

"Well, maybe 'relics' is the better word. Like the little chopped-up pieces of saints they keep in churches. Except Boris does musicians."

"So what's in the box, then?"

Jacobus gleefully detected growing unease in Yumi's voice, and it wasn't the result of the bumpy train.

Jacobus leaned in, so that no one else in the train would be privy to his treasure. "Paganini's finger!" he whispered. "Dedubian guaranteed its authenticity. Gave me a great deal. You have any idea how much these things are worth?"

"No!" said Yumi. "Jake, you're teasing me."

"Open the box if you don't believe me," said Jacobus, sounding offended. "Or don't you want it?" He held both hands out to Yumi, bestowing his priceless treasure upon her. Gingerly, she removed the lid from the box and found herself peering at a wizened finger nestled in a bed of cotton discolored by reddish-brown disinfectant. She recoiled in horror.

"Oh, my God!" she shouted. "It's a finger!"

"*Shh! Shh!*" whispered Jacobus, loud enough for anyone in the train to hear. "Of course it's a finger. I told you. *Paganini's* finger. Now touch it. It'll bring you good luck. The lawsuit will go away. Kortovsky will show up. That's what these things are for. Go ahead. Touch it!"

"You've got to be kidding me," said Yumi.

"And I thought you were a brave one," he said with deep disappointment.

36

He knew Yumi would never retreat before a direct challenge. He heard her breathe deeply. Several times. He continued to proffer the box, cradled in his hands, arms extended to her in supplication. Finally, she said, "Okay, Jake. I'm ready. You're sure it's all right, then?"

"What do you think, it going to jump up and poke you in the schnoz?"

With great reluctance Yumi extended her right index finger to touch its counterpart in the box. Upon making contact, Paganini's finger jumped to life and began wriggling and writhing. Yumi screamed, Trotsky barked, and Jacobus cackled in delight, pulling his finger out from the hole in the bottom of the box. Tears streamed down both of their faces, but for different reasons.

"Jake, how could you?" said Yumi. She punched him in the shoulder. "I hate you!"

Jacobus's laughter turned to wheezing, and it was only after several minutes that he finally was able to mouth an apology.

"Had to do it. It was a trick"—wheeze—"my brother Eli pulled on me when I was a kid. All my life I've been waiting to do it to someone else. Didn't mean to hurt your feelings, but it's a good one, don't you think?"

"I think you're a doddering, nasty old man," said Yumi. "But, yes, I suppose it's a good one."

"I agree with both of your opinions," said Jacobus, and spent the rest of the train ride teaching Yumi his boyhood songs, doing his best to make sure Yumi would never say "I hate you" to him again, even in jest.

Chapter Five

I n the previous year, Cy Rosenthal's burgeoning law firm, Palmese, Leibowitz, and O'Neil, or PLO, as their adversaries called it, had moved from the increasingly dilapidated center of town to the ground floor of a shiny new three-story office complex in a trendy new minimall off Hempstead Turnpike. Inspired by their eminent neighbor, the stores bookending the law office—a deli on the left and an art supply store on the right—named themselves Cut the Baloney and I Been Framed, respectively. The firm maintained friendly reciprocal business arrangements with the two stores, hanging cut-rate but tastefully framed reprints of Chagall and Monet on its walls. And it was a tongue and Swiss (thinly sliced) on pumpernickel with a sour pickle on the side from Cut the Baloney that now lay on a sheet of waxed paper on Jacobus's lap as he sat in the corner listening to the ongoing discussion. That he was permitted to attend the meeting was in itself the outcome of arduous negotiation.

Cy Rosenthal was only slightly less surprised and disappointed by Jacobus's presence than he was by Kortovsky's absence. The alliance between Rosenthal and Jacobus had been an uneasy one in the Allard murder case—at one point the two geriatrics had engaged in an ineffectual fistfight which left both of them winded if unharmed—and in the present situation Rosenthal expressed the opinion that having Jacobus around would prove to be a distraction and a nuisance. But Yumi had threatened that if he was not permitted to attend the meeting, Rosenthal might as well cancel it because she wouldn't remain there another minute without him. Rosenthal counterproposed that Jacobus could stay as long as he kept his mouth shut.

Jacobus made a last and best offer, arguing that if Rosenthal didn't want him to talk, he would have to be provided with something to prevent him from doing so. Thus the tongue sandwich, to be paid for by the law firm, to which Rosenthal acceded.

"I wish I could trade you for Kortovsky," Rosenthal said to Jacobus after dispatching the office gofer, "because I don't know how we can come to a resolution with this lawsuit either without his presence, or with yours." Then, addressing the three members of the New Magini String Quartet who were seated around the circular conference table, he added, "That being said, time is of the essence, and we need to proceed to the extent possible and then interface with Aaron as soon as we can contact him. Are there any objections to moving ahead?"

"Whatever," said Annika Haagen. "This is so typical of Aaron. He'll just have to accept whatever we agree to. After all, it would be three to one."

"So, tell me, vhat is this deal?" asked cellist Pravda Lenskaya. After how many—ten years—in the U.S., thought Jacobus, she still sounds like she just got off the boat.

"Let me first summarize for you Short's stated position, as communicated to me by his lawyer, Lew Carino," said Rosenthal.

"Why? Has it changed in last four years?" snorted Lenskaya.

"I'm afraid not," said Rosenthal. "I only bring it up to make the comparison with his new proposal. This we've known: Short asserts that he was unfairly and illegally fired from his position in the Magini String Quartet, which, he claims, used spurious and trumped-up reasons of musical incompatibility in order to dismiss him. Carino further contends the stated reason of incompatibility was actually a subterfuge for the true motivation, a calculated strategy to enhance the marketability of the group by replacing him with a younger, more attractive female."

"This is redeekooloos!" said Lenskaya. "I may be woman, and maybe once I was young, but attractive? Ha!"

Jacobus noted that neither Haagen nor Yumi commented. Was it because there was some truth to Carino's statement about the quartet's motives, or awkward politeness at Lenskaya's self-deprecation? He squirmed in his chair, resisting his natural inclination to speak out. Instead he dropped a few morsels of his tongue sandwich on the ground to keep Trotsky quiet. Rosenthal apparently had witnessed both actions.

"What's the matter, Mr. Jacobus?" asked Rosenthal. "You've been suspiciously quiet. Dog get your tongue?"

"There's a fine line between being a good comic and a good lawyer, Rosenthal," said Jacobus. "Sad to say you're not close to the line from either direction. Why don't you just stick to business?"

"I'll take that as a no," said Rosenthal, clearing his throat. "Carino qualified his comments," he continued, "by stating that his client has no intention of impugning Ms. Shinagawa's artistry, which, though he believes is of the highest caliber, is irrelevant to his complaint of the unjust and unwarranted action against him. To back up his claim," Rosenthal went on, "Carino cites a market study done by the quartet's manager, Sheila Rathman, undertaken at the behest of Aaron and Annika, which concluded that the New Magini String Quartet was lagging in audience appeal to affluent males in the twenty-five-to-thirty-four-year age bracket, and was losing market share for both live performances and recordings, *especially* live performances, to visually attractive all-female groups like the duo pianists Katia and Marielle Labèque, or the Eroica Trio. And, Carino adds, it is his client's conviction that the covert long-term plan was to replace Pravda as well with someone more compatible with their marketing objectives."

" 'Objectives'?" asked Lenskaya. "I never heard this 'objectives.' Vhat is this market study?"

"It was nothing, Pravda," said Haagen. "Honestly. It was simply that Crispin became intolerable. He was like a cancer for us. He was always complaining that his ideas about how things should go weren't being considered. But they were. We just didn't often agree with him."

Jacobus was considering putting Haagen's comments under the "protest too much" category when Rosenthal interrupted her words and his thoughts.

"That's easy to say but more difficult to prove," Rosenthal said. "The question is, are you willing to risk going to court to make your case?"

"Why wasn't I told about this market study?" Yumi quietly interrupted.

"Because you weren't a member of the quartet when it was done," said Haagen. Her brusque tone suggested to Jacobus that either she was getting tired of being badgered on the issue or had more of a personal bone to pick with Yumi.

Haagen caught herself and continued less cattily. "Besides, we didn't want you to think that you had been selected to replace Crispin for any reason other than that you were the best choice."

When Yumi didn't respond, Rosenthal continued.

"Let me refresh your memories as to what is on the table right now and then convey to you what Carino says his client is willing to do.

"Crispin Short is suing for wrongful termination, breach of contract, deprivation of livelihood, slander, emotional distress, punitive damages, and legal fees, of course. If his suit is successful, the quartet would be liable for approximately seven point five million dollars. Since the quartet is a 503(c)(3) nonprofit organization and the four of you act as officers of the board of trustees controlling all of its assets, that money would essentially have to come out of your pockets."

"We've known this," said Haagen. "We would lose our homes. Our instruments. Everything."

"Reedeekooloos!" echoed Lenskaya. "And vorse than money, we lose reputation. And when we lose reputation, we lose future, then no more money."

"What is the proposal?" Yumi asked quietly.

"I'll skip the legalese," said Rosenthal, "but essentially Short will drop the suit entirely, excluding legal fees, if he is promptly reinstated."

Jacobus heard Yumi's quick intake of breath.

"Yumi would lose her job," said Haagen.

"That's for all of you to decide," said Rosenthal. "I'm just the messenger."

"Excuse me, Counselor," said Jacobus, swallowing the last bite of his sandwich. "Mind if I say something before all of you devour each other?"

"We had a deal, Jacobus," said Rosenthal. "You butt out."

"Has my presence been a distraction or a nuisance?"

"No."

"Have I kept my mouth shut?"

"For the most part, yes."

"So I've kept my end of the bargain, and now it's my turn. There's one little item you're forgetting about."

"What's that?"

"Kortovsky. Even if all three of you charming young ladies decide on a response to Carino's proposal, without Kortovsky—who I assume is not only the first violinist but the president of the board as well—it can't be legally binding. If Carino's a good lawyer, he would never go along with it unless it was airtight. And if Yumi were so greedy as to insist on keeping her well-earned job, then the vote could be two to two. Am I right, Counselor?"

"So what is it you're suggesting, Jacobus?"

"How prompt is 'prompt'? When does Carino need to know?"

"By Thursday, the day of the Schubert performance."

"Thursday!" exclaimed Lenskaya. "Four days? That's all?"

"That's the offer," said Rosenthal. "The quartet must agree to reinstate Short so he can play that engagement. It apparently is important to him. I can't tell you all of my negotiations with Carino, but that was the one item he said Short wouldn't budge on."

"So I would say it behooves you," responded Jacobus, "to find Mr. Kortovsky. Put the word out. Call the cops. Whatever. But you better do it toot sweet."

Rosenthal was the first to reply. "Based upon Aaron's standard MO as I understand it, Jacobus, there's no reason to suspect foul play, hence, no reason why we would want the police involved, or why they should have any interest in being involved. Even if we did have grounds for suspicions, the quartet has been on a month's vacation after an international tour. Kortovsky could be anywhere. Nevertheless, I grudgingly admit you have a point that the clock is ticking. So, Mr. Jacobus, since it was you who insisted on attending this meeting and you who couldn't resist getting your two cents in—both against my explicit protest—and you who have a track record—checkered though it may be—of recovering missing violins and their owners, maybe it behooves *us* to have *you* be the one to find Mr. Kortovsky.

Toot sweet."

Jacobus and Yumi waited at the train station for the trip back to the city. It had begun to drizzle again. They sat on a peeling wooden bench under an overhang that had begun to drip over the edge. Trotsky, straining at the end of his leash, tried to catch the drops in his open mouth, all at once. Jacobus cursed himself for having opened his own mouth in Rosenthal's office. He had continued to argue that it would make more sense to have the police locate Kortovsky, but Rosenthal countered that he could still be on vacation for all they knew. That would hardly spark the interest of the NYPD, which had enough definitely missing persons in its own jurisdiction to worry about. And certainly, the quartet didn't need any further bad publicity. Jacobus knew Rosenthal was gaining the upper hand, and after spewing forth a few more obscenity-laced "buts," finally was thrown to the mat when Rosenthal, who knew Jacobus's pressure points—damn those lawyers—suggested that the successful outcome of his efforts might enable the quartet to settle quietly out of court, thereby making Yumi's future much less bleak.

Though Jacobus no longer had the energy to pursue an enterprise of this type on his own, he could depend upon Nathaniel to use his investigative expertise to supplement his own effort. The conundrum, though, was that if he found Kortovsky, and the other members decided to throw Yumi to the dogs in order to settle the suit, it might mean the end of her tenure with the quartet.

Having reluctantly accepted his new assignment, his first question had been, "How the hell is it possible none of you know where Kortovsky is?" The silence that followed suggested to Jacobus that they were staring at him openmouthed, as if that was the dumbest question imaginable.

"Mr. Jacobus," Haagen said with soft remnants of her Danish accent, "we all lead our own lives, the four of us, even when we work every day together. And since we've been on holiday for so many weeks, well..."

"So, how do you schedule rehearsals? How do you know when you have a damn concert?"

43

"Sheila the manager," said Lenskaya. "Sheila gives us schedule. We have a question, we call Sheila."

"Nah...nah...nah...like hell you will," followed by a nearby telephone being slammed into its receiver brought Jacobus back to the present, with his ass on a wet bench.

"Got any change?" Jacobus asked Yumi. "I want to call Nathaniel before the train gets here."

Yumi, who had been humming "Turkey in the Straw," memorizing the words Jacobus had taught her on the way out to Long Island, rummaged through her purse. Among her wallet, keys, and the box that had sheltered Paganini's finger, she gathered a handful of change.

"Do you need me to take you to the phone booth?" she asked, handing him the money.

"Nah, Shakespeare back there gave me the coordinates loud and clear. Don't worry, just take the mutt." He handed her Trotsky's leash and walked to the location of the previous conversation. "I'll try not to fall on the tracks."

Jacobus dropped in the coins, felt the buttons on the phone, and punched in the numbers. He asked Nathaniel to call Sheila Rathman and to have a chat with Pravda Lenskaya. For the latter task, Jacobus figured that Nathaniel, who had been the cellist in a trio with Jacobus in their younger days, might be able to create a rapport with a kindred spirit and thereby extract some worthwhile information.

"Jake, you forgot to ask me one thing," said Nathaniel.

"Yeah? What?"

"You forgot to ask, 'Nathaniel, could you please help me locate Aaron Kortovsky?' "

"Well, you have something better to do?"

"Actually, yes."

"Cancel it, then."

He hung up.

Chapter Six

Jacobus wiped up the remaining gravy in his bowl with a piece of white bread. Limited somewhat by blindness but more by indifference, Jacobus was a horrible cook. He enjoyed good food, as he defined "good," but had no interest in spending the time to prepare it. He preferred complaining that there was never anything to eat in his house. But as bad as his own cooking was compared to Nathaniel's, the isolation of his own hovel in the Berkshires nevertheless beckoned to him. Though by no means a nature lover, he appreciated the psychological buffer the forest surrounding his home provided from situations like the one in which he was presently enmeshed. Ziggy Gottfried had once said, "How I yearn for the exhilaration of solitude," or something to that effect, and at that moment Jacobus had almost felt sympathy for that little bastard. In the old days Jacobus stayed at a budget hotel while in the city, preferring inexpensive seclusion to enforced companionship, and though his proclivities hadn't changed, his ability to get around on his own, especially with the mutt, had, so he had grudgingly accepted Nathaniel's invitation to spend the night at his spacious, if unkempt, apartment on Ninety-sixth Street.

"Let me get you some more stew before you wear a hole in that bowl," said Nathaniel. "I spoke to Rathman today, and I have an appointment to see Lenskaya at her house in Flushing tomorrow morning."

Jacobus heard the clatter as Nathaniel lifted the pot off the stove, followed immediately in Pavlovian predictability by the clicking of Trotsky's claws on the old parquet floor as he slid into the kitchen from the living room.

"Atta boy," said Nathaniel. "Here's some for you, too."

"You waste good food on that mongrel? I'm meeting Haagen at Dedubian's tomorrow. She's got some viola business with him. What's in the stew?"

"Mama's recipe. Originally it was squirrel, but I use rabbit. "

"Squirrel, huh? Why don't you just go shoot some in Central Park? She and I are doing lunch, then they have a rehearsal tomorrow afternoon with that egomaniac freak, Power Ramsey. What did Rathman have to say?"

"Mostly what everyone else said. She's command central for the group. She had notified everyone by phone and email about the rehearsal schedule, so Kortovsky certainly would have known."

"And when's the last time Rathman heard from him?"

"Just before the end of their summer concert tour. He told her he was planning on going rock climbing in the Andes—"

"Rock climbing!" interrupted Jacobus. "Jesus Christ! No wonder he's missing! What kind of musician goes rock climbing?"

"One with strong hands and a death wish maybe," said Nathaniel.

An image popped into Jacobus's head of the corpulent virtuoso Isaac Stern hanging by his fingertips at the edge of a cliff, his trademark towel still draped over his shoulder. Stern lets go of the precipice with one hand in order to wipe the sweat off his brow with the towel... Jacobus, wondering how such an image would enter his perverse cranium, and why, even more, he would find it humorous, shook his head to bring himself back to reality, not caring to imagine the denouement.

"What's so funny?" asked Nathaniel.

"You wouldn't want to know," said Jacobus.

"Just before the tour," Nathaniel continued, "he even bought some state-of-the-art high-tech gear at a place called Future Tents near his brownstone on Columbus. I found the salesperson who sold the stuff to him. She remembered him and said she gathered from the questions he asked that he knew what he was doing. She also mentioned how much she appreciated his 'buns of steel.' "

"Well that's dandy, but what if Kortovsky got his ass stuck in a crevasse? How do we find out?"

"I suppose we could call the American embassy down there," offered

Nathaniel, "but we don't even know which country he'd be in. The Andes are pretty big."

"And that's the last Rathman's heard?"

"Yep."

"Doesn't Rathman, as their manager, book their travel?"

"I asked her that. She does for her other clients, but the guys in the New Magini all fly separately and stay in different hotels. She said it was easier all around for them to make their own arrangements and send her the bills for reimbursement. Besides, it was the last tour of the season, and she wouldn't have made their vacation arrangements in any case."

There was silence. Jacobus chewed appreciatively on a morsel of rabbit, imagining it was squirrel. Though his sense of taste was compromised by his cold, he relished the savory combination of meat with the boiled pearl onions and turnips in a sauce of red wine, rosemary, and..."

"What's the secret ingredient?" he asked.

"Huh?"

"In the stew."

"Oh, yeah. Juniper berries."

Jacobus gave silent thanks to Nathaniel's mother from the bottom of his heart.

"Maybe we could call the police in Lima," said Nathaniel. "That was their last stop, wasn't it?"

"You speak Spanish?"

"No."

"So what are going to do, dial the number and pant?"

"Maybe they speak English."

"Well, suppose they do. What are you going to ask them, 'Excuse me, señor officer, you don't know us but could you please help us find a violinist who might be missing, but then again, might not? He may be up in the mountains somewhere, but he also could be anywhere between the South Pole and the North Pole?"

"But," countered Nathaniel, "what if you said, 'We have reason to believe a world-famous American musician, who has been missing for several weeks, is still in Peru and his last known location is Lima, where he still might be? And if you don't cooperate with us we'll be forced to contact the American embassy and register a complaint'?"

Jacobus sat back in his chair with the sigh of someone who had eaten well and in copious quantity, a sigh of satisfaction tinged with regret that reminded him how he felt at the conclusion of Brahms' Third Symphony. He wiped his mouth with his sleeve and unbuttoned his pants.

"Well, if you put it like that... You remember that *Times* story? They mention the name of a cop?"

"Don't know. You didn't let me read past the first sentence, but I have the article right here."

"I thought I told you to throw it in the fire."

"I must've missed," said Nathaniel.

"What are you, blind?"

"Bad aim."

"Read me the whole damn thing since you've got it."

He heard Nathaniel flatten out the crumpled newspaper. Bad aim!

"An uneasy quiet reigns over Lima where a body, apparently the victim of torture, was discovered only two blocks from the presidential palace in the Plaza Mayor, reviving nightmares of drug wars and political killings in this strife-weary country. None of the Peruvian drug cartels, which have until now limited their activities to the difficult terrain north and east of the capital, have so far claimed responsibility. Nevertheless, fears of their expansion into the heart of the teeming capital have sent a tide of concern rippling through corridors of local and national government. At the same time, human rights organizations, led by Amnesty International, have stepped up their campaign to hold these very administrators accountable for political reprisal, fearing a return to Peru's wholesale and at times arbitrary violence of the 1980s, spurred by the war between the Maoist Sendero Luminoso, or Shining Path, and the oft-times heavy-handed administration of president Alberto Fujimori.

"The killing is being investigated by the chief of police in Lima, Colonel Espartaco Asunción Ochoa Romero. Popularly nicknamed Oro, a contraction of his surnames that also means 'gold,' for his glowing record of successfully prosecuted arrests, Col. Ochoa Romero commented that he will approach the investigation as 'one more homicide in our city of eight million people, where a crime occurs every three minutes. We do our best to solve them all.' "

"So, what do you think?" asked Nathaniel. "I didn't know Lima had eight million people."

"Eight million minus one, you mean. What the hell? You find the phone number of this Spartacus Ocho and I'll make the call. Tomorrow. Now I've gotta pass out from gastrointestinal overabundance."

Chapter Seven

TUESDAY

The next morning Jacobus and Trotsky saw Nathaniel off at the Ninety-sixth and Lexington subway stop, where he embarked upon his visit with cellist Pravda Lenskaya in Queens. Jacobus grunted his promise to call the Lima police with the number that Nathaniel had obtained after laboring for an hour with international operators, one of whom fervently insisted that, since she could find no listed number, Lima could not possibly have a police force. After Jacobus's appointment with violist Annika Haagen, he and Nathaniel would reconvene at Carnegie Hall for the quartet's two o'clock rehearsal, where they would compare notes.

Dragged back along Ninety-sixth Street by Trotsky, Jacobus was just a few steps from Nathaniel's apartment when he was distracted from his mental machinations by the familiar jingling of a tin cup at ground level and made an arc around the beggar.

"Spare some change for the blind, my friend?" The cup jingled again with a rarely requited optimism.

"Forget it," said Jacobus. "And I'm not your friend."

"Ain't you got no symphathy, fella?" he asked, indignation leaching through slurred speech.

"I ain't got no 'symphathy' for drunken bums," mimicked Jacobus.

Jacobus extended his cane to bypass the beggar. The path seemed clear, but suddenly he went sprawling, entangled in the beggar's outstretched legs, and landed painfully on his hands and knees. Trotsky began to bark, making the sound of a hacksaw biting through plywood comparatively easy on the ears.

A pedestrian hollered, "Hey, mister, control your animal!" A little girl shrieked at a frequency almost too high for even the dog to hear.

"Clumsy asshole," said the beggar, his voice choked with street living. "Serves you right. That mutt eat better'n I do."

Jacobus's palms were scratched by the cement and his hip throbbed.

"Count your luck I'll never know what your face looks like."

"What do you mean?" asked the blind beggar. Then in a moment of revelation through his personal fog, he exclaimed, "So you're blind, too, huh? Well, you deserve it!" he said, and spat.

Jacobus felt for his cane, pushed himself awkwardly to his feet, and wiped off his pants. He homed in on Trotsky's bark and managed to grasp the leash close to his collar before the dog ran off. Then, with great deliberation, with the tip of his cane he probed the space in front of him until he found the seated beggar's chest and leaned into it, pinning the beggar hard against the side of the building, undecided whether to push even harder.

"Hey!" screamed the blind beggar. "Are you crazy?"

"Rot in hell," Jacobus said and released the pressure.

He entered Nathaniel's apartment and slammed the door behind him, trembling with rage. Part of it was the humiliation of being seen, helpless, on his hands and knees. The other part, he knew, though he tried to deny it, was that when he had the end of his cane pressed against the heart of the blind beggar he was attacking himself. No matter what he had accomplished, no matter what he had done to overcome his affliction, in everyone's eyes he was the blind beggar. If the cane had been a spear, he would have killed him. Jacobus poured himself a cup of lukewarm coffee from the coffeemaker, spilling half of it on the kitchen counter, considered the hour of the day, and added a thumb of Jack Daniel's. Two thumbs. Fuck the cop in Lima. Fuck Kortovsky.

He decided instead to try to get WQXR on the radio. Maybe some music would make his day endurable. He knew the general vicinity of Nathaniel's kitchen radio and fumbled around the counter for the correct appliance. Damn! So many fucking Nathaniel gizmos. Jacobus didn't know whether he was turning on the radio or the toaster oven.

After several abortive attempts with knobs and dials, he slammed whatever appliance it was that had not cooperated and gave up.

"Dammit," he said. "Somebody's trying to tell me something."

Downing his coffee, he dialed the memorized fourteen-digit phone number Nathaniel had unearthed. A recorded voice told him he was an idiot for having dialed the 0 after the country code. He roundly cursed the voice—that it was recorded was neither here nor there—before strangling the receiver. He poured himself another coffee and Jack Daniel's, but without the coffee, and tried again, this time without the 0. After the eleventh ring he was about to hang up when he heard several clicks and then a voice.

"Oro."

"You speak English?"

"Yes, sir. How can I help you?"

"You the police?"

"Once again you are correct in your assumption, sir."

"I'm looking for a missing person."

"No doubt."

"How's that?"

"If he wasn't missing, surely you would not be looking for him."

"Are you from New York City, by any chance?" asked Jacobus.

"I have not yet had the pleasure of visiting that legendary metropolis. Why do you ask?"

"Because that's where the biggest wiseasses are from."

"If that is true, señor," said Ochoa Romero, "then you must hold the key to that fair city. So perhaps you will be kind enough to tell me your name and your concerns."

"The name is Jacobus, but I'm not as sure about the concerns." Jacobus spent the next several minutes explaining the situation. That he wasn't even certain Kortovsky was actually missing made it difficult for him to present a convincing case for the officer to do anything at all.

"Well, Señor Yacovis, I must tell you that here in Peru we have many people who we know with certainty are truly missing and it is with great difficulty that we occasionally succeed to find them. Sometimes they are never found, and sometimes they are found but I am sorry to say no longer having the capacity to appreciate our worthwhile efforts.

"Tell me, señor, what was the date anyone last heard from this Kortovsky?"

"July twenty-sixth."

"So you are telling me that for a month the missing man has not been missed?"

"Hey, who do you think you are? Gabriel Garcia Márquez? I thought you were a cop."

Ochoa Romero chuckled. *"Discúlpeme.* I will dispense with the metaphysic. Now, please tell me, where was Señor Kortovsky staying in Lima? Perhaps we can find out where he went from there."

"Damn," said Jacobus. "I don't even know that."

"You will find out and call me back. *Buenos días,* Señor Yacovis."

"What about a photo?" stammered Jacobus, grasping at straws. "I could tell his manager to send one down."

"A photo? What a considerate idea from a blind person, señor, but that will not be necessary."

"What do you mean? How the hell did you know I was blind?" asked Jacobus, primed to be re-ignited.

Ochoa Romero laughed.

"I am no Inca clairvoyant, if that is what you are thinking. It was only that I was fortunate enough to attend the memorable concert of the New Magini String Quartet here in Lima, and in the program notes was the biography of the lovely *segunda violinista,* that young Asian woman, Miss... One moment, I have it right here."

"Shinagawa. Yumi Shinagawa," Jacobus said, his patience waning.

"Yes, of course. Miss Shinagawa, which mentioned you as her illustrious teacher. That is how I know about you, and of your special gift."

"Gift?"

"Yes, your blindness. My grandfather, César, was also blessed with that gift, and it was he who taught me how to truly listen to music with only my ears and my heart, and no doubt it is one of the reasons why you have become such a perceptive teacher."

Tell the blind beggar he should be grateful for his gift, thought Jacobus.

"So, I gather you've got a photo of Kortovsky from the program book," he said.

"A splendid one, *gracias*. A handsome man, Señor Yacovis. A handsome man. Peru is not a country of tall, blond men, señor. The ladies must beware, *por cierto*. And the quartet, they played like gods. Or, shall I say, one god and three goddesses. Never has Lima seen such excitement since Peru vanquished Chile, one to nil, scoring a beautiful goal in the eighty-eighth minute to claim the South American *fútbol* title nine years ago. I myself was at the *estadio* with my aged grandfather—"

"He teach you how to listen to soccer with your heart?"

"He felt the pulse, Señor Yacovis. *La energía.* So much so that after the match he collapsed with joy and later expressed dismay that he had been successfully resuscitated, complaining he had lost his opportunity to die a happy man.

"But this is not why you called. We were talking about your missing Señor Kortovsky and his string quartet. I must say that although their Beethoven took the audience to its standing ovation—it was *el famoso* opus 59, *numero tres,* and the closing fugue was miraculously exciting—I was not, how shall we say?—so swept off my feet. *Discúlpeme.*"

"And why was that?" asked Jacobus with an edge. He considered Beethoven to be the greatest composer, and what could an opinionated cop know about music?

"For me, the heroism of Beethoven's music tells us what humanity *should* be, which no doubt is wonderful, but *un poco* utopian for me. That is why I prefer Mozart, because he tells us the way humanity really is. As a policeman, that is what I see every day. That is my life. And the utmost clarity with which he presents his musical ideas brings comfort to me, who has always to unravel what is murky and dark. That is why I preferred the Mozart that the quartet played on the first half. Yes, it is my favorite. Until later then,

54

Señor Yacovis."

"And which Mozart quartet would be your favorite?" Jacobus asked, but Oro had already hung up.

Chapter Eight

Jacobus, bolstered by the increasingly salubrious weather, walked to his rendezvous with Annika Haagen at the celebrated violin shop of Boris Dedubian at the Bonderman Building in the Midtown Manhattan. Before closing the apartment door behind him, he shouted to Trotsky, asleep on Nathaniel's king-size bed, "Guard the house."

Walking along Ninety-sixth toward Fifth Avenue, he steeled himself for another encounter with the blind beggar and felt vaguely deflated when, passing the spot of their earlier confrontation, the rattling of a tin cup was replaced by the groan of a bus leaving the curb. To make absolutely certain that he wasn't about to be ambushed, he reconnoitered with his cane, probing the area where the beggar had been. Nothing. Not even trash. Jacobus began to wonder whether the confrontation had been in his mind only, and whether he was losing his sanity in his old age, but his chafed palms provided evidence he wasn't totally mad. Yet.

From a missing beggar, his thoughts turned to a missing violinist. What had he learned, if anything, from his conversation with Ochoa Romero, that pampas ass? Not much. There was as much chance Kortovsky was assaulting a liverwurst sandwich right now at the Carnegie Deli in New York as assaulting the peak of Mount Fujimori, or whatever it might be called, in the Andes.

Such musings occupied Jacobus's mind as he meandered down Fifth Avenue along Central Park, until a squeal of car brakes and a blaring horn as he took a step into the intersection at Seventy-ninth Street provided a reminder that it was time to turn his daydreaming from Kortovsky to

56

Haagen.

Yes, he had met her a few times after the quartet's concerts, but this was the first time he and she would actually engage in anything other than the usual loathsome postconcert chitchat. He had always admired Haagen's playing, her determination not to be overwhelmed by the more prominent voices of the quartet—the first violin and cello—and her ability to bring out the musically tantalizing but often obscured inner voice of the viola part. Her tone, lush and sensuous, was matched, according to those who described her to him, by her Scandinavian beauty and her riveting stage presence. Jacobus suddenly barked out a raucous laugh—as he did so, he could hear the pace of the pedestrians near him pick up—hell with them—recalling a line by veteran *New York Times* music critic, Martin Lilburn, who had provided the most apt and succinct description both of the typical viola part and of Haagen's overall artistic personality in one of his rare displays of levity: "Annika Haagen can even make 'oom-pah' sexy."

Jacobus tried to imagine her looks based on her sound, but visual images of any sort had almost ceased to exist for him. At this point in his life, people were how they sounded and how they smelled, and occasionally what they felt like. Taste had not been a viable option for some time. Nevertheless, he entered the Bonderman Building entertaining himself trying to visualize a woman with a beautiful viola sound, and who, as Aaron Kortovsky's wife, might know something of his whereabouts. And more to the point, how it could be she did not know.

He pressed the button of the recently installed stainless-steel, automated elevator for the top floor, the sole longtime occupant of which was Dedubian et Fils Violins. As it ascended, with speed and silence, he recalled the old days: the vintage Otis elevator, manually operated by his onetime friend, Sigmund Gottfried. He could almost smell the polished woodwork, the soothing sound of the well-oiled wrought-iron door as it caressingly slid open. Ah, Ziggy, if only—

"So, Mr. Jacobus," came the Danish-inflected voice. "Here you are."

"Huh? Oh, Haagen. Ready to go? " asked Jacobus, holding the elevator door open.

"I am sorry, but no. I arrived here a little late. Traffic on 684 was just ridiculous. And parking! *Pffff*! And now Dedubian keeps me waiting and waiting. He has been on the phone since I got here. Shall we leave now? I don't want to keep you."

"What do you need to do?"

"Just an update on my insurance appraisal for my Gasparo. It should only take a minute. He knows the instrument well. After all, I bought it from him way back when I was still a student."

"Nah. We can wait."

"Thank you."

Haagen took his arm and escorted him from the elevator, across well-trod antique Oriental rugs and around the massive French Renaissance central table on which lay an assortment of eighteenth- and nineteenth-century violins, to a pair of frilly, overstuffed Victorian chairs in a corner of the ostentatious, spacious showroom. Jacobus caught the fragrance of her floral perfumed soap and heard the muted, intimate sounds of prospective buyers trying out six-figure fiddles in side rooms, and of other customers negotiating the sale, repair, or appraisal of their instruments in quiet confidentiality. He wondered why, after all these years selling tens of millions of dollars' worth of these pretty-sounding wooden boxes, Dedubian still hadn't retired to his beloved condo in Montreux. Business must be in his blood, Jacobus considered, just as blood was also in his business.

"It's a real racket these dealers have with the insurance companies, isn't it?" Jacobus said to Haagen.

"You mean with the appraisals?" Haagen asked.

"Yeah, they get you coming and going. The insurance companies want you to get an appraisal every two or three years or else they won't acknowledge appreciation for the instrument during the time between valuations."

"Yes, somehow they are unwilling to connect the dots," Haagen said, continuing his thought. "And at the same time, the dealers are only too happy to write the reappraisals for you, since they already have the information they need about the instruments, but don't mind charging you a hundred dollars for the new piece of paper with their signature."

"Exactly," said Jacobus. "They don't make you get your house reappraised every time you—"

"Excuse me," Haagen said, their conversation interrupted by an unexpected sound, jarringly inconsistent with their surroundings—an electronic version of the idée fixe from *Harold in Italy*, the unique symphony/concerto for viola that Berlioz composed for Paganini.

"My cellphone," said Haagen. "Please excuse me a moment."

While she conversed on the phone, Jacobus wondered what Berlioz would have thought to hear his genius reduced to a sissified, mechanical jingle? Where will music be in a hundred years? he mused. Will humanity reminisce nostalgically of the oldies but goodies of elevator music? "Hey, you remember that 'Guantanamera' recording when we strolled down the frozen foods aisle at Price Saver?"

"...so it's good news, Mr. Jacobus," said Haagen, interrupting his ongoing internal diatribe, "and bad news."

"What's good news?"

"Sheila managed to get Ivan to fill in for Aaron today and to do an outreach with us tomorrow. Smetana quartet."

"Ivan Lensky? Pravda Lenskaya's son?" asked Jacobus.

"Yes. He's a terrific violinist, and of course he knows our quartet very well..."

She left the sentence dangling.

"But? What's the bad news?" coaxed Jacobus.

"There's a reason they call him Ivan the Terrible."

A terrific violinist, yes, thought Jacobus. But he was well aware there was some major baggage there. It was Ivan Lensky who had finished second to Yumi when the quartet was auditioning candidates for Crispin Short's vacated position. Only months before the audition, Lensky had been a finalist at the Tchaikovsky Competition in Moscow, not winning a prize but playing well enough to secure a recording of the Dvořák Violin Concerto with the Prague Philharmonia. Doubtless, winning neither a top competition prize nor the position with the quartet had been a major blow to his ego, and to his mother. Surely, as Lenskaya got older, she'd want to resurrect the musical style established by the original quartet members, the style that had first brought the quartet to world prominence. Yumi, as she had related to Jacobus, believed it had been her ascendance over Ivan Lensky in winning the position that initially caused Lenskaya's icy standoffishness. Jacobus wondered why Ivan, after being rejected in favor of Yumi, would now consent to participate in their rehearsals. And how would Yumi respond to having someone she had defeated playing first fiddle to her second?

"I know what you are thinking," said Haagen. "But don't worry. Sheila told Ivan it was just temporary until Aaron gets back. Ivan is a strong violinist, but he's got that traditional Russian take-no-prisoners way of playing and would never be a good fit for the quartet. But for today and tomorrow, it seems a good compromise."

"What's the outreach?"

"We do little demo-performances at schools. We wanted to cancel this one because of Aaron's situation and with the concert on the Thursday, but Sheila said we had to do this because we get a grant from the city and if we cancel we'll lose the grant, and these days we really need the money. So it's good Ivan's available."

"Where is it?"

"Rose Grimes School. Up in Harlem."

"Yeah, I know it. BTower's school. Yumi teaches there."

Haagen didn't reply—it wasn't a very interesting conversation, anyway—so they continued their wait in silence, hoping that Nature would qualify their absence of verbiage as an example of a vacuum to be abhorred and would draw Dedubian into their presence. Several minutes later, Haagen gave up the experiment.

"Sometimes I think maybe I am paranoid, but ever since Crispin sued us it seems we've been treated like this. Like dirt. I'm afraid if he wins this thing, our careers might be over."

"Aren't you being a little melodramatic?"

"Maybe. But maybe not. You know, when these dominoes start to tumble in this business, who knows when they stop?"

"Pardon me for saying so, but you should've expected push-back when Kortovsky made Short's firing public. That's not the way it's done, even if it was justified. You have to admit, hostile takeovers in this business puts all of you in a very bad light."

"Maybe so. But we tried everything with Crispin, to make the separation easier. But he said 'You'll have to fire me to get rid of me,' and then when we did he went to the media like that." She snapped her fingers. Then she laughed.

"That's funny?"

"No. Just that when I snapped my fingers, Boris appeared."

Jacobus heard the familiar, cultivated voice approach that could be any accent or no accent, a voice that could charm or belittle, whatever was necessary to make a sale.

"Ah! Jake," said Boris Dedubian. "So good to see you again." He felt his hand clasped by one larger and softer than his, but the ensuing handshake, Jacobus noted, demonstrated a lack of enthusiasm inconsistent with his words. Interesting, too, that the appointment was with Haagen, yet Dedubian had greeted him first. Before Jacobus could return the greeting, Dedubian continued.

"You know, I still have that exquisite Guadagnini that you loved."

"That was two years ago. I liked the violin—it's a great violin—but I have no interest in buying it, and it's Ms. Haagen who's here to see you, not me."

"Ah, yes. Annika. Sorry to keep you waiting so long. Is there something I can do for you?"

"Boris, I just need an update on my Gasparo. I've brought it."

"Let's take a look, shall we?"

Jacobus heard Haagen remove the instrument from its case and hand it to Dedubian for inspection.

"Ah," he said after a few moments. "And when was the last time you had it appraised with us?"

"Five years. I know that's too long to wait, but—"

"No, no. No problem." There ensued a silence that to Jacobus seemed too long for a cursory reappraisal of a familiar instrument. Finally Dedubian continued. "I don't think its value has changed."

"What? I don't understand," said Haagen. "How is that possible? Every good instrument has gone up fifty, sixty percent in the past five years. And this is a 1580 Gasparo, the greatest viola maker ever, and it's in amazing condition. You've told me yourself it's never been cut down to size, like most of his other instruments. No bass bar crack. No sound post crack. This should be worth three hundred thousand, easy!"

There was a long, awkward silence.

"Well, now that I look at it carefully, Annika, I'm not even so sure any more whether this is a genuine Gasparo. What you say—that such an old instrument has never been cut down—that makes me suspicious whether it's original. You know there were so many later makers who copied his style. And four hundred years ago! Look at these f-holes. Gasparo's would have been longer than these."

"But I bought this from *you*! It's got papers from Laszlo Novak!"

A certificate of authenticity from a guy like Novak was worth its weight in gold, thought Jacobus. But once the guy was dead, it went from twenty-four to fourteen karats.

"Well, poor Lazlo's passed away, hasn't he? I would suggest you keep my previous appraisal, so I don't have to say in writing what I now think this instrument is, a nicely done nineteenth-century Saxon or Tyrolean copy of a Gasparo. Sixty, seventy thousand, tops. If you want to sell it back to me, I'd be happy to give you your money back for what you paid me for it."

"I can't believe this!" said Haagen. To Jacobus, she sounded on the verge of hyperventilating. "But, the sound! It has such an incredible sound!"

"That all depends upon who is playing it," said Dedubian. "Doesn't it, Annika, dear?"

"Kortovsky's got an Amati, right?" Jacobus jumped in. Partly he wanted to prevent Haagen, who had just witnessed her nest egg go Humpty Dumpty on her, from attacking Dedubian. Not that he was a peacemaker; in fact, he was enjoying their little tiff. But he wasn't sure yet whose side he needed to be on, and also he was interested in the timing of this reappraisal. Maybe she and Kortovsky were trying to push the valuations as high as possible in the event that Short's suit was successful, so that if and when they had to sell their instruments to pay up, the pain would be substantially eased. That might account for her level of distress. Sometimes Dedubian could be sweet-talked by a pretty face into giving a high appraisal; today he seemed to be having no part of it. That was also interesting. "When's the last time Kortovsky got his violin reappraised?"

"Sorry, but I can't tell you that, Jake," said Dedubian. "Privileged information."

"*I'll* tell you, Mr. Jacobus," said Haagen, about to erupt. "Aaron gets his violins reappraised every year, and it's only because he's so fucking anal."

For some reason that Jacobus didn't understand, she was clearly not on Dedubian's persona grata list. It did not require an expert in the subtleties of human nature to sense that Haagen was about to explode, so Jacobus suggested it was time go to lunch. As they departed, he could hear Dedubian saying, "Is there anything else I can do for you, dear?" Fearing what her response would be, Jacobus grabbed her by the arm and pulled her into the waiting elevator.

Chapter Nine

J acobus suggested one of his favorite New York eateries, Fat Chance, that boasted "down-home suth'n cookin." The specialty of the house, Kissin' Kuzzins, oysters wrapped in bacon, dipped in cornmeal batter, and deep-fried, served with homemade succotash, made Jacobus salivate just thinking about it. Jacobus's recommendation, though, was vetoed by Haagen, who objected to the astronomical cholesterol level of the menu, so Jacobus, in consideration of her frazzled state, acquiesced to her request to go to Yu and Miso, an unpretentious but well-regarded Japanese restaurant just across from Lincoln Center.

Haagen ordered the bento lunch box with miso soup and green tea. Jacobus, spurred on by an energetic chorus of slurping from various points in the restaurant, rekindling nostalgic memories of his concert tours to Japan in his younger days and his more recent stay at Yumi's grandmother's home, ordered tempura soba with a Sapporo beer. Since the way they eat noodles in Japan imitates the sound of a herd of African elephants at a quickly drying watering hole, they must be serving the real thing here, he conjectured.

He let Haagen take the lead in the conversation, reluctant to let go of a pleasant past for a troublesome present.

"I can't believe he did that to me," Haagen said, in a daze.

"Hey, dealers can be pricks. We all know that," he said in commiseration.

"Yes, but first the lawsuit. Then Aaron missing. And now this. It's hard to take."

"About Kortovsky. Aaron..."

"Mr. Jacobus, let me be candid. Aaron is a shit and I'm having a bad day. If it weren't for needing him because of this deadline on the lawsuit, I couldn't care less where he is or when he returns. He's always been this way."

"I understand, Ms. Haagen, that Kortovsky may always have been 'this way,' but you're his wife. How can you not have some idea what he'd be up to?"

"Wife, yes and no. And please call me Annika. Both and neither. We are married, but we live separate and— how shall I say?—open life styles. One of my parents was Danish and the other Finnish, so that's not such a big deal for us as it is here in your country. We both have that need to be individuals, you know, and Aaron for his adventures."

"Like rock climbing?"

"I wasn't thinking of that, but yes."

"Doesn't that kill his hands?"

Haagen laughed.

"Is that some sort of Scandinavian punch line?" asked Jacobus, annoyed.

"Just the opposite, I think. I'm sorry to laugh, but when he was a student he cultivated a reputation for having incredibly strong fingers, and liked to show off the grooves on his fingertips of his left hand to the other students. It was so Aaron."

"Yes," said Jacobus, "that was certainly a badge of honor when I was a kid. The deeper the groove, the longer it was assumed you'd practiced. But in the long run it's not the best way to play. It only really shows that you're pressing too hard. "

"Tell that to his fingerboard," said Haagen. "Or my arms. Not that I minded at the time."

She laughed again, but this time it was more to herself.

Haagen was spared further explanation with the arrival of their lunches. Jacobus, always appreciative of a well-prepared tempura soba, used his nose to locate the small bowls of sliced scallions and peppery seasoning, and added them—extra today, to help clear his sinuses—to the bowl of buckwheat noodles and breaded prawns swimming in a rich broth. He found himself back in the soothing comfort of Japan, where he had the friendship of his old counterpart, Max Furukawa, and Yumi's family. Yumi's

English granny, Kate Padgett. A true musician. The only woman in the world who ever understood him; loved him, maybe. Why he didn't have it in him to reciprocate, especially when they were in the hot tub together…

"Are you listening to me, Mr. Jacobus?"

"Of course I am. I heard every word you said. About Rupert."

"Rupert? Prince Rupert?

"Yes, *that* Rupert."

"But that was five minutes ago. I was asking how you liked the soba."

"Oh. It's delicious. *Oishii*, as they say. But, isn't he a little young to be going to boarding school?"

"Perhaps. But with Aaron and my schedule—"

"And lifestyles."

"Yes, and lifestyles, it would be so much worse for PR—that's his nickname, PR—to be stuck at home with a nanny all day. At least he can be around children his own age, and the Collective Reference Academy has a wonderfully creative program. You've heard of it? It was in the *Times*."

"Collective Reference?"

"Yes. There are no real classes. Instead, every student brings his or her own personal daily experiences from the outside and then they discuss them. There's no instruction in the traditional sense at CRA. The teachers aren't even called teachers."

"What are they called then? Babysitters?"

"Facilitators."

Jacobus, inhospitably, conjured up the Scrabble board, appending the P in PR to the end of CRA.

"The school's not far from my house in Mt. Kisco—that's why I moved there, along with it being impossible to afford anything in the city—and it's holistic and gender neutral."

It wasn't part of his job description to figure out what the hell that meant, so Jacobus only asked, "You see him much?"

"Not often. Not because I don't want to, but CRA discourages short, random contact between students and parents. Studies have shown visits like that only confuse the children."

66

"And what does the boy do during the summer, Annika, play Frisbee on the quadrangle?"

"So, okay, it's a little strange, Mr. Jacobus, but maybe we're all a little strange."

Jacobus noted he was getting her a little hot under the collar, which he liked, because he found that when people were frazzled they were more likely to speak spontaneously and, as a result, truthfully. He had used that tactic with countless students, and though it might not have endeared him to them, it at least got them out of their shells. When he had tried it with Yumi at her first lesson, it almost ended up being her last lesson as well. But that was years ago, and water under the bridge...

"And if we lose this lawsuit," Haagen was saying, "I'm sure I won't be able to afford CRA along with anything else. To answer your question, though, summer is when the quartet is either at festivals or on tour, so I take PR with me for those things."

"Does Kortovsky ever take him?"

"No. He says it interferes with his independence."

"Did you take PR with you on the South America tour?"

"Absolutely! Prince Rupert had a wonderful time, except..."

Except! thought Jacobus. Maybe now we'll get somewhere.

"Except what?" he asked, leaning forward.

"Except for the guinea pig," Haagen said.

Jacobus returned to his slouch and with his chopsticks made circles in his bowl of broth.

"What happened? Prince Rupert was attacked by a guinea pig?"

"No. He saw people *eating* guinea pigs!"

"Eating them, eh?"

"We try not to eat meat—for ethical and health reasons. They served them lying on their backs."

"Talented waiters in Peru, eh?"

"Not the waiters. The guinea pigs were served on a plate, lying on their backs with their little legs in the air."

"Better than standing up, though, I suppose."

"Don't joke. PR was traumatized for days."

"I hope he got over it."

"Eventually. The two of us hiked the Inca Trail to Machu Picchu. That helped a lot. He loved all the stories about the wars between the Spaniards and the Incas, and he got to pet a llama! It was so experiential."

"Very sweet. And what did you do with your viola on your trek? Carry it on your back and play 'Cóndor Pasa' around the campfire?"

"Mr. Jacobus, your sarcasm is so charming. No, the quartet has a special instrument trunk. It's got padded compartments, one for each of our cases, and each compartment has its own combination lock. InHouseArtists sends one of their management interns to our last concert and escorts the trunk back to their office in New York. Then we can return whenever we want and our instruments are waiting for us, safe and sound."

"And when you were in Lima, did you and PR and Aaron stay in the same hotel?"

"God, no! Aaron always likes to stay downtown. He says it has the pulse of real life."

"Something wrong with that?"

"Downtown Lima is old and run-down and not very safe, especially for women and children, and especially after dark. What Aaron really means is that it's got the pulse of real whores. PR and I stayed in Miraflores, a half hour outside the center. It's got nice hotels and shops and the ocean."

"Do you know which hotel he stayed in?"

"No."

"You, his wife with his kid, in the same quartet on the same tour, and you don't know where he stayed?" He immediately regretted not being able to keep the exasperated disbelief out of his voice.

"You seem to be having some difficulty understanding, Mr. Jacobus," Haagen replied. "Let me make it clear for you one more time. Not only don't I know where he stayed, I didn't want to know. Maybe Sheila knows, but I don't ask. Really, I make it my effort to *not* know where he stays. I know exactly who I am, and I know exactly who Aaron is, and I know it is better this way. How's your lunch?"

Unlike Haagen, Jacobus didn't want to change the subject. "So that's the story between you and Kortovsky. But what about the others? What about Yumi?"

There was a pause. Was it for her to sip her tea, or was it for her to choose her words carefully?

"I don't dislike Yumi, Mr. Jacobus, and I know she's a former student of yours, but we try to stick to business and not let any personal entanglements get in the way. Yumi has fantastic technique and she's so musical—I'm sure she got a lot of that from your teaching—but we all have our own personality. It's difficult enough as it is for a viola and second violin to play together in a quartet even when there are no distractions, shall we say."

"The last part is certainly true," said Jacobus, "but I don't buy the 'personal entanglements' stuff. Surely there's somewhere in between being buddy-buddy and not on speaking terms. Something like peaceful co-existence. It's known to exist."

"Well, I think you're aware of the situation Aaron put us all in when Yumi joined the quartet."

Yes, Jacobus had been told by Yumi, but he didn't respond to Haagen, waiting to hear what she would say. He took a swig of his Sapporo.

"Perhaps you aren't then," she continued. "Shortly after Yumi started with us, we were on a cross-country tour. Everyone was very nice to her because she was a welcome change from Crispin. She was so much easier to get along with and she was willing to learn. One day I heard her talking to Aaron. Her voice wasn't her normal voice, probably because it wasn't a normal conversation."

"Go on."

"She told him that she wouldn't tolerate his sexual advances, whether verbal or physical—it sounded to me like it had been both—and either they would have to stop immediately, or she would quit and call an attorney. She told him that in order to retain his respect and the respect of the rest of the quartet, their relationship had to remain professional, and only professional."

That was the advice he had given Yumi, Jacobus recalled, but this was the first he had heard it related back to him. Yumi had rarely mentioned the incident since.

"I'm not an eavesdropper, Mr. Jacobus, but Yumi's tone was not calculated to be confidential. Quite the opposite. So when I heard that conversation I confronted Aaron. That he would cheat on me and take advantage of a young woman in her position, who we had just hired. Aaron exploded. I suppose he didn't care to be raked over the coals by two women in one day..."

Jacobus pictured Haagen smiling over that thought. He picked up his bottle of Sapporo. Somehow, it had gotten empty.

"...but what he said to me was that I was being naïve thinking that Yumi was still a schoolgirl, that she was just an innocent bystander."

Jacobus slammed the bottle to the table.

"I see you also assume Yumi still is a schoolgirl, Mr. Jacobus. Maybe she was when you first taught her, but she's now a grown woman, and a very attractive one at that.

"I don't know if there was any truth to Aaron's excuses or whether he was just lashing out, which wouldn't surprise me, but I decided to take the advice Yumi gave to Aaron, to keep the relationship professional, and only professional."

"What about your 'open lifestyle,' Annika?" countered Jacobus. "It sounds like you want it both ways."

"You're wrong there, Mr. Jacobus. Outside the quartet, that's one thing. We all have our own lives out in the real world, to do as we please. To be free of the music that binds us together with our every breath. But when it comes to playing in a string quartet, Mr. Jacobus, you don't shit where you eat."

"Hence the current relationships."

"Hence is right, Mr. Jacobus. You know, I think it's time to go the rehearsal. I need to get there early to warm up. Shall we walk together?"

Jacobus reached for his wallet.

"I'll take care of it, Mr. Jacobus," said Haagen.

"That's very kind of you."

"That's not the reason."

70

"Why then?" asked Jacobus.

"Because I don't want to owe you anything."

They began their walk down Broadway in silence, Jacobus on Haagen's right. Since Broadway is a diagonal street, it creates little triangular islands as it intersects the otherwise squared grid of Midtown Manhattan's streets and avenues. Approaching the first mini-oasis, Jacobus smelled the aroma of Middle Eastern grilled meat and onions from a vendor's stand—too soon after lunch, he thought with regret—and heard a flock of strolling, cooing pigeons, their wings intermittently fluttering, an indication of someone tossing breadcrumbs in their midst.

"Dylan! Don't touch them! They've got germs!" said a woman in the horrified tone of someone fearing an outbreak of the bubonic plague.

"Tell me about this marketing study Rosenthal mentioned," Jacobus said, thinking about the flock of wild turkeys that roamed his woods, and wondering if they too had germs.

"Oh, that. As I said at the meeting, it was really nothing."

"It didn't sound like nothing the way Carino lasered in on it. It sounded more like something."

"Look, we would never, ever try to fire Pravda. She is our anchor. She's our connection to the past. It's just when Pravda decides to retire, we ask ourselves, what will we do next? What must we do to make ourselves marketable without compromising our artistic integrity? Because these days, for good or bad, the former has become an essential part of ensuring viability. If we have no viability—in other words, if we fold—it doesn't matter how much integrity we have, does it? And what Crispin has done is twist this around in his mind so he can believe that this—this market study—is the reason we fired him."

"Just out of curiosity, Annika, is Crispin Short an attractive man?"

"If your definition of 'attractive' is a pudgy, pasty, five-foot-tall bald Englishman," she said. "I can guess what you're thinking. 'Wouldn't someone rather pay for a ticket to see an Asian beauty in a tight dress?' But please remember that we didn't know what the results of the study would be when we asked Sheila to do it, so how could anyone accuse us of intentionally forcing Crispin out of the quartet? And should Yumi be penalized because she happens to be good-looking? And plays better than Crispin? Ouch! Crispin!"

"He couldn't have been that bad," said Jacobus.

"No. It *is* Crispin. What are you doing here, Crispin? Let go of my arm. Have you been following us?"

"Why is Lensky playing with you now, love?" came a whiny voice from the other side of Haagen. It was also panting, suggesting to Jacobus the degree of exertion required of pudgy, pasty Short to catch up with them.

"It's none of your business who plays with us. You should know that by now," said Haagen.

"How'd you know Lensky was going to play with them?" asked Jacobus. Short ignored him.

"But it *is* my business, Annika darling. Or weren't you listening to Carino's offer yesterday. I get reinstated, you're off the hook. Otherwise, you get the hook. It would be wonderful to play with you again, Annika, in every way, but you don't have too many chances left. Fair warning. Off to the solicitor. Ta-ta."

"Disgusting, jealous little man," Haagen said after a moment.

"Jealous?"

"Oh, nothing. Let's forget him. Please."

"The joy of quartets," said Jacobus, making Haagen laugh in a joyless sort of way.

"Have you heard the story of when Crispin broke Aaron's bow at a rehearsal?" she asked.

"No! Shit!" Jacobus said in disgust, the scent of the souvlaki replaced by another.

"Yes, it's true!"

"No," repeated Jacobus. "I just stepped in dog shit."

"So you have." This time Haagen's laughter was genuine. "Here, let me help you." She escorted Jacobus to a nearby bench, took off Jacobus's shoe, found a stick, scraped out as much of the offending excrement as possible, discarded the stick in a trash can, and replaced Jacobus's shoe on his foot.

"That's one of the advantages of living out in the country," he said. "You can let your dog out to crap in the woods. I'll be smelling this for the next week. What were we talking about?"

"I've forgotten."

"Whatever. Are you rehearsing the Smetana quartet today?" he continued.

"No, just Schubert. Why?"

"You mentioned you were doing it for an outreach. I've always enjoyed your playing of the viola solo in the beginning of the Smetana. Better than Trampler, Hillyer, even Michael Tree in my humble opinion. You play it with balls."

"I appreciate the sentiment, Mr. Jacobus, but I find your choice of words insulting."

"Oh?"

"Yes. Half of the life force of this earth is the feminine. We're as capable as men are of expressing power and passion, as you've just acknowledged. I could just as appropriately tell you, Mr. Jacobus, that you play with cunt. Now, don't you find that disgusting and offensive?"

Jacobus laughed. "You have a point," he said.

She added, "You may want to come tomorrow to the Rose Grimes and hear our Smetana program. It's one we've done a lot for students, and I'll admit that it is my favorite viola solo."

"Because it's so passionate?" asked Jacobus.

"No," said Haagen, "because the others have no choice but to follow me!"

Chapter Ten

Haagen opened the Fifty-sixth Street stage door for Jacobus. It had been more than a decade —could it really have been that long?—since Yumi first played on the Carnegie Hall stage at a Victoria Jablonski master class and with such unforeseeable consequences. Jacobus shook his head at the irony that after that first disastrous performance, here was Yumi now, a veteran of this legendary stage. Though he hadn't been to the hall for a few years, it was as if he were visiting an old friend's familiar living room.

As he stepped inside, he heard a voice. "Yeah, buddy?" it said. Ah! The security guard, with the tone of voice that almost unaccountably aroused in Jacobus a spontaneous rage, the voice that had no comprehension of the value of what it was guarding, that treated encroachers on its turf as an a priori enemy engaged in class warfare, that relished the abuse of insubstantial authority for no good reason and no good end. It reminded him of his parents' fate. But here at Carnegie Hall!

"There's no panhandling on these premises," the voice persisted.

Jacobus raised his cane.

"Who the—"

Jacobus felt Haagen's hand on his arm. "It's okay, officer," she said, interceding.

"And who may you be, Annie Sullivan?" said the guard. Jacobus heard a second male stifle a laugh. A stagehand perhaps.

"That's very witty," said Haagen. Before Jacobus had a chance to tell the guard to go fuck himself, she continued. "My name is not Annie Sullivan. It is Annika Haagen," she said politely. "The violist of the New Magini String Quartet. This is my colleague, the renowned teacher, Daniel Jacobus. We're here for a rehearsal. Now it's your turn to tell me your name, because I'm going to have you fired."

Jacobus heard the buzzer as the inner door into the hall was unlocked. He felt Haagen take his arm in hers. "Schmucks," she said in her lovely accent, as she led him along the carpeted corridor into the near-empty main hall.

Afternoons at Carnegie were usually quiet affairs, empty but for musicians rehearsing or hall employees picking up last night's programs or dusting off the seats. Today Jacobus sensed a good deal more bustle–lots of shuffling around, mezza voce conversations, equipment being hauled and hoisted.

"What gives?" asked Jacobus. "What's all the commotion?"

"Getting ready for the big production. This is our first rehearsal with combined forces. Dancers getting into position. The film screen's being hooked up at the back of the stage with lots of wires. I hope it doesn't fall on us."

"What film?"

"I'm sure Power will tell you all about it," Haagen said.

The ghosts of all the great—no, greatest—musicians who came from around the world to make their names in this place must be rolling in their collective graves, Jacobus thought. From the world premiere of Dvořák's "New World" Symphony in 1893, to this multimedia travesty! Maybe they should have torn down the place back in '60 and saved it from this fate.

"If you see a black man out there in the seats, that's my friend Nathaniel," said Jacobus. "He might've arrived by now."

"A large black man?" asked Haagen.

"Extra-large."

"With white hair?"

"Jesus! He's got white hair?"

Haagen led Jacobus about halfway down the hall. Nathaniel, typically, was sitting one seat in from the aisle, in order to accommodate Jacobus's preference to sit directly on the aisle, where he wouldn't have to trip over

75

other concertgoers, making a nuisance of himself. Haagen excused herself to go warm up before the rehearsal.

"So how was Flushing?" Jacobus asked Nathaniel without preamble.

"Flushing? I just got back from three hours in Mother Russia!" said Nathaniel. "You should see Lenskaya's house. Every inch is loaded with stuff—there was an army of those Russian dolls that fit inside each other."

"Matryoshka."

"No, it's true! And the Fabergé eggs too. Not the real, expensive stuff. Just low-cost, souveniry. Keepsakes, but, Mama, you cook make a million Egg MacMuffinskies with them. From the outside you think, now here's just another modest semidetached house in Queens. But then you go inside with the rugs and the heavy curtains and the old furniture and the cut glass and all the tchotchkes—"

"That's Yiddish, not Russian," said Jacobus.

"Maybe, but they were still tchotchkes!" said Nathaniel. "One interesting thing was all the autographed photos in her study. You know I like that stuff. Must have been a hundred. Black and whites of her with musicians she played with in Russia. David Oistrakh, Sviatoslav Richter, Kurt Sanderling. Even Dmitri Shostakovich. You name it."

"Mstislav Rostropovich?"

"Last but not least. Seeing the two of them together in a photo, it's no surprise they nicknamed her Mrs. Slav."

"I thought it had to do with the way she played."

"I'm sure it does, and if she were male she probably would've been as famous a cellist as he is. But I must say, even though she's a little younger, the resemblance is pretty striking."

"Too bad for her. He's got an underbite like a piranha. She's probably not too thrilled with a nickname like that."

"Actually, she said she thinks 'Mrs. Slav' is pretty funny. And a compliment. In fact she was telling me, as we drank tea from her samovar—"

"You must be kidding."

"—she was saying that she emulated Rostropovich in all ways. He was a national hero—"

"Till he defected, anyway."

"Cynic. Even so, his passionate musicianship, his technique, his overall approach to the cello were contagious. She even uses the same type of bent endpin he does."

"The kind that makes the cello look like a narwhal?"

"Yeah. I never went for that when I was still performing. I tried it, but it made the cello more parallel to the floor so my left arm got sore extending it forward rather than down, which, it seems to me, is much more natural."

"Why do they bother with it, then?"

"The advantage is that your right arm can work with gravity to get the bow into the string, making it easier to get a big sound. I suppose if you're a career soloist, it might make sense. But she's thinking of switching away from it."

"Why?" asked Jacobus. "She getting tendinitis in her left arm?"

"Yes, but not for that reason. Some cellists say the brand of endpin she uses gets stuck when you slide it back into the instrument when you finish playing and are putting the cello back in the case. Maybe that has to do with the bend. Lenskaya said hers has been such a pain since she got back from the tour, it's giving her tendinitis just trying to maneuver it."

"You cellists, with the endpins! At least that's one thing violinists don't have to worry about."

"You might want to try it. Just stick it through your neck. It'll help you hold up your fiddle."

"Thank you for your suggestion. No wonder you went into insurance. Do you have anything worthwhile to share?" asked Jacobus, getting impatient. "Anything about Kortovsky? Remember *him*?"

"Not really. She talked my ear off about the good old days when they were starving under Communism and how, after rehearsing in the orchestra all day, they'd rehearse quartets at three in the morning with candlelight when it was twenty below and the wolves were howling outside the door, but she didn't seem to want to talk about the current situation."

"So, nothing interesting?"

"Well, maybe, two things, but they have nothing to do with Kortovsky.

Guess where the original Magini Quartet's from?"

"Russia."

"I mean where in Russia? The original group, with Lenskaya, Vissman, Vladimir Greunig, and Lipinsky."

"I give up. Moscow."

"Nope."

"St. Petersburg."

"Guess again."

"For Chrissakes, Nathaniel. Chernobyl! They were based in goddam Chernobyl! Okay?"

"Jake, pipe down! They haven't even started rehearsing and you're gonna get us kicked out. But you got it! That's where they're from. Everyone thinks Moscow because they studied there when they were younger, but they all had homes in Chernobyl. They were on tour in Europe in '86 and were thinking about seeking asylum because they're Jews—"

"Wait a second," said Jacobus. " Lenskaya's not a Jewish name."

"No, but her husband's a Jew. Was. That made her Jewish as far as Big Brother was concerned. When the reactor blew while they were on tour, that just iced the cake. They were afraid to go back for political *and* health reasons."

"But what about the husband?"

"His name was Yurlinsky. Marin Yurlinsky, an engineer at the plant. According to Lenskaya, he tried to warn his superiors that there was a danger of a catastrophe. Shoddy workmanship and shoddy oversight. Needless to say, they didn't listen to him, and afterwards to cover their tracks they sent him back into the contaminated site to restore order."

"And?"

"And he died within four months, of radiation poisoning. All the other workers who went in and died became heroes. Yurlinsky became disappeared."

"Any pictures of him on her walls?"

"I don't know. Could be. There were a bunch of framed black-and-white photos in one of her tchotchke cases. They looked like family stuff. Might've been her and her husband with two little boys, but the pictures were kind of old. They could've been friends or relatives."

Jacobus heard footsteps, heavy and officious, approaching. Someone familiar with the territory. Maybe they would be getting kicked out.

"What was the second thing?" asked Jacobus.

"What second thing?"

"You said there were two interesting things."

Jacobus felt a tap on his shoulder.

"Excuse me, sir. The two of you can't sit here. You'll have to move."

"C'mon, Jake," said Nathaniel.

"And why is that?" asked Jacobus. Notwithstanding the recent exchange with the security guard, Jacobus was incapable of allowing the owner of a voice in charge to take it for granted that he was, in fact, in charge.

"Because these seats are for the dancers."

"I always thought dancers dance. Since when do dancers sit?"

Another voice entered the conversation.

"Is there a problem, Mehmet?" said a voice that sounded higher up the food chain. Overtly cultured, thought Jacobus. Elitist, almost. Authoritative, though.

"This gentleman refuses to vacate," said the voice called Mehmet.

"We're guests of the quartet," said Nathaniel in a tone that suggested hope for reconciliation without contradicting his friend's intransigence.

"Ah, you must be Mr. Jacobus and Mr. Williams," said voice number two. "I'll take it from here, Mehmet. Just tell Jonel and Fern to sit one row up… Better make that two." The voice called Mehmet was now footsteps called Mehmet, and Jacobus heard them draw away toward the stage.

"My apologies for the upset, gentleman. My name is—"

"Power Ramsey," said Jacobus.

"How did you ever know that?" asked Ramsey.

"Good guess, I guess."

"Well, I hope you'll enjoy our little production, here. In all the years I've been director of The Movement I don't think I've ever been so excited about an event."

"Tell me about it." Jacobus intended his tone to be dismissive, but Ramsey's next remark was right at his ear level, so Ramsey must have missed the sarcasm and instead knelt down to respond. Losing my touch, Jacobus thought.

"No doubt you know 'Death and the Maiden' far more deeply than I," said Ramsey. "In fact, when I began to conceive this piece I came to think of myself as Everyman—"

"That's hard to believe."

"Well, perhaps Everyman who also knows how to choreograph."

"Dancingman, shall we say?"

"Shush, Jake," said Nathaniel. "Let the man talk."

"And it occurred to me that Schubert's music was so profound, so powerful, that it could accommodate a multidisciplinary treatment and not be marginalized in the process."

"Hence the dog and pony show?"

"An amusing euphemism. My vision is to universalize the music's life-and-death embrace, so the big-screen montage of photochoreography—"

"Slide show."

"Oh, no, Mr. Jacobus. No, no. A slide show would be demeaning. Photochoreography is an art unto itself. It has as much ebb and flow as music, as dance, as—"

"Talking. Go on."

"Yes, our montage will be of moments frozen in time—"

"Snapshots."

"—of genocide. World War II, Cambodia, Rwanda—that tragedy still so fresh in our minds and hearts. Millions, young and old, consumed by death before their time. Sometimes graphic, sometimes subtle, depending on the course of the music."

"Of course."

"And then, because Death is no stranger, and the bringers of death are so often among us— are they not?—the dancers will emerge from the audience itself."

"That wouldn't be because backstage at Carnegie is too cramped for dancers, would it?" asked Jacobus.

Ramsey forged on, apparently undaunted by Jacobus, who was increasingly exasperated that his jibes hadn't been sufficient to get this guy to shut up.

"They will be strategically seated in dozens of loci around the hall—including the very seat in which you now find yourself, Mr. Jacobus—emerging from their positions only in the final movement, their bodies fully covered in formfitting white Lycra. As the music shifts from timbre to timbre, multicolored lighting will irradiate their costumes, transporting them through the entire spectrum, a metaphor of the passage from life to death, through light. And the coup d'grâce, Mr. Jacobus: One by one each dancer will select an unsuspecting partner from the audience to join in a dance of deadly embrace, culminating in a collapsing human spiral directly in front of the musicians at the same instant the music and photochoreography end."

"Deadly embrace is right," said Jacobus. "You get enough of those overweight investment bankers doing their dipsy-doodles, and one of them'll either have a heart attack or their BO will asphyxiate the whole audience."

"Thank you for that word of caution, Mr. Jacobus. I'll be sure to take it to the planning committee. For now, though, the plan is for the hall to go completely dark for a frightening moment to set the stage, so to speak, for an archival film of Marian Anderson singing 'Death and the Maiden.' I don't know if you've ever heard it—it's recently been rediscovered and reprocessed—but it gives me the heebie-jeebies every time I see it. Once that's over, the lights will come on and—"

"Why all the dohickeys?" asked Jacobus.

"Meaning?"

"The dancers, the light show, the...photochoreography. It's like tarting up the *Mona Lisa* in mascara and hot pants. Don't you think Schubert's music would be better served to be heard without any distractions? After all, you said it was because the music was so profound and powerful that you were attracted to it in the first place. Why diddle with perfection?"

"Mr. Jacobus, music and dance have been inextricably intertwined for eons, ever since the caveman struck two sticks together to create rhythm for sacred movements—their rites to keep the predators at bay, the fire going, the gods appeased. It has remained thus ever since. One discipline lends itself to the other. Rhythm and movement. As for the light and the visual, just picture in your mind's eye, if you will, Neolithic man dancing around the fire. The reflection of light on the cave wall. The primordial essence. I have tried to capture it. What is more basic than life and death, Mr. Jacobus?

"Some people call my multidisciplinary work 'enhancements.' I fancy calling them 'enchantments.' Some people have called me an artist of vision—"

"Which leaves me on the outside looking in," Jacobus interrupted. "No hard feelings, but I'll have to pass on the enchantments and settle for only the music, and it sounds to me like the quartet's starting to tune up for it right now."

"Ah, yes! So they are. Excuse me," said Ramsey. "I would love to tell you more about my..."

"Vision," said Jacobus.

"Yes, but now I must rush off."

"Sorry you've got to go."

Once the sound of his footsteps disappeared, Jacobus said to Nathaniel, "See, blindness has it rewards. He can shove his photochoreography up his—"

"So let me tell you the second thing in fifty words or less before the quartet starts rehearsing," said Nathaniel. "Lenskaya has a garage attached to her house. Coming from inside it I heard one of the songs from 'Winterreise.' I thought it was the recording of Goerne singing and Brendel on piano."

"Someone has good taste. So what?"

"Jake, it was Schubert's 'Winterreise' coming out of a garage! In Queens!"

"Which song?"

"Not sure. There are twenty-four in the cycle. It's hard to remember them all."

"Sing the melody."

"All right." Nathaniel cleared his throat and discreetly hummed a plaintively despairing melody in a lustrous tenor, beautifully in tune, with a mellow, deeply felt vibrato.

"My, you're in fine voice."

"I've been singing in a gospel choir," said Nathaniel.

"Since when?"

"Since we got to know Rose Grimes. She really loved her choir so I thought I'd try it out. I go every Sunday morning."

"You really like that stuff?"

"No, I just sing it because I'm an oppressed, six-figure–earning black man. Actually I hate it. Any more stupid questions?"

"That was pretty dumb, huh?"

"Uh-huh. For your information, I've also been teaching cello and music theory at the Rose Grimes School."

"No shit. I thought you locked your cello in the closet for good, years ago."

"I did, until Yumi and BTower talked me into dusting it off and giving some of those Harlem kids lessons. BTower was right; between him on violin and me on cello, that's about half the professional black classical musicians in the city. He said he thought I'd be 'an inspiring role model.' "

"I wouldn't go that far."

"Well, you wouldn't be the one to talk, then, neither. So do you know the song or not?"

" '*Eisenamkeit*,' " Jacobus said. " 'Loneliness,' " whereupon he immediately supplied the text in German, then in English: " 'As a dark cloud passing through serene skies, as through the fir tops a feeble breeze blows: Thus I wend my way with heavy tread through bright and joyous life, alone and ungreeted. Must the—' "

"Well, I'll be amazed and blessed!" said Nathaniel. "How did you know that right off the bat like that?"

"When we were students at Oberlin?"

"Yes?"

"There was this girl I was trying to impress."

"Helen?" Nathaniel guessed, thinking of Helen Kaufman, who had been the pianist in their trio for many years.

"Nah, another one, a singer," said Jacobus, already ruing having brought up the subject. "Paula something. She loved Schubert."

"Nice voice?"

"Big tits."

"Oh!" said Nathaniel. "So did you impress her?"

"Not enough."

Like a vicious saber cut, the first five notes of "Death and the Maiden" sliced through their conversation, bringing their ability and desire to talk further to a swift halt. Jacobus could tell from the first extended phrase that Ivan Lensky was a violinist to be reckoned with, adept at combining virtuoso technique with musical personality. He could tell from the second phrase, however, the truth of what had been said about Lensky as a chamber musician. Lensky seemed to have little notion that center stage was no longer his, refusing to allow the inner voices, the second violin and viola, to take over the reins when the music called for it. Was this a case of inflated ego, or, Jacobus wondered, was it simply artistic intransigence? As the music progressed, Lensky seemed to be trying to make the point that he was the star and the others the supporting cast. Not only was that kind of musical narcissism the kiss of death for the psyche of a quartet, it made it almost physically impossible for the musicians to hear what they needed to in order to play together. Butting heads with Kortovsky, the reputed arch-manipulator, would have created a combustible relationship. Jacobus now understood the wisdom of the selection of Yumi over Lensky for the second-violin position, even though as a soloist the latter might be able to pull off the Tchaikovsky Concerto with greater dazzle and panache. But Lensky apparently couldn't tell the difference between a concerto and quartet.

Extrapolating from Lensky's playing, which combined raw power with less enviable unrefined musical glossiness, Jacobus pictured a young, strongly built man, maybe late twenties. From his ostentatiously confident facility combined with blatant disregard for the other musicians, Jacobus envisioned someone of overt egotism, someone who liked—Jacobus corrected himself—someone who *needed* to be noticed above others, so to his mental image Jacobus tossed in a black turtleneck and a gold Rolex.

At first, what little discussion among the quartet that was audible to Jacobus was perfunctory, limited to very basic issues of ensemble and intonation. Jacobus could think of several reasons for the laconic exchanges: One, they were simply sticking to the game plan of coordinating the music with all the "enchantments"; two, they knew that as soon as Kortovsky returned they wouldn't have to bother with Lensky anyway; three, it was a wasted effort to get Lensky to change; and four, they didn't like talking to each other to begin with.

Little by little the comments among the quartet became more and more pointed and animated, and as a result, louder. Most of it was between Haagen and Lensky. Yumi said little. Lenskaya nothing at all.

"Why you make ritardanda?" argued Lensky, finishing off the Italian words that ended in *o* with a heavily inflected Russian accent, so that ritardando became ritardanda. "Is impossible to play spiccatissima when you make ritardanda." To Jacobus's ear, the comment was not so much belligerent as it was surprise that the three others weren't doing Lensky's bidding.

"Ivan," said Haagen. "We've decided to play that *on* the string. We like the notes a bit longer so you can actually hear a tone. That might be why you thought it was getting slower, but that's the way we've done it for years. After all, it's Schubert." There was a moment of dramatic silence. "It's not Rossini."

Ah, thought Jacobus, actually rubbing his hands together in anticipation. Now it begins! Throwing down the gauntlet, and so soon! He knew those last three words by Haagen, "It's not Rossini," were a thinly veiled and no doubt intentional insult to Lensky's musicianship, suggesting he didn't understand the difference between Schubert's dark profundity and Rossini's opera buffa congeniality. Haagen had probably taken that brief pause to decide whether or not it was worth firing the shot off the bow. Would Lensky take the bait or would he respond diplomatically? If the latter, the rehearsal could probably proceed constructively, but Lensky would lose face. From what he'd constructed of Lensky's personality, if the other three musicians had been men, Lensky might have been inclined to back down, but...

"I see," said Lensky. "What you say is, Schubert is Schubert. Rossini is Rossini..."

Maybe I was wrong, Jacobus thought.

"And shit is shit," Lensky added.

Ah.

Distracting Jacobus from the main event was the approach of the cosmetics counter from Bloomingdales.

"Mr. Jacobus?" He felt a light touch on his shoulder.

"Yeah." His eyes began to tear and his tobacco-frayed lungs began to wheeze. Even his congested nose was no match for the excessive perfume that was now giving him an allergic reaction from hell.

"I'm Sheila. Sheila Rathman. InHouseArtists."

He regretted having to turn his attention from the rest of the quartet's love spat, but he could predict a stalemate. In any event, he needed information from Rathman.

"May I have a seat?"

"As many as you want."

Rathman's polite titter conveyed some uncertainty whether his intent had been facetious; regardless, he did detect her fragrant self waft to the seat in front of him.

"I just wanted to find out if you've made any progress finding Aaron," she said, with more than a little concern. Must've just heard the exchange between Lensky and Haagen, thought Jacobus, which would add to any manager's ulcer.

"Not really."

"None at all?"

"What do I look like, *Have Gun, Will Travel*?"

"Well, is there anything you can tell me?"

"There are some things you can tell *me*. Number one, you told Nathaniel that the last you heard from Kortovsky was at the end of the tour."

"Yes."

"When at the end of the tour?"

"After the last concert. The one in Lima."

"What did he say?"

"He didn't really say anything."

"Then what didn't he really say?"

"It wasn't a phone call. It was an email. Two emails."

"Whatever. Honey, you want to obfuscate, fine. But go waste someone else's time. I want to listen to a little Schubert."

"Let's just say they were personal messages, then," said Rathman. "But Aaron indicated he was planning on being back by now."

Jacobus, well-disposed to stubbornness and sensing there was more Rathman had to say, persevered through an increasingly uncomfortable silence, during which the quartet had stopped playing. Either they were taking a short break or, possibly, a permanent one.

She gave in and filled the void. "But I've deleted the messages."

"Well," said Jacobus. "I don't know anything about computers or these emails, but I presume in this day and age they can be undeleted. After all, this ain't Watergate and you're not Rose Mary Woods. So we'll need to see the email, and we'll need to find out if he sent or received emails or phone calls to or from anyone else after his little love note to you."

"I don't think that's possible," said Rathman.

"What don't you think's possible? That they can be undeleted, or that there were communications after his little love note?"

"Please don't refer to it that way," Rathman said. Jacobus could almost feel the heat from Rathman's cheeks leach through and melt her makeup. "It really wasn't like that. But what I mean is that we don't know his user names or passwords to get into his server. Maybe if we could figure these out—"

"I don't know what the hell you're talking about, but you better get someone on that right away." Nathaniel. Yes, he was the one who could do that task.

"Hey, Nathaniel," Jacobus shouted, but his voice echoed in the hall with the only response being an anonymous voice shouting back, "Quiet!" When the hell had Nathaniel left?

"Is there anything else, Mr. Jacobus?"

"You need to open Kortovsky's instrument trunk."

"I'm sorry. We can't do that."

"Hey, do you want to find out where he is, or are you trying to make sure he stays MIA?"

"It's just that we don't have the combination—"

"Drill."

"The insurance company won't let anyone other than the owner open the trunks. It will void the policy, and if the instrument has been damaged… And it's an Amati!" she said, as if that explained everything. "Why do you need that, anyway?"

"According to Haagen—you know, his wife—if the members of the quartet were planning on vacationing at the end of the tour, they would put their instruments in the trunk to be picked up upon their return. If they were planning on coming back right away, they would more likely take the instrument with them on the plane. So if Kortovsky's fiddle is in the trunk, there's a greater probability that he actually did go off rock climbing. If it's not in the trunk it might be more likely that he's holed up in this neck of the woods because he would have taken it on a plane with him."

"I'll see what I can do."

"You do that. One more thing, since you've been so helpful."

"What's that?"

"What hotel was Kortovsky staying at in Lima?"

"I don't know."

"Oh, please."

"Really. I don't. The musicians book their accommodations themselves and send me the bill for reimbursement later."

Jacobus fumed, trying to figure how he was going to tell Ochoa Romero he couldn't discover even the simplest information, but apparently Rathman thought his silence meant he wasn't buying her answer, so she added, "I can tell you where the other three stayed because they sent me their receipts, but I can't tell you Aaron's."

"Thanks. You've been a doll."

Suddenly someone grasped the back of his neck with extraordinary strength and twisted it in directions Jacobus didn't think anatomically possible, reminding him why he would never go to a chiropractor.

"Ha!" laughed the voice that belonged to the hand that now released its powerful grip.

Jacobus recombined the voice, the accent, the strength, and the attitude.

"Ah, Lensky," said Jacobus. He rubbed the back of his neck. "What a pleasure."

"So, Mr. Jacobus, you like Sheila? She can make a man happy. Ha-ha!"

"I have to go," said Rathman.

Jacobus heard the seat on which Rathman had been sitting spring up with a thump and her footsteps retreat with far greater alacrity than when she had arrived.

"So, how you like quartet?" Lensky continued, with the accent on the *quar* and a *v* instead of a *u*. "Schubert, what great composer! Like Shostakovich. You and I know this. We are colleagues. We are *moo-zee-shns*. I know all about you. You understand this." He slapped Jacobus on the back hard enough to leave fingerprints and laughed. Jacobus checked his dentures to make sure they hadn't fallen out and prayed he might survive Lensky's sense of humor.

Jacobus had no idea what Lensky knew "all about" him, but he let that pass, along with his chutzpah to refer to Jacobus, about forty years his senior, as his colleague.

Rather, he asked, "Seems you had a slight disagreement with the violist."

Lensky laughed again. "Bah! What they know about *ar-teek-uh-lay-shn*? Schubert, he writes dots. Da! Da! Da! Staccatissima! This is important. They play woo-woo-woo. This is not staccatissima. That is borscht. My mother, she knows right way, but doesn't play."

"Why not?"

"Because then she lose her job. This is the way things work. I say you more but now I go work."

"Yeah? What you say me?" asked Jacobus, testing how far he could push Lensky's insensitivity.

"Ha!" said Lensky. "You have accent, too! I know, for example, where is Kortovsky."

"Really?"

"Sure, but you meet me later. Seven o'clock."

"Sorry. Have to walk dog." That was a lie, but he would want to talk to Nathaniel before meeting with Lensky. "Make it nine. Where?"

"My friend, he has place for drinking. Private. Musicians only. Guys. Forty-eighth Street and Ninth Avenue. Downstairs. Name Circle of Fifths. My guest."

Before Jacobus could respond, a massive whack on his back propelled him forward. If he hadn't instinctively put his hands in front of him, his head would have been driven into the back of the seat so recently vacated by Rathman.

Forceful though the shove was, in Jacobus's mind it wasn't close to being sufficiently violent to have elicited the scream that immediately ensued. From his limited experience with screams, they meant one of three things: pain, fear, or revulsion. This one, from the vicinity of the stage, didn't sound like pain. Rather, it seemed to contain equal parts of fear and revulsion. Maybe more revulsion. He heard footsteps approach him down the aisle, first walking fast, then running, then slowing down to a walk again.

"Mr. Jacobus—"

It was Ramsey.

"Please come with me," he said, apparently forgetting, or ignoring, Ivan Lensky. "Yumi has found something in Annika's case."

"What? A dead viola?"

"No," said Ramsey, as if Jacobus's suggestion was serious. "No, it is something dead. That's true..."

"Come on, Power. You've got the gift of gab. Spit it out like a good boy."

"It's an appendage..."

No. It couldn't be, thought Jacobus. It just couldn't.

"What kind of appendage?"

"It's a finger."

It could.

Chapter Eleven

"All I wanted was to hear a little Schubert," Jacobus lamented. And where the hell was Nathaniel? Momentarily disoriented, he felt a strong grip on his arm.

"Let's go," said Ivan Lensky, "we go see what was," and ushered Jacobus through the burgeoning chaos toward the backstage area. Panicked dancers from The Movement flitted around them, careening into each other like so many leotarded bumper cars. One of them, maybe it was Fern, whispered to another that she had been told "by Conrad" that Power Ramsey had planned the whole scenario with a fake finger to put everyone on edge for the performance. "You know, like bring us closer to the *d*-word." Wishful thinker, Conrad.

By the time they arrived backstage, the police, amazingly enough, were already there. Lensky deposited Jacobus in a chair against the wall in between the curtain ropes and sandbags. Before departing to find his mother, he reminded Jacobus to meet him later at the Circle of Fifths. "This," he said, referring to the current chaos, "is all part of Kortovsky big plan. I say to you tonight."

The next voice directed at him was all too familiar, and though Jacobus would have chosen to ignore it, he knew it was futile.

"Why am I not surprised to see you here?" the voice said, with a combined inflection of Manhattan, Jewish, and cop.

"Perhaps, Detective Malachi, because nothing would surprise an investigator of your talents."

"Do I detect a note of sarcasm?"

"You're the detective. You figure it out."

"Lieutenant," a young Hispanic voice interrupted. "We've got the lady that found the finger."

Jacobus jumped in. "Was it a real finger?" He immediately knew he sounded like an idiot.

"No, Jacobus. It was a pretend finger. That's why we're here on this pretend assignment."

Jacobus heard the other cop stifle a laugh as he continued. "We're still looking for the one whose case it was in. Hogan? Hagen? But here comes the other one."

"Well, if it isn't Miss Shinagawa!" said Malachi. "I should've guessed. I should call the two of you Smoke and Fire."

Jacobus said, "I should call you—"

He felt Yumi's dexterous hand cover his mouth. She said, "You wanted to talk to me, Lieutenant?"

"I need to ask you a few questions."

Yumi remained silent, so Malachi cleared his throat and asked, "What were you doing inside Haagen's case?"

"I needed to borrow some rosin."

"Where was yours?"

"I forgot it. I left it at home."

"Go on."

"I answered your question."

"Why did you need rosin? Why did you need *her* rosin?"

"I just got my bow rehaired—"

"By who?"

"By Tom Stevenson—"

"You'll give us his address. Go on."

"And when you get new hair you need a lot of rosin, otherwise you don't get a sound from the violin. It doesn't grab onto the string. So I needed more rosin."

"You don't need to instruct me about rosin. I used to play the violin."

"Like hell," muttered Jacobus.

"What was that?" Malachi asked. Receiving no response, he continued. "I also know that violin and viola rosin are different. So why didn't you borrow Lensky's?"

"I hardly know Ivan."

"You're just borrowing rosin. It's not like you're sleeping with him."

"She's not sleeping with Haagen, either, Sherlock," Jacobus burst in. "But she's worked with her for years and felt more comfortable borrowing her fucking viola rosin."

"Look, Jacobus—"

"Why don't you just ask everyone around here to show you their goddam hands and see who's missing a finger instead of wasting—"

"It's okay, Jake," said Yumi. "The rest of the rehearsal's been canceled anyway. We've got time. What else would you like to know, Lieutenant?"

"Why didn't you ask Haagen if you could borrow the rosin?"

"She was still onstage talking to Pravda. I didn't think it was necessary to disturb them over such a small thing."

"Tell me what you did after you opened the case."

"I didn't open the case."

"Then how did you get the rosin? Levitation?"

"That's a toughie," laughed Jacobus derisively. "You've been watching too many reruns of *The F.B.I.*, Malachi. Obviously, the case was already open."

"Shut up, Jacobus."

"Hey, is Efrem Zimbalist Jr. your role model? Good-looking guy! Did you know," Jacobus continued, "that his father, Efrem Zimbalist, Sr., was a renowned violin teacher at the Curtis Institute? It's true. Look it up."

"There are two differences between you and Zimbalist, Sr.," said Malachi.

"Really! And what would those be?" asked Jacobus.

"He's renowned and dead. But pretty soon there'll only be one difference. He'll still be renowned. Now, Miss Shinagawa, how did you get the rosin?"

"There's a compartment in the case for extra strings, rosin, mutes. Accessories. I opened that up and..."

"And saw a finger."

"Yes. It was disgusting."

"And you screamed."

"Of course she screamed!" said Jacobus. "What the hell would—"

He felt her restraining grip on his arm, not so soft this time.

"Yes. I suppose so," she said.

"Well, everyone else in the hall says you did, so I'll suppose that too. But you did something before you screamed. Didn't you?"

Yumi did not respond.

"Miss Shinagawa, you were seen doing something before you screamed. What was it?"

Still Yumi paused. This time Malachi waited.

"Yes, I suppose I picked up the finger."

"You were seen holding the finger. Were you picking it up or were you placing it in the case?"

"Malachi!" said Jacobus.

Malachi ignored Jacobus. "Let's say for the sake of argument you did pick it up. You're telling me you saw that disgusting, repulsive dead finger, picked it up, and only then screamed? Why did you have it in your hands, Miss Shinagawa? To examine it? Maybe you know the party to whom the finger belongs?"

Jacobus now understood Yumi's reticence. She had been trying to protect herself, and him.

"She thought it was a joke!" he exploded.

"What?" said Malachi, the surprise in his voice genuine. "I know you classical musician types have a warped—"

"Just shut up for a minute," said Jacobus. "I'll explain."

Jacobus told him about the prank he had pulled on Yumi in the train. Yumi added that when she first saw the finger in Haagen's case she assumed it would be some kind of variation of the joke, that maybe Jacobus had been part of it. That is, until she actually picked it up and saw that it was real. And dead.

"So that's your explanation," said Malachi, "why your fingerprints will now be found all over the finger."

"And why the finger's prints will be found on Yumi," said Jacobus.

94

"That's not funny," said Yumi and Malachi in unison.

"Where's Haagen?" Malachi continued.

"I don't know," said Yumi. "I put the finger back in her case. I guess I didn't want her to know I'd seen it, but it was too late. She heard me scream and came backstage. Then when she saw it, she just turned and left."

"Leaving her precious viola in the case?"

"Along with the finger. Yes."

"I assume it's a valuable instrument."

"I believe so."

"How likely is it, Miss Shinagawa, that a serious musician would walk away from her priceless instrument, to which she is no doubt closely attached, leaving the case open with all this commotion? As we know," he said, his voice insinuating, "even Stradivarius violins have been stolen right from their cases."

"Yeah," said Jacobus, "and we also know that Yo-Yo Ma once left his Stradivarius cello in a taxi, and that's a skosh bigger than a violin, so get off it. You know, I'd give you the finger except someone's already done me the favor."

"We found this, Lieutenant." It was the voice of the young Hispanic cop.

"Tell me about it," said Malachi.

"It's her handkerchief. Haagen's. The Russian lady, the cello player, ID'd it. We found it in the bathroom."

"How long's it been there?"

Yumi interjected. "Annika uses that to cover her chin rest when she plays—it's silk—so she won't get a blister on her neck. She's got sensitive skin. She had that during the first part of the rehearsal."

"So when she sees the finger she goes to the ladies' room with her handkerchief to do what? To gag? To puke? To freshen up? Any signs of vomit, Ortiz?"

"I'll take a look," he said, without enthusiasm.

"You do that. What else?"

"That's it. No one's seen her. They all came running here, along with the security guard, when they heard the scream."

"Security guard see anyone suspicious? Anyone unauthorized?"

"Yeah, we asked him that. Only this blind guy here."

"Okay, keep looking."

"I say the concert should be canceled," Jacobus said.

"Why?" asked Yumi. Jacobus discerned a distinct tone of protest in her voice.

"Because when you find a finger in a viola case, this is not a good sign. It doesn't matter who put it there. Whether Haagen did, or Kortovsky did, or Short did, or even you did. It doesn't matter because the meaning is the same. It means danger. Maybe a warning that someone doesn't like what is going on. So for everyone's safety, I repeat, the concert should be canceled."

"Are you sure," asked Yumi, "that you're not just making up a reason because you're so opposed to the production?"

"What are you talking about?"

"Only that you're so traditional when it comes to how music should be performed that you'd come up with just about any rationale to prevent a different approach. You just seem so obstinate—"

"Traditional! You make that sound like an obscenity, Yumi."

"—that you'd even let my career go under the bus if you could get this concert canceled."

"Excuse me," said Malachi. "As much as I'm enjoying listening to your little spat, I'm going to let the two of you have some private time to work things out, but I'm sure we'll be chatting again."

Malachi left to coordinate the search for Haagen with Ortiz. Jacobus, with a vague thought in his head, asked Yumi sotto voce, "By any chance, could you tell if the finger had been dead for a long time? Or was it a new dead finger? No, I'm not joking."

"How do I know? It was gross and all shriveled up and had turned disgusting colors. Why does it matter?"

"Well, if it's been dead for about a month, and she's had it in her case that long, then maybe—"

Jacobus felt a hand on his shoulder. Larger, stronger even then Lensky's, but gentler.

"Where the hell've you been, Nathaniel?" asked Jacobus. "Coney Island?"

"All that tea at Lenskaya's added up, Jake. I been on the can."

"The ladies' room by any chance?"

"Hell, no! What's up?"

Chapter Twelve

By the time they got back to Nathaniel's ninth-floor apartment, Jacobus had filled him in. "So while you were pishin', Rome could've burned and you'd still be holding your dick."

"It was only fifteen minutes," Nathaniel protested.

"Fifteen, eh? Time flies when you're having a good time."

Jacobus heard Nathaniel switch on the light and immediately backed up against the wall for support, bracing himself for the onslaught. The clattering of claws on the wood floor accelerated with frightening speed as Trotsky barreled into the hallway and leaped on Jacobus, knocking off his dark glasses with a prehensile tongue.

"Get the goddam gorilla off me!" Jacobus cried.

"Down, boy," said Nathaniel, firmly but gently easing the dog of Jacobus. "Can't help lovin' dat man," he crooned.

"Shows you how stupid he is," Jacobus said. He bent down to retrieve his glasses, miraculously intact.

"Want me to walk him?" asked Nathaniel.

"Yeah, or if you want, you can just drop him out the window, but first get me Crispin Short's phone number. Maybe it wasn't a coincidence that Short harassed Haagen an hour before the fickle finger was found in her case. And I'm wondering whether this has anything to do with Kortovsky. And why no one knows where Haagen is. And while you're at it, find out whether Prince Rupert really did go with her to Peru."

"Prince who?"

"Her kid. There shouldn't be too many Prince Ruperts who had a plane reservation to Lima in the last few months."

Nathaniel found Short's number in the phone book and recited it to Jacobus. After waiting until Nathaniel's muttering died away along with the mutt, he dialed the number but got only Short's answering machine, which said, in part, "Please direct any business or legal queries to my attorney," without mentioning the attorney's name. Very helpful. What was it? Marino? Carino? He dialed information, and after seven or eight unsuccessful efforts finally obtained the number for Lewis Carino, attorney. He got hold of Carino just as he was hurrying out the door to go home to his seventeen-room colonial in Chappaqua. In thirty seconds Jacobus managed to convince Carino of the benefit of a meeting with Short as soon as possible the next day, since until they discovered the whereabouts of half the New Magini String Quartet it would be difficult to come to a resolution of the suit, and the sooner they did this, the sooner Carino could make his yacht payment. Carino said he had a fifteen-minute slot the next morning, as long as they could meet in his office.

Jacobus hung up, satisfied, and prepared to make himself a cup of coffee.

The phone rang almost immediately, and Jacobus figured it was Carino calling back to cancel, but instead of a voice saying, "How dare you insinuate my client was involved in alleged criminal activity," a familiar voice said, "*Buenas tardes*, Señor Yacovis."

"Oro?"

"Yes I am!"

"How'd you find me?"

"After all I am a policeman, am I not? I desired to be sure you are really you when I speak to you, so I discovered your home phone number, only to be disappointed you were not there. Then, I think, who can I trust? So I call your local police force—"

"Roy Miller?"

"Exactly so."

"He's also my plumber."

"Ah, the true Renaissance man, this Señor Miller. He tell me your friend's name in New York, this Señor Williams, so I try *cinco, seis, seite*, Nathaniel

Williamses, and here I am. Now that I know you are the *verdadero* Maestro Yacovis, I can talk to you with more free."

"Two questions. How do you know maybe I haven't broken into the *verdadero* Señor Williams's apartment and killed him?"

"It is unlikely, wouldn't you agree, that you would answer the phone and ask me such a question if you had? And the second question?"

Smug little son of a bitch.

"Why is it important you had to confirm I was the *verdadero* Señor Yacovis?

"Ah! You have quite the perspicacious! This I will answer in good time, señor. All in good time. *Pues*, Maestro, now that we have completed the preliminaries, can you report to me the residence of Señor Kortovsky in Lima?"

"No, godammit. I'm working on it, though."

"Please, don't let it trouble you, Maestro, because I, Espartaco Asunción Ochoa Romero, have made this discovery."

"Really."

"I must admit, I had some little luck. After the concert of the New Magini String Quartet, I desired to obtain the musicians' autographs on my program."

"How lucky can you get?"

"Ah, you underestimate my difficulties! Let me read you what our music critic, Flor Vivanco, wrote in *El Comercio*: '*Esta ciudad, nunca antes habia escuchado una representación del Cuarteto de Cuerdas opus 59, número 3 de Beethoven que estuviese tan lleno de electricidad y poder sísmico controlado.*' "

"Well, that's *grande*," said Jacobus, "except that the only word I understood was 'Beethoven.' "

"*Discúlpeme, Maestro*," said Oro. "Let me try the translate: 'Never had this city heard a performance of Beethoven's String Quartet, opus 59, number 3 that was so full of electricity and controlled seismic power.' "

"Okay, Oro," Jacobus interrupted, cursing himself for not making his coffee sooner. Could he, a blind man, make coffee with one hand while holding the receiver with the other? He might have to chance it. "As you said, we've completed the preliminaries."

100

"But Maestro, it is important you know about this concert."

"Why?"

"All in good time, I repeat you."

"Alright. It's your peso."

"*Sol.*"

"No, Daniel."

"Not your name. The sol is our currency. Not peso."

"Whatever."

"Yes. As I say, when the concert ended, there were the choruses of 'Bravo! Bravo! Braaaaaaavooooooo!' and there were the chain reactions of cheers of a less coherent nature, which you could almost not hear over the rhythmic foot poundings that rattled the floor. From my balcony seat I saw the wife of *El Presidente* standing in her privileged box. I must say it amused me to see the first lady, so ardent a patroness and defender of the performing arts in our cash-poor country that she had been nicknamed *La Maestra*, stomping her feet along with the masses while at the same time, her entourage of political correctness must be remaining neutral.

"At this point I say to myself, I must go now if I want my autographs, so I begin to push through the standing people. I glance at the stage; they are still bowing, but it occurs to me something curious of a juxtaposition which is this: the quartet, they had played together with precision almost superhuman, but as they now took their respectful bows they seemed to accept the accolade of the audience as individuals, not as a single entity. Each looks in a different direction, but none at each other. The first violinist gazes up at the balcony, how you say, in search of the adoring feminine eyes. Yes, the second violinist, your young *Japonesa*, she had worked the hardest and had a smile on her face, though even from my great distance, it looked like the *artificial*. The violist looked like she couldn't wait to leave. A pity. She is very beautiful. But I give her the benefit of the doubt. It was their last concert of their tour. Maybe she had a plane to catch. The cellist, the heavy one, she looks down at her shoes as if saying to the audience that perhaps their adulity was not to be warranted, but she, too, maybe the most, knew Beethoven."

"Well, *muchas gracias,* Oro, for telling me nothing, but I've got a hot date with Señora Folger."

"*Discúlpeme*, Maestro. Of course you know what it is like to receive the adulity of the concert. This is not of noteworthy to you, but please, if you permit me to relive this experience I would be most grateful. It is possible I will never hear such a concert for the rest of my life, and *¿quien sabe?* it may turn out to be important—"

"—all in good time."

"Precisely."

"Go on, then. You were talking about the cellist's adulity."

"Gracias, Maestro. When the applause momentarily subsides as the quartet exited the stage, I say to myself I must hurry, but the audience was not satisfied. The applause reorganizes with its own energy. It became a rhythmic pulse, like the palpitating heart. This almost never happens here, so the musicians must return to the stage, making more of the screaming, and the rhythm disintegrates into the sound of torrential rain against the window. This sequence repeats itself, six times, seven times, eight times; little by little the people become exhausted and enter into the aisles, making my progress to the backstage area very like rush hour.

"Finally, as the audience became aware the quartet would not return to the stage yet again because they come out without their instruments, the lights of the house rose and the audience groans disappointed—no encore. Well, I say to myself, now I must push. I give some several people my small elbow, but then there is the final obstacle, a young man like the size of a mammoth who is limping and seems not to know whether he was coming or going. I say to myself, perhaps God does not want me to have my autographs. I cannot see around him, but finally I make a small avenue, only to find that *La Maestra,* protected by her numerous bodyguards, has made the more efficient passage to our destination. Now I would have to wait my turn, and who knew how long that could take?

" 'What?' I heard the first lady exclaim in a most un-first-lady-like tone. 'Very well. If there *is* a next time.' And then the entourage exited with a most unanticipated alacrity.

"Now I am first in line! I poke my head into the backstage area, which in the Museo Nacional makes many dimly lit poor alcoves, like where the moles live, but I see no one but the stage manager.

" 'César,' I said. '¿Que pasa? I want to congratulate the musicians.'

" 'I am sorry, Colonel,' says César. 'Like I told *La Maestra*. They're gone.'

" 'Gone? So soon?' I ask.

" 'Yes, and maybe my job with it. *La Maestra* was not happy. They just took their cases and left. They didn't say a word. Americans.'

"I had no time to reply to his one-word editorial, which, knowing César, would undoubtedly be the beginning of a lengthy political dialectic about how America was adding South America into yet more *Estados Unidos*. César, he likes to talk. But I think, maybe I can catch them. 'What direction did they go?' I ask.

" 'They went in every direction, like the compass.'

" 'What does that mean, César? I don't have time for the riddles.'

" 'They each went a separate way,' César said. 'They didn't even look at each other.'

"So I race out the stage door into the darkened street, but all I see is the audience on the cloud of the euphoria, and the idolized musicians were nowhere to be seen."

"So you didn't find out where Kortovsky's staying."

"Oh, but I did, Maestro! I am very determined. I go back to César and ask which taxi company the quartet uses, and César says to me, 'Embassy Company.'"

"How would he know?"

"Here in Peru we have many taxi drivers. Taxis are very cheap, but some of them are not to be trusted. We have many tourists who take the *tico* and then—"

"*Tico?*"

"Yes. They are a very small taxi, about the size of a bread box, but not as comfortable or safe. Sometimes the tourists get robbed, or charged too much, or taken somewhere they don't want to go. Sometimes the *tico* breaks down and the passenger has to push. So the *museo* arranged a secure company for the musicians. I call the company and find out the drivers who pick up the musicians, and call the drivers."

"And?"

"Binjo! Señor Kortovsky stay at Maury Hotel. A very nice establishment that, how shall we say, somewhat basks in the warmth of its former glory."

"You mean it's a dump."

"No, no, Maestro, not at all! It no doubt still has the *dignidad* and the *majestad* like the rest of the area around the Plaza Mayor. The Spanish balconies from the sixteenth century, the cathedrals, the... Well, I am sounding like a travel guide, am I not? And after all, the Maury was the first to make the pisco sour."

"First or last, if they made the piss go sour, it's a dump."

"No, no, sir! Pisco! Pisco! You misapprehend my accent. Pisco is our national drink, like grappa in Italy or aquavit in Denmark. The pisco sour combines the alcohol with the limone, the sugar, and the egg whites with the crushed ice. Sublime!"

"Sounds sub-lemon to me."

"Ah, you will see. Perhaps one day I will have the honor of pouring a pisco sour for you, Maestro."

"I doubt it. So what about Kortovsky?"

"Señor Kortovsky apparently checked out a few hours after his concert. This I learned from Señorita Angelita Flores, the receptionist. We are beginning to make the progress, no?"

"Is that it?"

"Well, I have a question for you, Maestro."

"Yeah?"

"How was it you knew to call me in the first place?"

"There was an article in the *New York Times*. About a drug killing. It mentioned your name. Why do you ask?"

"When you asked me why I had to confirm your identity, I told you 'all in good time.' Do you remember this?"

"Vaguely. It seems long ago."

"Well, now, I suppose, is the good time. You see, Maestro, the unfortunate individual who became a corpse seems to have made this transition approximately the same time Señor Kortovsky was at the Maury Hotel.

"Big deal. As you said, Lima's got eight million people."

"Exactly so, Maestro. You are so perceptive. It is for this very reason why it may be more than coincidence that the body was discovered one block from the Maury Hotel."

Chapter Thirteen

"You think Kortovsky had something to do with a drug killing?" asked Jacobus. "How do you know how long the body's been there? You think it's Kortovsky?"

"These questions have not been so easy as you would expect, Maestro," said Oro.

"Why not? You said you've got his photo. You saw him in person."

"You see, here in Lima we have the humidity. We also have the vulture, the ant, and, unfortunately, the rat, in greater abundance than we wish. So after a certain time this combination of natural forces makes use of the photo of the person who is now the corpse, let us say, unprofitable. It could be Señor Kortovsky, or it could not. If not, we must find where he is to see whether there is some involvement."

Jacobus, who knew little about the decomposition rate of corpses, conceded a month might be a reasonable ballpark figure for some quality rotting time, so the person could conceivably have been offed around the date of the quartet's concert.

"What about clothing? Was the corpse wearing white tie and tails by any chance?"

"That indeed would have provided us with direction and the corpse with, shall we say, *dignidad*? But I am sorry to say that either our victim walked to his doom in what you call his suit of birth, or the killer removed the clothing afterward. I suspect my second theory is more the probable."

"The newspaper said it was a drug killing and the body had been tortured."

"Well, perhaps they said that, and preliminary indications would suggest

106

there is some truth. I, myself, was not involved with the original investigation."

"So you're not convinced?"

"Let us say that there are factors to be considered."

Jacobus, tired of being led in circles, bristled that he was being treated like an algebra student lectured by Einstein.

"Well, I have a little information I'd like to share with you," he said.

"*¿Sí?*"

"Our dead amigo wouldn't happen to be missing a finger, would he?"

There was silence at the other end.

"Hello? Hello? Oro, are you still there?" Jacobus chided.

"Tell me why you ask this, Maestro."

"Is it true? *¿La verdad?*"

"I'm sorry to say, no, it is not."

"No?" Jacobus had been sure.

"Technically, no."

"Spit it out, professor."

"Actually, he is missing *four* fingers. Of the left hand." There was a pause. "Plus, the appendage unique to the male species....plus a face."

"Torture."

"It would *seem* so. The body was discovered tied to a chair on the second floor of one of our elegant Spanish colonial structures. The ground-floor *tiendas* in that building sell sweets and tourist items, and there is a commendable *cebichería*. The upper floor, however, like many such *edificios*, has long been abandoned to the elements. The police searched for the missing body parts among the garbage and broken glass with no success. Perhaps we may now know why. *Por favor*, tell me how you know of the missing finger."

"Well," began Jacobus, "all I wanted to do was to listen to a little Schubert…
"

When he finished recounting his story, Oro said, "*Gracias*, Maestro. You and I, we make the good partner. But does this Lieutenant Malachi know about the missing Kortovsky?"

"Not much, but he will soon enough."

"Please allow him to wait. Because we don't know for sure who the corpse is, or if your finger comes from my hand. And as you correctly surmised from my voice inclinations, though it appears so, our friend may not have been tortured by his killer after all," said Oro.

Jacobus thought about this and did not respond. He didn't enjoy being baited by anyone in authority, including this haughty cop, and so decided to inflict a little silent torture upon Oro. It didn't take long.

"Señor Yacovis? Are you there?"

"Yeah. I'm here." Did he detect a note of exasperation in Oro's voice? "I didn't hear you ask me a question."

"Most people would inquire after such a statement. After all, our friend was speared through the abdomens, his fingers cut off, his head almost so, and his face disfigured."

"So you're saying their meeting wasn't in the nature of a friendly get-together," mocked Jacobus.

"Ah! You jest, señor," said Oro, but Jacobus could tell he had him on shaky ground.

"Or, the disfigurement occurred *after* death," said Jacobus, having concluded that from the beginning.

"*¡Sí!*" said Oro, reassurance flowing through his one syllable, which he extended like a sigh. "That is my current hypotheosis. I will not go into forensic detail, but the investigation report tells me there was much blood released from the stab wound to the abdomens, but very little from the face and the neck, and almost none at all from the amputation of the left hand and the sexual organ. You are very perspective, señor."

"*Gracias.* But it's just simple logic to conclude that if he was all chopped up like chicken liver but hadn't been tortured, that it must've happened *after* death."

"So now our questions are—"

"One, why would our friend have been mutilated ex post facto?"

"*Sí.* For torture to be effective it is recommended that it take place while the victim is still alive. Otherwise it is difficult to elicit the kind of information, or send the proper message, that the executor would wish."

"Well put, Marquis de Sade. And the second question would be whether Kortovsky's the butcher or the meatloaf. Or neither."

"And once we can answer those questions," said Oro, "we shall know for certain whether Señor Kortovsky is still funct."

"I'd say he's probably fucked one way or the other," said Jacobus.

"No, Señor Yacovis! Funct! Funct!"

"What the hell's 'funct'?"

"Is it not the opposite of 'defunct'?"

"Whatever makes you gruntled."

There was a silence.

"Sí, *Maestro*. But I do fear for Señora Haagen to have that finger found in her case. Such a beautiful violist!"

"Her playing or her looks?"

"Sí. *Buenas noches*, Maestro."

Chapter Fourteen

Jacobus, with assistance from Nathaniel, descended the four slippery steps from the sidewalk to the Circle of Fifths. The evening air had grown damp and breezy, and, probing with his cane, Jacobus felt more than a few clotted leaves that had found refuge in the stony stairwell.

When Nathaniel pulled open the heavy steel door, Jacobus was engulfed by a rush of stale air on which wafted the combined aroma of cigars, alcohol, and frying grease, and the sounds of animated conversation and a quartet—violin, trumpet, piano, and string bass—playing unadulterated East European folk music—all in all the sensory equivalent of Trotsky's assault on him three hours earlier.

Jacobus was lifted off the ground and his left cheek was slapped three times in rapid succession.

"Ah, Daniel, my dear friend!" said Ivan Lensky, as if the smells and sounds had materialized into his form.

"If that's how you treat your friends," said Jacobus, "then I can only imagine how—"

"And you must be Williams Nathaniel," Lensky continued with unabated enthusiasm. "Come. I am Ivan. Ivan the Terrible! Ha! We make extra room for you. Double extra! Then we drink!"

Jacobus felt himself being led along a circuitous path, noting that Lensky's speech was slightly slurred, either from drinking already embarked upon, or from a heretofore unknown dialect from the Caucuses.

"What are we doing? Taking the Great Circle route?" Jacobus asked. "Or are you not able to walk in a straight line?"

"Ha! Very good! I see no one can fool you. Place here was organized by Russian musicians who had idea—fifths in music and fifths in drinking go good together."

"Perfect, in fact."

"Ha!"

Jacobus winced, anticipating another whack on his back that, to his relief, did not come.

"So in music we have circle of fifths, and we add one sharp each time: C–G–D–A—"

"Yes, Ivan, I've learned my key signatures—"

"So here bar is in circle, and as you go around circle we drink one fifth, then two fifths, then—"

"What happens when you get to C-sharp major?"

"No one makes it to C-sharp major." Lensky sounded serious. "Just like in music!" He burst out in laughter, and to emphasize the almost nonexistent humor of his joke, hit Jacobus on the back with a thundering wallop. "Here we are."

As Lensky eased him into a creaking wooden chair, Jacobus heard two men at the table speaking Russian.

"Daniel, Williams, these are my friends, Vladimir Greunig and Yosef Lipinsky. They are like my fathers."

The two surviving members of the original Magini Quartet, not counting Pravda Lenskaya. Yosef Lipinsky, second violin, and Vladimir Greunig, viola. Jacobus had always admired their musicianship, more even than the current ensemble which bore the quartet's name.

"Honored, gentlemen," he said.

A glass thumped in front of him.

"We, too," said one of the voices, high-pitched and anxious.

"Enough of the flattering, Yosef," said the second. "Now we drink."

Jacobus heard his glass being filled. It sounded like a large glass.

"What key are we in at the moment?" Nathaniel asked.

"Only two sharps—D major," said Yosef Lipinsky.

"For the moment!" said Greunig. "*Bud'mo!* Long life!"

111

"*Budyem!*" said Ivan Lensky and Yosef Lipinsky. "Health!"

Jacobus and Nathaniel echoed the toasts and drank. Vodka. Good vodka. Straight and cold.

"We were just saying Kortovsky plays like shit! He *is* shit!" said Greunig, with the depth of one of those Russian bassos that defies the limits of human anatomy.

"Now, Dimi! Daniel and Williams are our guests. We must be polite!" said Lipinsky.

The contrasting voices reminded Jacobus of Schmuyle and Goldenberg from Mussorgsky's *Pictures at an Exhibition*.

Another glass was poured. "*Budyem!*" Jacobus said, lifting it.

"What is important, polite or truth, eh?" said Greunig. "You tell us, Jacobus Daniel. What is more important, polite or truth?"

"Truth, of course."

"Ah! You see, Yosef? Truth, of course! Yosef, you are like little mouse. Always sneak up behind us when we practice concertos and pluck out accompaniments, *pizzi, pizzi, pizzi* on your violin with your little mouse smile. No wonder you lose your hair. Polite shmolite! Why you no play concerto yourself? First should be truth, *then* polite. You are true friend, Jacobus Daniel."

"But the truth is," said Jacobus, his tongue already loosening, "we're like Kortovsky. We're shit too. The only difference is, someone else's shit always smells worse than our own."

"Ha!" said Lipinsky. "Vladimir, your true friend here is also wise man. But sadly, it is true, it was Kortovsky ruin us."

"Not again, please, Uncle Yosef," said Ivan. "You cry in your beer."

"You talk to your elders like this, Ivan? I don't cry...and it's not beer."

"How did he ruin you, Mr. Lipinsky?" asked Nathaniel.

It was Greunig who responded. "Kortovsky wasn't the first to ruin us. Only the best. First were the Communists. When we toured in Soviet Union, it was Party that made our schedule. We travel for six, seven weeks to the republics. Bus, train, boat, once in a while plane. We stay in shit hotels made of cinder blocks with no heat and we eat shit food—"

112

"When available," Lipinsky squeaked.

"Yes, when available," repeated Greunig, with a growling chuckle. "And we play every night, also with no heat."

"And no money," added Lipinsky.

"What good was money," Greunig countered, "when there was nothing to buy?"

Lipinsky squeaked out what Jacobus interpreted to be a laugh, but it came out sounding more like a hamster being squeezed by a six-year-old.

"Do you remember how we washed our clothes?" Lipinsky said. "Let me tell you! After one week of tour we put on all our clothes, go into the shower that was always cold, and rub our clothes with soap, then take off top layer, then do same with second, then take of third—"

"I get the idea, Lipinsky," Jacobus interjected. "Seven days without washing, no doubt, makes one weak." No one laughed. "But," he continued, "you did tours around the world. You were always the headline quartet for any series. You must've gotten something out of that."

This time both Greunig and Lipinsky burst out laughing, though the former almost drowned out the other.

"You're a funny guy," said Greunig.

"Yeah, and a true friend. Tell me what's so hilarious."

"Funny," said Lipinsky, "because even though on our international tours we had steak and clean sheets, we were prisoners."

"How so?"

"First of all," said Greunig, "KGB was with us whole time. Room next door. First row, balcony. Check-in at airport. So we couldn't talk to nobody."

"And second of all?"

"Our families were hostages," said Lipinsky, and Jacobus could almost hear Lipinsky's voice break.

"It's okay, Josef. It's okay," said Greunig. "They knew we wouldn't defect, or talk, like I talk to you, Jacobus Daniel, because we knew what they would do to our families if we did. I think that's really what killed Osvald, a sweet man. Too sweet. The doctors said heart attack, but I think it was fear. I think it was stress. I think it was sadness."

No one talked for a while. The little band, oblivious to the old musicians' sorrow, kept up peppy folk music in the background. A foreign television show droned on. The only sound at their table was of glasses being set down with a hollower ring than moments earlier.

"They wouldn't even let us take our good instruments overseas," said Lipinsky.

"Your Maginis?"

"Ha! Ha! again, Mr. Jacobus. We never had Maginis. This was propaganda. This was big joke: Magini Quartet and no Maginis! At home we had playable instruments. But even they needed a lot of repair. And on tour, even your worst student wouldn't be seen dead with what we play on."

"Where are you families and your instruments now?"

"After Chernobyl—"

Jacobus heard a sudden clatter of glasses, plates, and silverware—maybe something was spilled—and a heavy thud in the middle of the table.

"*Khashi!*" said Ivan. "You try, Daniel, Williams?"

"Why not?" asked Jacobus. "What's in it?"

"Never mind. It's Georgian. Perfect with vodka. No hangover! Guaranteed! You try."

Jacobus felt for his spoon, dipped it into the soup bowl in front of him and made contact with a floating gelatinous lump that he first pinned against the side of the bowl, then with a deft maneuver so it wouldn't slide off scooped it into his spoon, splashing only an insignificant amount of the broth onto the table.

Swallowing the contents he felt briny grease scald the inside of his mouth and gullet. What remained on his throbbing tongue was a small mass of fat that bore vague hints of beef and garlic. He downed the rest of his vodka in an effort to extinguish the third-degree burn in his esophagus.

"You like?" asked Lipinsky.

"What's the meat?"

"Maybe beef. Maybe finger!" said Greunig, with a laugh. "Maybe not."

"I think we now go to A major," said Ivan, saving Jacobus from having to respond, though he couldn't.

Nathaniel escorted Jacobus, his legs beginning to respond semi-independently from each other, to the next table. "Where's my *khashi?*" he asked. Glasses were filled.

"*Budyem! Bud'mo!*" the Russians said.

"Budyems up!" said Jacobus just before he belched.

Jacobus, feeling bleary, needed information before he passed out. He knew at some point, probably soon, he was going to. What were their names again? Ah, yes. Glasnost and Perestroika.

"So tell me, Glas...boys, why is Kortovsky shit? How'd he ruin your quartet? To my ear he sounds fine."

"*Blyad!* Who says about sound?" asked Greunig.

"Not so loud, Dimi," whispered Lipinsky. "It's very bad word," he continued to Jacobus. "It means whore."

"But we use it like American 'fuck,' " said Greunig. "Nice and indignant. So I say it softer for Yosef. *Shhhh! Blyad.* Lots of people sound fine *and* are shit. But we didn't know this in beginning."

Lipinsky said, "In beginning, after poor Osvald die, may he rest in peace, we decide we hire Aaron Kortovsky, good young violinist—Ivan was still too young, unfortunately we know that now—and then we will train him to be like us. We have reputation. We have our special..."

"Style," said Nathaniel.

"Yes, style. And no. More than style. We *understand* the music. The right way for Mozart, Beethoven, Shostakovich."

"There's a lot of composers between Beethoven and Shostakovich," said Jacobus.

"We know right way for that, too," said Greunig.

Jacobus was starting to feel annoyance creep through his alcohol-induced haze.

"You have to admit, Vlady," he said, "there's more than one right way to play music."

It was as if he had just called Jesse James a cheater. All sound came to a halt. He waited.

"Mr. Daniel," said Lipinsky, "we rehearse Shostakovich quartet number eleven with Shostakovich himself. Forty-six times we rehearse before we perform! We memorize every Shostakovich quartet. Do you think Aaron Kortovsky's right way is better than our right way?"

"Point taken, Uncle Yosef," said Jacobus. He picked up his glass. Empty again! "But I must say—Don't shush me, Williams Nathaniel! Let go of my arm!—I am not the world's biggest Shostakovich fan. I mean, it's okay to hate Stalin, okay? He was a *baaaaad* man. And to express that hatred, okay? But in every fucking piece he wrote? I mean—"

"*Poshel ty na khui*," mumbled Greunig, with menace. "Go fuck–"

"Ha!" said Ivan, delivering another whack to Jacobus's back. He was getting used to this. "Good joke, Daniel! And now, E major."

Jacobus removed his glasses and rubbed his eyes, trying to stay awake. Where are my glasses? he wondered. Always losing them. Ah, here they are, in my hand.

"Kortovsky has a sound," said a voice, either Lipinsky or Greunig. Now they were starting to sound so alike. How did they do that?

"And plays so in tune it's frightening," said another voice.

"Okay. In tune. But that is all," said another.

"No, that's not true. He has one other thing. He is political. I thought here in America I would be free, but Kortovsky knows pressure."

"You couldn't take heat, Yosef."

Jacobus heard Lipinsky fumble with his glass. "*Za uspekh nashego beznadezhnogo dela*," he said, slurping its contents.

"Huh?" said Jacobus.

" 'To the success of our hopeless cause.' You are right, Dimi. I don't like heat. Every day the small insults. The quiet intimidation: 'Yosef, maybe you should put on new strings. Yosef, it sounded so good…last year. Yosef, are you sure you feel well?' Life wasn't the same. So I leave."

"Then we hire the blonde."

"Kortovsky's girlfriend," Jacobus elaborated, proud of himself for being able to stay on top of the conversation's intricacies. He even remembered what "blonde" meant.

But where, oh where, has my Annika gone? Oops, someone was talking to him.

"...no, my friend. The *Englishman's* girlfriend. She plays good. Maybe not like Yosef—right, Yosef?—but good. Maybe now Kortovsky's happy. For year, two year, okay. Then, little by little, they give Pravda and me the Yosef treatment—"

Ivan Lensky interrupted. "Today, Annika blonde, she say to me, do I know Smetana Quartet? 'What!' I say. I say to her, 'I know both Smetana quartet, both Janáček quartet, *all* Dvořák quartet, because my coach was Borodin Quartet in Moscow and they know Czech music better than New Magini will ever!"

"See?" said Greunig. "This what I mean. What do I need this for? I ask me. Good old days are gone. So one day we rehearse and Kortovsky go to bathroom. So I go to bathroom on his music and leave. Bye-bye."

A tear of laughter brimmed up from Jacobus's left eye and formed a rivulet over the bridge of his nose. Guided by the rim of his glasses, it merged with the tear from his right eye to form a little puddle on the table, upon which he suddenly realized the right side of his face rested. Abruptly, without missing a beat, the tears of joy became tears of grief. Why was he thinking about his older brother, Eli. Why? Then he heard it, behind the conversation, behind the sporting event being broadcast in a language that had no vowels, his heart had been listening to the folk band playing its rendition of Dvořák's Slavonic Dance no. 2 in E Minor. He had played the violin-and-piano arrangement of that poignant dance with his brother Eli. Eli, the one with the real talent. It had been the last music they had ever played together, for their parents the night before Jacobus left for Europe to study in the United States before the war.

It was to be the last time he ever saw any of them. His parents had died in the camps. That was a fact. But where was Eli? Jacobus had searched, but all traces were swallowed, engulfed by the voracious gut of the Holocaust. Missing. He could have been dead for fifty years. He could still be alive. For all Jacobus knew, Eli could be the blind beggar on the street.

What does "missing" mean? Missing to whom? Eli could be searching for *him*, in which case Jacobus would be "missing."

"And Lenskaya?" he simpered. "Is she missing? Like Kortovsky?" He wasn't sure anyone heard him, though. "Why didn't she quit?"

"After I leave, the Englishman come. Was what Kortovsky wanted all along. He hire Haagen to get Short because he think, 'He and I, we are the same.'"

"But that turned out to be problem, not solution. They were same! Same ego!"

Someone was laughing. Far away, it seemed.

"—so funny?" Jacobus managed.

"Uncle Yosef says Annika didn't think they were same. Is funny."

"*Obviously* same. Annika *obviously* didn't think they were same."

"Here's to Annika!" blurted Greunig. "*Shtoby myaso bylo I khui stoyal!* To the hope that there will always be meat and our pricks stand tall!"

"So Crispin, now he lose music war to Kortovsky. He lose politic war to Kortovsky. And he lose Annika war to Kortovsky. But he's not smart like me. When I lose, I leave. Short doesn't leave. He gets fired. Boom! He is very angry."

"Maybe he should drink more!" blurted Jacobus, receiving howls of laughter and a whack on his back that seemed to him to have been endured by someone other than himself. Poor guy. Poor Pravda!

"Lenskaya! Lenskaya! Why'dn't she quit?"

Jacobus felt another cheek next to his, sharing his spot on the table top. Cheek to cheek, are we? A well-shaven cheek. Cologne and garlic.

"After they kill my father in Chernobyl," whispered the voice, "my mother stop arguing. She has life but lost soul."

I really should shave more often, thought Jacobus. Not easy to shave when you're blind. No one understands. Fuck the razor blades! Cut my throat that way. Electric safer, safer. But boy, do you look stupid if you miss a spot!

"Where's Kortovsky?" shouted Jacobus as loud as he could. "I want to know! Where the hell is Kortovsky?"

"Jake," said a voice jiggling his shoulder. It was a familiar voice this time. "We best be going while we can still move."

"But we're only on E major!" Jacobus explained rationally. He would make it clear enough for even a schoolchild. "We still have B, F-sharp, then R, then

118

double Yoohoo, then"–Jacobus began to giggle–"Special K." He burst out laughing.

"That's what I mean. Let's go."

Jacobus felt himself being lifted up. One of his friends on each side of him. He had been so comfortable. Where were they taking him? To Kortovsky? His feet were running but they were not reaching the floor. People laughing. Old friends. New old friends. He was glad they were happy.

"Toodle-oo! Toodle-oo!" Such nice people.

The voices were so far away, talking too fast. Why didn't they slow down for him? He heard garlic-and-cologne use the word "Vaseline," and his big, black friend—he had his name on the tip of his tongue—reply with "oat car."

Infinitely somber, he began to sing the melody to "Death and the Maiden" with a new text: "Va-se-line oat-car, Va-se-line oat-car." Annika! Yumi! Jacobus loved them both.

"Hey, Ivan the Terrible! My big black friend tells me...in other words, who, who the hell's listenin' to *Wintereisse* in yo mama's garage? Yo, Ivan? Who the hell—"

"Peter the Great," came the chuckling response. "My baby brother. But he is not listening. He is singing."

"You have a brother, too? Like me? Pretty damn nice voice, my friend tells me!" sang Jacobus. "But can he sing 'Vaseline oat car,' I ask you? And who's playin' *piana* in the garage? Sweeascheslavic...Rikter?"

"No, that baby brother too. He's talented one in family."

"Uh-huh?"

Then, as Jacobus was being dragged, he heard someone snoring. He wasn't sure, but it might have been himself.

Chapter Fifteen

WEDNESDAY

His dream was making no sense. The ringing. A heavy weight pinning him down as he lay on his left side. Something wet and slivery penetrating deep into his right ear.

"Get off me, you goddam mongrel," Jacobus growled. The admission of his consciousness, though, only spurred Trotsky's enthusiasm. The licking spread to Jacobus's unshaven face, as he struggled to answer the phone.

"Yeah," he said with all the vitality of his withered tomato plant. His head felt like a football kicked by Lou "the Toe" Groza and his stomach as if that had been its destination.

"Hi, Jake!" It was Yumi. "Coffee?"

"Bring it here. I can't move. Literally."

"Are you okay?"

"Why? What else could 'can't move' possibly mean?"

Yumi laughed. "I guess you are, then. Can I bring anything else? I'm going to Lower Crust."

"Doughnut."

Yumi began to sing the ditty Jacobus had taught her on the train to the tune of "Turkey in the Straw": "Oh, I went into a doughnut shop to get a bite to—"

"Shut up! I mean," he continued in a more palliative tone, "you can tell me why you're so goddam cheery when you get here."

He hung up, the cue Trotsky was waiting for to eat the telephone, and hunched his way toward Nathaniel's bathroom, his hand against the wall for guidance and to keep him upright. " 'No hangover. Guaranteed,' " Jacobus grumbled in an imitative Russian accent. "My ass."

He risked scalding himself on Nathaniel's temperamental shower that on occasion would either sputter like the last drop of a canteen in the desert or, with the pressure of a riot control hose, gush superheated water from some secret nuclear-powered heating device that only New York City knew about. After scrubbing off enough of the previous night's debauch, he managed to stand erect. He fumbled through Nathaniel's medicine cabinet and found what he hoped were aspirin, swallowed a few, and returned to his bedroom where he donned one of Nathaniel's flannel robes, which would have fit Trotsky and him combined. Shaving was out of the question.

When he answered the doorbell, he wordlessly gestured to Yumi not to talk to him but to just hand him the coffee, which she did with practiced understanding. With his other hand he found her arm and guided her to the kitchen table. There he sat and sipped the life-giving caffeine that gradually brought him back from the precipice of a vegetative state.

Halfway through the coffee he reached out his hand and said, "doughnut," and felt an old-fashioned plain cruller silently placed in his palm.

"Ah, good girl," he said, but immediately regretted even such a modest utterance, as the pain in his head vengefully reasserted its dominance.

With the cup now half empty, Jacobus knew he could dunk the cruller, confident it would not overflow. One. Two. Three, he said to himself silently, and removed the cruller. Any more than three seconds and it would become saturated and fall apart in his hand. Any fewer and it would not have absorbed sufficient caffeine. When the pastry was finished, Yumi handed him a napkin, with which he wiped his mouth and fingers.

"Now," he said as softly as possible, so softly that he could feel Yumi's sweet breath close to his face in order to hear him. "You've got news to tell me."

Yumi spoke just as quietly, and Jacobus thanked the powers of the universe for having provided him this one student out of all others. "Annika's okay," she said. "She was never really missing."

"*Mmm.* Go on. But please talk slower."

"She was just so disgusted seeing that finger there, she had to get away. She went to the bathroom backstage to wash her face and decided not to go back for her case. She knows it was stupid, but she just couldn't face it. She went to a bar where she had a few drinks and—"

"What's the name of the bar?"

"Um, she didn't say."

"And how do you know this?" asked Jacobus, still whispering.

"Because she called me from the bar."

"She called *you*?" Jacobus asked, again regretting the unintended increase in decibels. "That's a new one."

"I was surprised too," said Yumi. "But she said she wanted to get together and patch things up. That the shock of the finger made her realize that we need to work together to figure out what's going on."

"And?"

"And so she invited me to her spa over on Second Avenue, Perfect Finnish, for a massage and a sauna. She told me—"

"You were both naked?"

"That's what one usually is in a sauna."

"But she told me in so many words she was...you know."

"Bisexual?"

"Yeah. I hope she didn't harass you, give you the Kortovsky treatment."

"What if she did? I don't see the problem here, Jake."

These were uncharted waters for Jacobus, who couldn't recall the last time he had sex but nevertheless considered himself squarely in the heterosexual corner. It wasn't as if he had been incapable of sexual gratification—his misguided fling with Victoria Jablonski, his then protégée, was more than proof of that, though it happened only after she was the one to make the first move. On the other hand, he had faced the possibility of true emotional intimacy with Yumi's grandmother, the English woman, Kate Padgett, and found that that prospect paralyzed him. He knew to where it all traced back to— the Grimsley Competition, that swine judge, Feodor Malinkovsky, who called him into his office and...

"Jake, aren't you even listening to me?"

"So," he blustered, "what the hell *did* you discuss in the sauna?"

"I just said, we talked about how in Japan we go from a hot tub to a cool room, but in Finland they do the exact reverse, going from the hot room to an ice-cold—"

"Hey, you," said Jacobus, momentarily forgetting his hangover. "Don't jerk me around. You know what I'm talking about. What about the finger in her viola case? What about MIA golden boy husband?"

"I'm sorry, Jake," Yumi said. "I've left out the best part, and I probably should have started with it. That's why I guess I'm being a little defensive."

"So what's the best part?"

"Annika told me she hoped I wouldn't lose my job because of Crispin's lawsuit—"

"That's nice of her."

"And proposed the idea that if something terrible has happened to Aaron, where he couldn't play anymore—"

"You mean, if he's dead."

"Well, of course we hope not, but if it were something serious where he wouldn't be able to continue in the quartet, she said I could be the first violinist and Crispin could have his old position back."

The market study entered Jacobus's mind unbidden and the body in Lima, which he hadn't yet told Yumi about. Before he could think better of it, he said, "Yumi, I think you're being manipulated."

"Jake, something's bothering you and it's more than your hangover. Just spell it out please."

"Yumi, as you know, tact is not my strong point."

"This is already sounding bad."

"Yeah, but this is what I'm thinking. You discovered Annika's little secret in her case. What if ... what if that finger just happened to have once been connected to Kortovsky's hand? What if Kortovsky's no longer alive?"

"Jake! You're suggesting Annika killed him?"

"Just listen for a minute. Then maybe you won't think I'm totally meshuga. If she had killed him and you discovered some evidence to that effect, what would she do? She'd take off like a bat out of hell and figure out what to do next. And maybe she'd come up with an excuse why she left her precious viola there, which only a couple hours earlier she'd told me how dear it was to her, and figure out a way to make you her ally, or at least keep you quietly on the sidelines."

"The offer for me to be first violin."

"Offer? More like a bribe to keep your mouth shut. And the icing on the cake is that in return for her sexual favors—"

"Sexual favors! Jake, we were in a sauna!"

"That's just the first step."

"First step? First step to what? Are you crazy? I think that hangover has addled your brain."

"Don't try to flatter me."

"I'm serious. We don't even know that Aaron's dead, so why speculate? And why would Annika kill him anyway?"

"I don't know that she did, but *if* she did, I can think of several reasons, not the least of which is his philandering. Plus his domineering ways, plus his neglect of their child. And just maybe he did care that his wife is a dyke."

"I think that's enough, Jake. I don't care about your hangover and I don't really care about your opinion. Maybe it's time I did a little manipulating of my own. Artistic integrity, yes, but I don't have to be the Virgin Mary in order to maintain it. If Annika wants to kiss me, what's that to you?"

Jacobus turned his head away as he heard Yumi get up and walk to the door.

"Don't choke on your cruller," she said and closed the door behind her with intentional definition, but out of consideration for his state, not quite a slam.

Did I mishandle that? Jacobus asked himself.

When he heard the door reopen a half minute later, he said, "Personally, I don't care whether she's a dyke."

"That's good to know," said Nathaniel as he entered the apartment. "Are you by any chance referring to the busty lass who loved Schubert more than you?"

124

"What are you doing here?" asked Jacobus.

"If you recall, I happen to live here. Do I have your permission to come in to my own apartment? Lilburn has an article in the *Times* about yesterday. I brought you some coffee."

"And a cruller?"

"No, why?"

"Never mind. Let's hear the article. Wait! First give me the coffee."

Jacobus heard Nathaniel's bulk ease into the kitchen chair across from him, which gave but did not break, defying the laws of physics. " 'Digital Discovery Threatens Live Performance,' " he read.

"A finger. In a concert hall. With a viola case. The already precarious fortunes of the New Magini String Quartet took two turns for the worse yesterday. First, Aaron Kortovsky, the first violinist of the ensemble, was missing at the quartet's rehearsal at Carnegie Hall yesterday afternoon in preparation for a make-or-break performance there on Thursday night, and had to be replaced at the last minute by the young Russian violinist Ivan Lensky. The quartet's manager, Sheila Rathman from InHouseArtists, only reluctantly admitted that Kortovsky has not been heard from since their summer tour to South America.

"Far more troubling for the quartet, already beset by adversity and internal strife, was the discovery of a severed finger in the instrument case of quartet violist Annika Haagen. According to New York City police lieutenant Al Malachi, his forensic team has determined that the finger was roughly amputated from an unknown victim approximately a month ago. He went on to state that there is currently no reason to connect the finger with Kortovsky's baffling absence.

"Power Ramsey, artistic director of the internationally recognized dance company The Movement and of Thursday's Schubert extravaganza, which will include photochoreography and dance to supplement the quartet's performance of Schubert's 'Death and the Maiden,' in commemoration of that composer's bicentennial, stated unequivocally that the concert will proceed as planned.

"The future of the New Magini String Quartet, however, is not nearly as certain. With its string of misfortune, beginning with the messy public firing of former second violinist Crispin Short, followed in short order by his potentially devastating lawsuit, the New Magini's Thursday performance of 'Death and the Maiden' may also signal the death of a remarkable institution."

"That's all," said Nathaniel. He pulled out a notebook from a drawer in the table to take notes, and over their coffee the two of them went over as many possible, if not necessarily probable, scenarios for the appearance of the finger in Annika Haagen's viola case. Could it truly have been Haagen's doing, keeping Kortovsky's finger in her case as some kind of a ghoulish souvenir? Could it be the obnoxious, litigious Brit violinist, Crispin Short, who had swooped down upon Jacobus and Haagen only an hour before the discovery of the finger and issued not-so-veiled threats? Could it be Ivan Lensky, boorish, ambitious, cocksure, and more than disappointed not to have been selected as a full-time violinist in the quartet? Or could it have been Kortovsky himself, missing but nevertheless center stage, who planted someone else's finger? That's the theory Lensky had intimated at the Circle of Fifths, but he had been drunk, so how serious was that? If it was Kortovsky's doing, did the fingers belong to someone he killed in Lima, perhaps? If so, for what reason? Or could it have been someone else entirely, and for reasons they could not yet fathom?

"Well, we're certainly making tons of progress here," said Jacobus. "Is there anything you can tell me that doesn't end in a question mark?"

"I found one of Martin Lilburn's first articles in the *Times* about the lawsuit from a few years ago. Want me to read it?"

"Go ahead. Martin would be happy to know that at least two people read his stories."

" 'Bach, Beethoven, and Bad Times?' "

"I said no question marks."

Nathaniel ignored him and read.

"The New Magini String Quartet was named after one of the first great Italian violin makers, whose instruments are renowned for their beauty of tone, impeccable workmanship, and lasting quality. Though the renowned ensemble can lay claim to the first two of those characteristics, the third may well be in jeopardy.

"Second violinist Crispin Short, recently fired with unprecedented publicity by the other three members of the ensemble, has responded with similar wrath with a lawsuit of immense proportions and implications, one that has the potential not only to bring about the dissolution of one of the world's foremost quartets but also to permanently tarnish the careers of its individual members and empty their bank accounts in the process.

"Until the firing of Mr. Short, fourth son of English factory workers who, according to Mr. Short, grew up 'on the other side of the Tube' in London, performances by the quartet gave little evidence of backstage turmoil. Yet, according to the members of the quartet, trouble had long been brewing.

" 'Over time,' said first violinist Aaron Kortovsky, who was raised in Great Neck, Long Island, and studied at the Juilliard School and the Curtis Institute, 'it became clear that Crispin was not working in the best interests of the group. He has his own personal ambitions that gradually took precedence. He became increasingly vocal with his displeasure of our musical goals, to the point that it was impossible to rehearse constructively. We really had no choice but to dismiss him. Painful as this was, it's something that happens day in, day out with chamber ensembles, and for him to now sue us is not only baffling but despicable.'

"Annika Haagen, violist of the quartet who is married to Kortovsky, added, 'What will happen to music groups if we allow the courts to decide who we must play with? Music is such an intimate thing. Shouldn't we have that right? After all, we were here before Crispin.'

"Yet that may not be how the courts see it. It is certainly not how Crispin Short sees it.

" 'Kortovsky and Haagen have a private, personal agenda,' he stated, 'that has little to do with music and more to do with commercial success. They're looking for a sexed-up image so they can sell more tickets and more recordings and I just didn't fit into their profile, so I was made a scapegoat. I don't mind musical disagreements, but to publicly slander me is a different kettle of fish and requires an appropriately strong rebuke.'

"It was also confirmed that the quartet sent Mr. Short a notarized letter from their legal counsel, Cy Rosenthal, demanding that Mr. Short return all quartet music, his key to their rehearsal studio, and their business credit card within twenty-four hours or risk arrest. The quartet even changed their computer passwords, citing what they claimed to be Mr. Short's tendency toward vindictiveness.

"The one remaining member of the original Magini String Quartet, Pravda Lenskaya, was more philosophical than her colleagues.

" 'When we were in Russia, we had nothing, and we played for nothing except for the music, and our only enemy was government. Now here we are, free and making lots of money and big success, but maybe soon we end up out on street.'

"In the cloistered world of classical music, such sentiments, if expressed, are rarely heard beyond the practice room doors."

Jacobus chuckled. "That's it?" he asked.

"Yeah. What's so funny?"

"These Russian musicians. They go on and on about how they were persecuted in the motherland. How they were followed around by the KGB when they went on tours. How they didn't make enough rubles to buy a sack of potatoes, even if there was a sack of potatoes to buy. How they had to give up their instruments and their families, who were essentially held hostage, when they defected. Then they get here, faint when they see a supermarket that actually has food on the shelves, get a job, make a lot of money, and then tell everyone how great things were in Russia."

"Aren't you being a little harsh? I mean, especially with the Jewish musicians."

"Am I?"

"Pravda Lenskaya was telling me that when they were in Russia, they were always referred to as the Jewish quartet, not Russian. It was only when they came here that people called them Russian, and they would say, 'You mean us?' until they got used to it."

"So?"

"So all I'm saying is that with all they had to give up, maybe they just want to hold onto something. To make them feel better. When you think about what it was like back in the seventies and eighties in the USSR, and then with Chernobyl, that was kind of like the *Titanic* finally hitting the iceberg."

"Yeah, well. Whatever. Anything else, Boutros Boutros?" Jacobus asked, draining the last drops of his second coffee.

"That's it for now. I've got to get over to the music school or I'll be late. I've got a couple students today."

"Any good?"

"Too soon to tell, they're seven years old."

"Christ, how can you put up with that raspy, discordant noise?"

"Hello! I've been talkin' to you for years, haven't I?"

"Have a nice day," said Jacobus.

"Thank you."

"Hey, before you leave!" Jacobus said, reminded of something. "Speaking of funny names, what's a Vaseline oat car?"

Nathaniel laughed. "So you do remember something from last night! It's Otkar Vasalin."

"Oh, thanks. That explains it."

"Otkar Vasalin is a violin collector."

"Never heard of him."

"Not surprising. That's because he's not a dealer. He just collects. Very private. Very shadowy. Originally from one of the Baltic states—Latvia or Lithuania or one of those *ias*—then lived in Russia for a while, then moved around Eastern Europe, then when the whole ball of wax melted he moseyed down to South America."

"And how do you know about him?"

"There've been a few incidences of stolen instruments that people thought led to him that I had to track down for the insurance companies. But they were wrong; he keeps his hands clean."

"He knows a lot about violins, then?"

"Actually, he knows very little. He only buys instruments that have impeccable provenance. Never a question mark. Always very quiet, but always aboveboard. He pays top dollar. And he never sells. In a way, it's unfortunate, because every instrument that's taken off the market makes every other instrument more expensive. Even for him."

"Expensive is right. Where'd he get his money? Selling *blini?*"

"I don't know. Political wheeler-dealer, maybe. Why?"

"No reason. Why'd Lensky bring his name up?"

"He thinks Kortovsky sold his Amati to Vasalin when the quartet was on tour so that Short couldn't get his hands on it if the suit is successful. He thinks Kortovsky plans to live off the fat of the land in South America from the easy pickin's off the sale of the violin and that you'll never hear from him again."

"Well, it's a theory. What do you think?"

"It's possible, I guess. But that's a lot for Kortovsky to give up just to avoid a potential ruling against him. His family, his quartet, his—"

"Fame."

"Yeah. That too. Well, I gotta go. What are you doin' for the rest of the day?"

"I was thinking of taking Trotsky for a walk. In Queens."

Jacobus took another shower, turning the tap as hot as it would go and keeping his head under it for as long as he could tolerate it, the theory being that it would help drain his head of the alcohol and of the lingering congestion brought on by the Beethoven Ninth fiasco. Though it helped marginally in that regard, it failed to clear his head of the plethora of missing people running through his troubled thoughts—Kortovsky, his brother Eli, and an anonymous blind man. When he could no longer stand his head being scalded, he got out of the shower, dried himself off, and got dressed.

Chapter Sixteen

There was no response to Jacobus's bell ringing or repeated knocking at Lenskaya's front door, so he and Trotsky trudged up the driveway to the garage adjacent to the house. Jacobus kept his left foot on the grassy divider and his right foot on the cement lanes for the car tires as a way of confirming that he was walking in a straight line toward the garage, but also partly to maintain his traction from Trotsky, straining at the leash in his left hand while he carried his cane in his right. Jacobus felt the moisture from the tall, wet grass in the divider seep through the seams in his left shoe and up his pant leg to his shin. The grass hadn't been mowed for a long time, indicating to him that the garage was no longer used for cars.

An unseasonably cold, damp wind that blustered off the Long Island Sound bit at his ears. Because it was coming from behind him it was only when they were close to the door on the right side of the garage that he was able to hear the music. The voice, a mezzo-soprano of astounding clarity and virtuosity, was accompanied by a pianist, both sensitive and informative.

Jacobus raised his hand, about to knock, but then, so as not to disturb the duo, waited silently until the aria concluded—it wasn't Schubert by any means; it was Italian, definitely Baroque—whereupon he knocked tentatively on the door. Immediately the piano keyboard cover was slammed down. Heavy, impatient footsteps approached. The door was swung open and a menacing low growl, the opposite of the miraculous tessitura he had just listened to, began to emerge. Just as quickly, however, it vanished.

"Lensky? Peter Lensky?" asked Jacobus.

131

"Who's dis? *Moy malyenkiy!* Who's dis wittle woozie?"

Is this person insane? was Jacobus's first thought—he had been called many things in his life but never "wittle woozie"—until he heard Trotsky begin to groan like a bull walrus in heat, and by the rotation of the leash in his hand he knew that Trotsky was rolling on to his back in order to have his stomach scratched. Jacobus let the "Aw, who dis?" lovefest continue, hoping the man he presumed was Lensky would forget his earlier pique. Finally, the location of the voice, which had descended to ground level, rose back to human height, and above. Lensky's voice was a rich, resonant baritone.

"Yes, I am Lensky. And what is your dog's name? He is castrated, I see."

"We call it neutered."

"That is a strange name."

"No, we say neutered instead of castrated...so we don't hurt woozie's feelings. His name is Trotsky."

"Trotsky? After the Russian revolutionary?"

"No, because he can't runsky."

"I don't understand."

"Never mind."

"So, Mr. Jacobus, what can I do for you?"

"I didn't know we'd met previously," said Jacobus.

"Perhaps not face-to-face," said Lensky, "but my brother told me he had an enlightening conversation with you last night, and the Japanese girl has mentioned you to my mother."

"Girl? She's older than you are."

"That may be. You are looking for my mother, no doubt."

"I was hoping she'd be here. My friend Nathaniel Williams spoke to her yesterday."

"She is out, Mr. Jacobus. One of her shopping forays, no doubt."

"Forays?" asked Jacobus.

"She provides for my needs, shall we say. She doesn't believe I am capable of living on my own, and I don't try to dissuade her."

"Why would she think that?" asked Jacobus. "Shall we invite her in when she returns?"

132

"I prefer to maintain my privacy, but if she returns, we'll see. Why don't you come in where we can be comfortable?"

Jacobus couldn't form a stable mental image of Peter Lensky. His spoken voice, though a rich baritone, had almost feminine mellifluous overtones. His accent showed faint traces of Jewish-Russian heritage, but, from his singing most likely, also contained hints of German, maybe even Italian.

Peter Lensky ushered him to a plain wooden chair. Peter's hand, on Jacobus's arm, was as large and strong as his older brother's, but softer. At least Peter hadn't whacked him on his back. Yet. From the light, impatient arpeggios coming from the keyboard, Lensky had obviously returned to the piano bench.

"Where's your friend?" asked Jacobus.

"Friend?"

"The mezzo. That was pretty virtuoso stuff. Vivaldi?"

"Porpora. And there is no one else here. Except for you."

"You're kidding."

"Why should I lie?"

Jacobus shrugged. "You speak English a lot better than your brother, who's several years older," Jacobus said. "How's that?" Jacobus set his cane down next to the chair, but Trotsky having already usurped that spot, grabbed the cane between his jaws and began to gnaw on it. Jacobus didn't even try to yank it out and resigned himself to hear a snap any moment.

"I came to the U.S. in 1987 to be with my mother," Peter said. "She missed Russia, though Russia had no need for her except for their propaganda, and she missed family. She was expatriated, and with all of the quartet's touring she said she needed grounding, so I came. You should see her home. It is like a little Russian dacha. Here in Queens."

"Nathaniel told me all about it."

"Ivan stayed in Moscow and completed his music training. Real training. You can't find that quality of violin teaching in this country. Everything here is rushed. Superficial. Success before substance."

Jacobus held himself back from saying, "Thank you for your kind words," but instead said, "And no doubt singing helps."

"Singing?" asked Peter.

"With the languages. Nathaniel heard you singing Schubert. Just now I listened to Italian."

"Ah! Of course. Also there is French and English. Spanish. My native Russian, some Yiddish from my father. Yes, I know most of the languages. Ivan is not fluent in any spoken language, but he communicates well in the language of enthusiasm."

"Yes, I've learned that. So, what do you do?" asked Jacobus.

"What do you mean?" replied Peter Lensky. "I play music."

"Professionally?"

"Don't be absurd. I would not allow my music to be polluted by such a toxic cloud. Look at what concerts are these days. Look at my mother's quartet. They must play in any hall their manager books, regardless of the quality of the acoustics, of the lighting, of the stage, of the chairs they sit in, of the backstage facilities, of the lavatories, of the parking. They must play any program the presenter requests, which is usually drivel pabulum. They must play at a time which suits the public: in other words, late enough for the audience to have had time to stuff themselves at the local sushi bar but early enough so that it isn't too late for postconcert drunkenness, never mind that the musicians have to get up the next day at dawn and fly to the next city by the next afternoon for the next concert the next evening.

"And these are the *best* conditions! What happens when the lighting is bad? When the heat is not working or, in your death traps like Phoenix, when the air-conditioning is not working? When the acoustic is like playing in a cardboard box? When they have to play outdoors at these so-called festivals? Tell me, Mr. Jacobus, what is so festive when you have to perform the Pachelbel Canon in blinding heat and you sound like so many little tin cans as the sweat pours down your back?

"And who are they playing for? A bunch of illiterate monkeys! Consider this, Mr. Jacobus. Would you say Schubert and Beethoven and Mozart are great composers? That they have attained the highest degree of human accomplishment?"

"No doubt."

"Then what does it say about humanity when the response people have to this music, any music, is to slap their hands together; and the more they like it, the louder and faster they slap? This is the behavior of apes beating on their chests, not supposedly intelligent beings. And then, if the hand slapping is not sufficient to convey their excitement, they stomp their feet on the ground and even jump up and down, yelling incoherently. Can you imagine a greater extreme in behavior, Mr. Jacobus, than this bestial response to the most sublime human achievement? Must we pander to the beast in us?"

"You've got a point. Can't say I've ever thought of it that way."

"But this is not the worst of professionalism, Mr. Jacobus. This is not the worst."

"No? Sounds pretty bad to me."

"The worst is when the music itself becomes corrupted. When the purity of the musical vision becomes perverted by egomaniacal interests. When you add the light shows, the dancers, the videos, the—"

"The Power Ramseys?"

"Precisely. You understand. The Power Ramseys of this world have made my mother into a strumpet. And they call this 'professionalism.'"

Jacobus laughed. "Ah! Absolute Power corrupts Ramsey! I'd actually been daydreaming of writing a book along those lines, Peter. I was going to call it 'Crimes Against Humanities.'"

"We think along the same lines, Mr. Jacobus! I have already written such a book."

"Really! That's very precocious for someone so young."

"I have an old soul, or so I'm told. Translated into English it would be called 'Crimes Without Punishment,' but unfortunately for you it is in Russian."

"Too bad. By the time it's published, translated to English, and then Braille, I'll be dead."

"We'll both be, no doubt."

"So I presume you don't go to concerts, either," Jacobus said, after he stopped laughing. "What recordings do you listen to, then?" he asked, an aficionado, via old 78s and LPs, of the great violinists of the early twentieth century.

"Recordings, never!"

"Why not?" asked Jacobus. "You don't hear the kind of playing anymore that I heard when I was a kid. Kreisler, Horowitz, Heifetz. One can learn from great musicians of the past."

"One can learn from the music, not the musicians. It is all in the music. A piece of music is a life. It exists in time and space. With the first note it is born and with the last it dies. The Rewind button is the death of real music. If we were able to replay our lives over and over again, what a tragedy that would be, for it would make our real existence, the precious beauty of every moment, meaningless. When I hear music, true music in front of me, I see color. I see all colors. I feel the radiation of the vibrating air. It is an invisible force molding all life. But when I hear a recording, I see nothing. I feel nothing. Only blackness. No. A performance must live, then it must die, and that is why when it ends, there should be silence and contemplation, not the slapping of the hands. When I sing Schubert, I am the ichor of Schubert."

When Lensky began the gently pulsating eighth notes on the piano, Jacobus immediately recognized the song, even before Lensky began to sing in a glowing, radiant tenor. It was one of Schubert's great uplifting songs, "An die Musik," Hymn to Music, and within a few irresistible verses, Jacobus found himself humming along.

> *"Du holde Kunst, in wieviel grauen Stunden,*
> *Wo mich des Lebens wilder Kreis umstrickt,*
> *Hast du mein Herz zu warmer Lieb' entzunden,*
> *Has mich in eine bessre Welt entruckt!*
>
> *"Oft hat ein Seufzer, deiner Harf entflossen,*
> *Ein susser, heiliger Akkord von dir*
> *Den Himmel bessrer Zeiten mir erschlossen,*
> *Du holde Kunst, ich danke dir dafur!"*

In one way, thought Jacobus, it was just the opposite of "Death and the Maiden." In another way, though, it was exactly the same. It was not Death,

136

but Music, beckoning the singer into the next life.

> *"Oh dear Art, during how many gray hours,*
> *When life's savage cycle traps me,*
> *Have you lit my heart with warm love,*
> *And placed me in a better world!*
>
> *"Often, a sigh, released from your harp,*
> *And a sweet, holy chord of yours*
> *Has unlocked the heaven of better times for me,*
> *Oh dear Art, I thank you for this!"*

Jacobus had never heard a more blissfully moving rendition of the song. Peter indeed seemed to be Schubert when he sang it, and Jacobus was about to applaud gratefully at the song's conclusion, but caught himself just in time.

Finally, it was Peter who spoke first. "You said I was precocious, Mr. Jacobus, but Schubert was my age when he composed this masterpiece. It was also not long after when he died. I am but a servant of the master. Please wait here. I must ablute. I am wet."

"Go ahead and ablute."

While he was gone, Jacobus pondered Lensky's radical ideas about the state of music and concluded they were not so unlike his own. Maybe when he was younger he had shared Lensky's cocksure certainty of the truth of his convictions, though "younger" had been so long ago, he couldn't really remember. In any event, he never would have been able to express his thoughts with such eloquence.

He did remember, though, and would never forget the experience of 1931 when he was a youthful contestant in the Grimsley Violin Competition, which in so many ways was a perversion of what music should be about. Students who had been force-fed music for seven, eight, nine hours a day for months, like geese having gavage stuffed down their gullets to engorge their livers, only in order to compete against each other like pint-sized gladiators.

Children who were instructed to play music not *with* each other but *against* each other.

"Trotsky, what the hell are you doing now?" Jacobus said, as the tension on the leash pulled him off his seat like a daydreaming fisherman who had just hooked a marlin. He had no choice but to follow the dog to the piano, where he heard Trotsky sniffing animatedly around the piano bench. Jacobus, curious, followed suit, but with his sinus congestion wasn't able to smell much of anything, except perhaps some lingering body odor. "Well, he did say," Jacobus quietly said to Trotsky, dragging him from the piano, "he had to ablute."

When Lensky finally did return, it wasn't perspiration Jacobus smelled but the seductive aroma of ripe imported cheese.

"I like talking to you," said Lensky, "so I've brought us a meager repast. Some cheese, a little caviar, some biscuits, black bread."

"Peter, you know, I think you're being a little too hard on mama," said Jacobus, accepting his first tidbit. "After all, we're living in a capitalist society here and she needs to earn money to make her shopping forays so that you can stay here in your inner sanctum eating canapés and keeping your music pure."

"Money? One can survive without it. One can survive so many things. She has made her choice to play for the monkeys."

"Perhaps, but this is the real world we're talking about." Jacobus accepted proffered caviar on a cracker without any qualms and popped it in his mouth. "People have to make livings, and what your mother is doing is not coal mining. Yes, there is a difference between a recording and a live performance, but there is also a difference between an audience and no audience. There is a great mystery to music."

"We know this."

"But it's not the one you've been talking about. It's the one where thousands of people pay good money to sit in a room and watch other people create a highly complex set of vibrations. And of why those vibrations, which literally physically enter the bodies of those thousands of people, create a common subjective, visceral response, even if the music was composed three hundred years ago in some far-off country that the person in the audience has never been to. There's something mystical about this—maybe science will someday explain how it all works—you call it color, I call it a force—but for now it's definitely mystical, and your mother is creating a set of some of the world's greatest vibrations at an extremely high level. She can't help it if she's playing it for philistines. Could you pass a slice of the havarti?"

"Or *with* Philistines?"

"Look, Peter, everyone has their own taste," Jacobus said, swallowing. "There's no right or wrong in music. Let me take that back. There's a little bit of right and a lot of wrong, but there are no absolutes is what I'm saying. You might not go for the likes of Kortovsky or Crispin Short or—"

"It is intriguing, is it not, Mr. Jacobus, how an artist can at the same time have the capability to create something intensely beautiful, yet still have an off-putting, even repulsive personality."

"Like Short?" asked Jacobus.

"No. Not Short. He is a good, sincere musician."

"Really? I'm surprised to hear you say that, considering he's suing your mother."

"That's not his fault. That's the doing of Haagen and Kortovsky, and by making this all public, maybe they now cannot fire my mother as Crispin told me they would. But in the large scheme of things, someone like Kortovsky was small potatoes. I was thinking of great artists, like Wagner, like Beethoven, or even..."

"Or even?"

"Or even yourself."

"I suppose I should consider that a compliment," said Jacobus.

"Indeed, though to be honest, I haven't found you as repulsive as your reputation led me to believe."

"That's very kind of you."

"But I cannot say the same for Kortovsky. In Russia, many years ago, when my mother played the Schubert Quintet with the great Rostropovich, he wouldn't permit her to play the second-cello part. He made her play *first* cello, because he said when she played the slow movement it was like heaven opening for him. Every time they rehearsed it he would jump up, give her his bear hug, and kiss her on both cheeks. But what does Kortovsky say to her? He says, 'Play on the string. You're too soft. You're too loud. Your vibrato makes me ill.' What kind of treatment is this for an artist?"

"So, you have any ideas why Kortovsky hasn't shown up to mistreat your mother some more? They've got a dress rehearsal tomorrow afternoon, and if he doesn't make an appearance, it'll be your big brother again."

"My brother seems to believe Kortovsky is in South America."

"And what do you seem to believe?"

"I suppose he is off somewhere auditioning nubile, young cellists with large bosoms."

"Off somewhere? Can you narrow that down?"

"Nubile, young, *blond* cellists with large bosoms."

"Hmm. Could you pass some more of that caviar?"

Chapter Seventeen

The Rose Grimes School of Music is located in an old four-story brownstone just a few blocks north of Central Park in Harlem. The building had been slated for demolition, but with the intervention of several prominent local politicians running for reelection and well-connected board members, the school was able to obtain a grant from the city to renovate the structure. That the director of the school, the young African-American violinist BTower, had achieved worldwide celebrity as a concert artist also helped focus public attention on the effort to create a tuition-free after-school music program for underprivileged students, young and old.

The assembly gathered in the third-floor chorus room. Folding chairs had been set up for the guests; the approximately fifty students sat on the floor. Jacobus and Nathaniel had arrived there early and, after exhausting themselves climbing the stairs that still smelled of new paint in the as yet elevatorless building, were sitting in the back of the room catching their breath.

The New Magini String Quartet was introduced by BTower, who read a list of their accomplishments over the years—their tours, their recordings, their awards—and though the details meant little to the students who were by and large unfamiliar with names like Spoleto and Aspen Music Festival, EMI and DGG—in other words, the world outside their own neighborhood—the impressively daunting length of the list alone was sufficient to elicit enthusiastic applause.

The quartet's outreach program was in two parts. The first was a description of the story of the String Quartet in E Minor, entitled "From My Life," by the nineteenth-century composer, Bedřich Smetana. The second was to demonstrate how Smetana gave each of the four instrumentalists an opportunity to tell a different part of that story by taking over the leadership of the music. Because this was a program the New Magini String Quartet had presented this program many times, and because it was the first occasion for Ivan Lensky, it was left to the three women to deliver the scripted explanations.

They started with the story. How each movement of the quartet depicts a chronological autobiography of the composer's life. How the first movement represents the turbulence of Smetana's early years as a composer and his struggle to gain legitimacy for himself and for Czech national music in a country that had been under Germanic cultural and political domination for hundreds of years. How the second movement, rousing and exuberant, is a celebration of the Czech folk dance. How the third is a passionate love song to his wife. How the fourth begins with the celebration of Smetana as a beloved, revered composer in his homeland—a national hero, in truth—and the respect he gained for his music throughout Europe. But then how the triumph suddenly turns to tragedy with the playing of a piercing high E by the first violin, which represented the debilitating sound Smetana heard continuously in his head in his final years, a symptom of the syphilis that resulted in his loss of sight, hearing, sanity, and ultimately, his life. How, though biographical music is not unknown on the concert stage, this quartet, of a composer describing his own death, is unique to the entire repertoire.

By this point, the students were wholly absorbed by the story behind the music and were expectantly anticipating the demonstrations. Even Jacobus was eager to hear the performance. He knew the story backwards and forwards but had always enjoyed listening to the music simply because it was great music, especially with Haagen playing that viola solo in the beginning. He tried to get comfortable in the folding chair.

"Think BTower can get another grant for some decent chairs?" Jacobus whispered to Nathaniel.

"Shush!" whispered Nathaniel in response. "Just be happy you don't have to sit on the floor."

The quartet's violent E-minor downbeat, Allegro vivo appassionato, abruptly terminating their conversation, was followed by the undulating pianissimo eighth notes in the two violins and the long low E in the cello, setting the stage for the recklessly defiant viola solo for which Annika Haagen was perhaps the world's most compelling exponent. With her bow, Haagen bit into her strings, playing with a passion and intensity that always had the result of riveting and inspiring young audiences.

About thirty seconds into the music, Lensky stopped playing, followed shortly thereafter in disorganized fashion by the others.

"Have you got a problem, Ivan?" Haagen asked.

"Sorry to interrupt," said Lensky, "but you rushing."

The assembly, already silent, somehow managed to get even quieter.

"What do you mean? I'm the soloist and this is the way we've always done it."

"You play faster, faster. Is impossible to play together with bad rhythm. You must listen to others."

"That's ridiculous," said Haagen. "All you've got are damn eighth notes, and you're telling *me* that—"

"Students," said Yumi, quickly addressing the group, "this is a good example of what goes on in rehearsals. How every little detail of our performance has to be dissected and practiced until the whole ensemble reaches agreement. That's one of the things that makes string quartet playing such a wonderful challenge. We'll now go to the second movement, where the second violin leads a very upbeat, joyful Czech polka. But it's all on the G-string, which makes it very difficult, so listen very carefully and let me know if I do okay.

"Second movement," she said to the others and gave the upbeat before anyone had time to object. When they finished Yumi's excerpt, the students applauded, enjoying the rhythmic playfulness of the music. The quartet then played the third movement, Largo sostenuto, in which Pravda played her cello solo with the internationally renowned heartwarming soulfulness for which she had been dubbed "Mrs. Slav" and which provided the tonal foundation for the whole quartet, representing Smetana's own voice as he expressed his love for his wife.

The last excerpt, featuring the first-violin part flamboyantly performed by Lensky, started in the middle of the fourth and final movement, Vivace, where the music seems to be accelerating into a victorious ending but is suddenly interrupted by his fortissimo high-E harmonic. From that point the music turns ominously dark, reminisces dreamily on the composer's earlier life with brief flashbacks from the first three movements, then descends despondently into oblivion.

After the last long note disappeared into nothingness, they remained motionless in position, freezing the uninitiated audience from reacting to soon. The silence was broken by BTower's applause, followed by Jacobus, and then by the others.

There followed a short session during which the quartet answered questions, none of which they had not heard a hundred times before: How much does your instrument cost? How old were you when you started? How old are you now? How much do you practice? My brother plays the guitar.

There were two interesting questions. One was from a tall, elderly gentleman named Bailey Haskell, who had recently retired from a career as a prison guard and was just a beginner. He said that he had noticed the members of the quartet were all breathing together and wanted to know whether that was something that they worked on as a group.

Haagen responded to that one, talking not only about breathing but also about movement, and how, when a group achieved unanimity in how they wanted a phrase to sound, it was almost inevitable that they would breathe together. So it was actually the idea that comes first, and the physical manifestation of it that follows.

The second interesting question was from Yumi's young student, Louisa. Yumi was surprised but happy to see Louisa's hand shoot up and so called on her herself.

"Yes, Louisa?"

"Will I be able to play that song when I grow up?"

"You certainly will...if you work hard enough."

BTower then thanked the quartet for coming to the school, asked the students to give them another round of applause, and dismissed the assembly. He chatted amiably with Jacobus and Nathaniel as the three of them passed the quartet packing up their instruments, on their way to the stairs. They were about two flights down when Jacobus heard the quartet enter the stairwell above them; already there was some commotion, some heated discussion on. In the echo chamber of the stairway and with BTower talking to Nathaniel about the excellent progress the school was making, it was difficult for Jacobus to make out what was being said. Suddenly there were a series of shouts, then the ugly rumble of someone stumbling, falling down the stairs.

BTower and Nathaniel immediately turned and raced back up, Jacobus following as quickly as he could, one hand on the railing the other using his cane like an alpenstock to propel him upwards.

"Someone call nine-one-one," he heard Yumi order.

"No! No, it's all right. I'm okay," came Annika's voice. "Just leave me alone. *Pfff.* I only hope the viola is not broken."

"What happened?" Nathaniel asked.

"It was nothing. It was accident," said Pravda.

"What was an accident?" asked Jacobus.

"Annika and Ivan were arguing about what happened at the outreach," Yumi said.

"Not arguing," said Ivan. "Discussing. We were discussing. I say to Annika, so, maybe you think now I know Smetana Quartet."

"And Annika said," Yumi continued, " 'Yes, you do death very well.' "

"I thought it was funny joke," said Ivan.

"So he gave her a friendly pat on the back," said Yumi, "hard enough to knock her down a flight of stairs."

"Annika, can you get up? You've broken anything?" Jacobus asked.

"Nothing a stiff drink wouldn't fix," she said. "But please, someone check my Gasparo."

Annika's viola, strapped in and protected by a newfangled epoxy composite case, fared better than Annika herself, who suffered a twisted right

145

ankle and bruised left shoulder, but was otherwise reasonably intact. Ivan and Pravda continued to protest that it had been an accident, even as Yumi helped the limping Annika into a cab.

"A little tumble's not nearly as intimidating an experience as finding a finger in a case. Don't you agree, Ivan?" Annika asked. She rolled up the window and the cab drove off.

Chapter Eighteen

"More Tabasco?" asked Nathaniel.

Once it had been determined there was no medical emergency, at Jacobus's insistence he and Nathaniel went all the way back to Midtown. Jacobus had already been deprived of one opportunity to eat at Fat Chance and didn't want to risk missing it altogether. Plus, Sheila Rathman had called with "awesome news" and wanted to meet them somewhere in her vicinity.

"No, I'm okay," Jacobus replied to Nathaniel's offer. "I'm trying to be careful with my stomach." Jacobus felt for a Kissin' Kuzzin on his plate, using his sense of touch to distinguish it from the hush puppies, and submerged it into a bowl of tartar sauce.

"Have to say," said Nathaniel, "Ivan really moved up the chart of suspicious characters today. Annika called him on his masculinity and musicianship, but you wouldn't think he had to shove her down a flight of stairs to give it back to her. With her and Kortovsky having stood in his way from getting into the quartet, who knows what he might have done to Kortovsky?"

"Yeah, maybe. But it doesn't really make sense to me," said Jacobus. "My guess is that if he thought Kortovsky was out of the way, the next stop on Lensky's agenda would be to become Kortovsky's replacement as first violin. But if that's true, he'd want to kiss the fair Annika's ass, not bounce it down the stairway."

"Maybe he'd want to get rid of her too and bring back the old gang."

"Nah, I don't think so. Those guys're living in the past through a haze of vodka. They're no more capable of a comeback than I am. I'm thinking the accident with Haagen was just that, an accident."

"Speaking of whom, it wasn't so easy getting confirmation of her kid, Prince Rupert's, reservation to Peru," said Nathaniel, returning to the summary of the information he had obtained earlier in the day.

"Tell me what wasn't so easy about it."

"The first thing I did was call Sheila Rathman to find out from the invoices that Annika had submitted what airlines she flew on. That was the easy part."

"Where is Rathman, anyway? She's late. What was the hard part? How's your jambalaya?"

"Almost as good as Mama's, but I think this shrimp was frozen. Delta refused to give me the information since I wasn't an 'authorized party.' They also required the kid's ticket number. I told them if I had the ticket number, I wouldn't need to be asking them if he had a reservation."

"Sounds like an airline. Can you pass a napkin?"

"Plus, they needed his last name, and I didn't know whether it was Haagen, Kortovsky, or a combination of the two."

"So what did you do? Tell them off?" Jacobus asked. He took a final swig of Abita Turbodog, the house brew.

"No. That's something you would do. I called Sheila back and got the name of the hotel Haagen stayed in. The Marriott in Miraflores. I asked Sheila to call the hotel pretending she was Haagen, telling them that her son had left his precious Game Boy in the hotel room—"

"And they said they would look for it, but in the meantime they remembered the little boy very well and hoped they had a pleasant stay. Right?"

"Something like that. In any event, I'm pretty sure the boy was with his mother. Shall I order two more beers?"

"Only if you give me one of them. What about getting Rathman to open up Kortovsky's instrument trunk? Any progress?"

"Hold on." Nathaniel signaled for the waitress to bring another round. "She said she tried the insurance company, but they're balking. They told her that whether the violin is in the trunk or not wouldn't be conclusive enough to warrant making an exception to their policy—"

"That's ridiculous."

"Yeah, well. They're an insurance company. One step up from an airline."

Jacobus stopped eating. "I think he's dead," he said, the words escaping almost before the conscious thought.

"*Mmm*. The body in Lima?"

"Yeah. Just a feel. People are starting to refer to him in the past tense. Maybe that's why."

"There's nothing for sure that says he's dead," said Nathaniel.

"But there's nothing that says he's alive, either—"

"Mr. Jacobus! Mr. Jacobus! I've got some good news!"

Even if he hadn't recognized the voice, the perfume gave her away, so when, in an effort to be helpful, she redundantly said, "It's me, Sheila," he replied by saying, "It's me, Jacobus," which momentarily puzzled her into silence.

"You were saying," said Jacobus. "The good news? Remember? You gonna sit down?"

"Oh, yes. Yes! The first thing is that Power Ramsey said that since Martin Lilburn's article came out in the *Times* this morning, the box office phone has been ringing nonstop. It looks like the concert is going to be sold out!"

"That's great. Maybe if we throw in a few more vital organs it'll be standing room only."

"Do you think?"

"Never mind. You said that was the first thing. Is there a second thing?"

"Yes there is. We won't be needing to break into Aaron's trunk."

"Yeah? Why's that? Did you say 'Open, sesame'?"

"No."

"Okay, honey, spit it out. Tell me the good news."

"I just received an email from him!"

"Wonderful!" said Nathaniel. "We were starting to get worried that something had happened to him. Would you like something to eat, Sheila?"

"No thanks. I only have a minute, then I have to run."

Jacobus was surprised, and he admitted to himself, disappointed. All the theories he had devised, all the conversations with Oro, all the intrigue with Haagen–were they all just fanciful pipe dreams? Had he secretly been hoping for Kortovsky's demise so that he, the great Jacobus, could once again claim to have solved the insolvable?

"Hold on a minute. An email?" he asked. "What was in it?"

"Aaron says he's okay and plans on being at the dress rehearsal tomorrow afternoon. I've called Ivan and told him that we'll pay him for the rehearsal but his presence won't be necessary. And I know you're kind of the suspicious type, so I printed a copy and brought it to you."

"What about the two you deleted?"

"I have to confess to you, Mr. Jacobus, I wasn't being truthful. One of them is...not intended for public consumption, but I never did delete them. I printed them out because I was getting worried. But now that he's okay—"

"You have them here?"

"Why, yes."

"Hand them over."

"But—"

"Never mind *but*. Give them to Nathaniel to read. He won't broadcast it to the masses, if that's what you're worrying about. We're all grown-ups here."

Jacobus heard Rathman open her purse, remove some sheets of paper and hand them to Nathaniel. He then heard Nathaniel unfold them.

After Nathaniel finished reading, he said, "Well, the first one's a little spicy, but it's like Sheila said."

"And the second?" asked Jacobus. "Spicy?"

"The second was written a day after the first, and just reiterates that he'll be arriving for the first rehearsal. Cut and dry, just to confirm, I guess."

"You have the third one, you said?" Jacobus asked Sheila. "Read it. Please."

" 'Sheila, I was unexpectedly delayed in South America, and will be at the dress rehearsal tomorrow. Aaron.' "

"That's it?" asked Jacobus.

"Yes."

"How do you know it's from him? How do you know any of them are from him?"

"What do you mean? It's from him. It has his email address."

"When was the last one sent?" asked Jacobus.

"About three hours ago, but I just opened it an hour ago," said Rathman. "It had to be Aaron, because you need to know the quartet's username and password to contact me the way he did, plus of course he had my email address."

"Well, computers are not exactly user-friendly for blind people, and I'm no expert with these emails and all that username and password crap, but it's not like a letter where you see the handwriting or a voice on a phone where—"

"I think you're grasping at straws, Jake," said Nathaniel. "The likelihood of—"

"Have you written back?" Jacobus asked Rathman.

"Not yet."

"Do me a favor, hon," Jacobus said, trying to imitate the sound of what he supposed conceptually to be a supportively patient voice. "Shoot him off an email and ask him a question only he'd know the answer to."

"I don't see why—"

"Look," he interrupted, dropping any notion of cordiality. "We need to be sure it's Kortovsky who's writing because we still have someone's finger without the someone. Am I getting through?"

"What kind of question?"

"How the hell do I know? How many dimples on your ass? Or is that common knowledge?"

Jacobus heard the seat next to him pop up and the high heels click away faster than Secretariat at the Belmont.

"Good work, Jake," said Nathaniel. "You sure know how to get results."

"Fuck you too," said Jacobus. "And where the hell is our beer?"

Chapter Nineteen

J acobus was chewing on an extra antacid for good luck and was ready to sack out when the phone rang in Nathaniel's apartment.

"It's your new amigo," Nathaniel said, and handed Jacobus the phone.

"Oro, you have any idea what the hell time it is?"

"Eleven fifty-four, New York time, I believe. Did you know that the time in Lima is the same as–"

"Never mind. What do you want?"

"We have some complication. It appears, Maestro Yacovis, that we have perhaps been led down the false path. I assure you, though, that—"

"What do you mean, a false path? The corpse get up and run away?"

"I am glad to hear you have not lost your sense of humor, Maestro. Because I was finding some difficulty discovering anything about Señor Kortovsky after the night of the concert in Lima on July 27, I went back to the hotel for a further discussion with the receptionist, Señorita Angelita Flores. I asked to see the receipt that all guests are required to sign upon checking out in order to determine if there might be some informations that could be helpful."

"And the informations was not helpful?"

"There was no informations, Maestro. This was both unhelpful and helpful."

"I've got two questions."

"Yes, Maestro."

"One: Could you please stop talking in riddles and get to the point?"

"I will do my best. And the other?"

"Can you stop calling me Maestro? It's giving me a headache."

"What shall I call you then?"

"How about Jake?"

"As you please, Yake. So I will give you all the informations, and you decide if it is helpful or unhelpful…Yake. It seems that when Señorita Flores, who had the shift of the night when the Lima concert took place, noticed that Señor Kortovsky did not return while she was on duty. The next day his room was cleaned, but the day after that it was clear that nobody had slept in the bed. However, Señor Kortovsky's belongings were still in his room, and he had not checked out even though his reservation had expired.

"Señorita Flores properly had Señor Kortovsky's belonging transferred into the office by the house help, to remain there until Señor Kortovsky returned to claim them. These belongings were put into a corner where they would not be in the way of anyone, but at the same time, they were out of the view of everyone.

"When Señor Kortovsky did not return after several more days, Señorita Flores, who is a hard worker with four young children but no husband, was unable to resist the temptation. She removed the belongings of Señor Kortovsky and gave them to her cousin, José Carlos, who has a degree in architecture but who at the moment is a driver of the *tico*, to dispose of on what you call the black market. As a result, I could not find any information on Señor Kortovsky's receipt because there never was a receipt."

"Hey, Oro, you're sounding a little protective of hardworking Señorita Flores and overachieving José Carlos after they killed Kortovsky so they could sell his million-dollar violin, and computer, and high-tech mountain-climbing gear and live high off the hog. Why the warm and fuzzy?"

"That was my precise thought, as well, Yake, when Señorita Flores confessed to me."

"And?"

"Now I do not believe it is true."

"Why not? It fits, doesn't it?"

"Yes and no, but more no than yes. If they killed him, and if we assume the body one street away is that of Kortovsky, there was no reason to then

153

spend so much time removing the body parts and risk discovery. It would not fit their motive. Then, if we assume Señor Kortovsky was killed the night of the twenty-seventh, which I think we may now do since that was the last time anyone saw him, both Señorita Flores and her cousin have the good alibi. She was on duty and he was repairing his *tico* with his brother, Miguel. I believe they are innocent of murder because I talked to them. I also believe they stretched the law because they are poor, but they were most remorseful."

"It's not hard to be remorseful when the choices are going to jail for the rest of your life or being a millionaire."

"Ah, you are wise, Yake. Here in Peru there are not so many *ricos*. People with a little money, a modest house, have iron fences, alarm systems, floodlights, security guards, because too many other people with little money are envious. So no doubt there was the temptation. Yet I have not told you one important detail that you had all the rights to assume. They made some money selling Señor Kortovsky's mountain-climbing goods, *sí*; however, there was no violin and no computer, so they did not become the millionaires enough to kill for."

"How the hell do you know that? Did you look deep into their eyes and decide you could trust them?"

"This time you are incorrect, Yake."

"Then *how?*"

"I have my ways, Maestro. They have been persuaded to tell the truth, and you can trust me in this. They did not kill anyone."

In those few sentences Jacobus heard what Oro hid under his velvet-tongued civility—a cold-as-death ruthlessness that made him shudder. He knew better than to argue.

"Then where does that leave us?" asked Jacobus.

"There are two meanings to the American phrase 'check out,' are there not? One is to leave a hotel, the other is to die. Is that not correct?"

"Yeah," said Jacobus. "Where did you hear that?"

"*Cagney and Lacey*. I confess it is my favorite TV show. So entertaining. But I am taking up too much of your time."

"Yes, you are."

"Well, now that we know that Señor Kortovsky did not check out of the Maury Hotel, because there was no reason we know of for him to not check out, there is a greater chance that he is the corpse who checked out one block away."

"Unless he was the killer."

"That is always possible, yes, but if that were the truth, don't you think he would have returned to the hotel, checked out, and removed his belongings to continue life in an unsuspecting way? It is also possible he fled the hotel for a reason to which we are not the privy, but the location of the body suggests that is not the likely trail. No, more and more I fear that our victim is the person whom you seek."

"If that's true..." Jacobus mused. "Do you still have the corpse chilling out in a morgue somewhere?"

"I am sorry to say the body has been disposed of. If at the time we had known..."

"What about the autopsy report?"

"Yes. That we still have. Of course."

"I want you to check out if medical examiner noticed anything interesting about the right hand."

"The right hand. And for what purpose, Yake?"

"To satisfy my curiosity, let's say."

"I will investigate and tell you. You have my word. In the meantime, I will also speak to the bartender who served Señor Kortovsky several pisco sours with the mysterious stranger."

"Mysterious stranger!" bellowed Jacobus. "Why the fuck didn't you tell me this first? Who the hell is the mysterious stranger?"

"If I knew, then he would not be a mysterious stranger, would he?"

"Let's not get into that again, Oro," said Jacobus. "Just spit it out."

"Late that night, the night we presume Señor Kortovsky was killed, he and another yenkleman were seen in the bar by the bartender, who served Señor Kortovsky three or four of the Maury Hotel's legendary pisco sours."

"Enough of the travelogue, Oro, I just—"

"This time it is important, Yake, not just my pride of the nation. You see, one pisco sour at the Maury is *fuerte*, strong. Three or four would make someone not accustomed to its potency, how shall I say, assume the horizontal. And also, please note, the bartender did not say he served pisco sours to both yenklemen, only to Señor Kortovsky. Do you see now what I am thinking?"

"You think Señor X got Kortovsky drunk and then dragged him off in order to kill him."

"Precisely."

"Any idea who Señor X is, then?"

"Señor Equis? I am not sure, except that I am told he had a limp."

"The man at the concert! Who you bumped into!"

"Perhaps, but it is too early to conclude."

"Didn't the bartender see his face?"

"It was dark, and he had no reason to be interested. But I did not see his face either at the concert, only his back. But we will continue the search."

"Well, maybe I underestimated you, Oro. Maybe you will figure this out. Anything else?"

"Just one thing more, Yake.

"Oro, it's not Yake. It's Jake. With a *juh*, not a *yuh*."

"Of course, Yake. *Discúlpeme*. Before this mysterious man arrived, there was another person who met with Señor Kortovsky at the hotel after the concert. A young lady."

"Let me guess. Señorita Angelita?" Jacobus asked, enjoying the rhyme and the musical bounce of rhythm. Señorita Angelita. Señorita Angelita.

"I am afraid not. It was your former student, Señorita Shinagawa."

"Like hell it was," Jacobus exploded. "How do you know?"

"I had her photo, from the program. I showed it to many of the workers at the hotel. She was well recognized, even by the housekeeper who saw her going into Señor Kortovsky's room. We have a surprising number of Japanese people in Peru, Yake, but few as attractive as Señorita Shinagawa. And even fewer who have those marvelous green eyes. Certainly someone of her ancestors was not *un japonés*."

"English," said Jacobus. "Grandmother."

"Ah! Another mystery solved. But I must be very honest with you, Yake, and I tell you this even though I shouldn't because I have the high respect of you: Because of the information you have given me, I was required as a police officer to inform your New York City lieutenant, Lieutenant Malachi, of my information. He was very thankful."

"I'll bet," said Jacobus.

Chapter Twenty

THURSDAY

As he waited by the receptionist's desk in Lewis Carino's office, Jacobus made a fist, pounded his chest, and belched. Fond memories of Fat Chance. He didn't mind. What he did mind was being kept waiting for Crispin Short to arrive.

"When's he going to get here?" Jacobus asked the receptionist for the third time.

"I'm sure he'll be here any moment now," she said for the third time. "He's aware of your appointment. Would you care for a magazine?"

"You have a recent copy of *Modern Invalid?*"

He decided not to ask any more and sat there contemplating while the receptionist continued to do nothing of any appreciable value that he was able to ascertain.

"Ah, so there you are!" Short said when he eventually arrived. "Waiting long, have we?"

"Yes, we have," said Jacobus.

"A bit hot under the collar, are we?"

Jacobus did not respond.

"Mr. Carino gave us a conference room," Short continued. "He decided that since you haven't brought a lawyer it would be better if he left us to our own devices and found something else to do."

"Like boff his receptionist?"

"We take a jaundiced view of the legal profession, do we now?"

"Me? Not at all. I'm just trying to figure out what purpose Miss Efficiency has for taking up space in the office."

"Yes, that is a bit of a mystery," said Short. "One of the trappings of success, I suppose. Can't begrudge anyone that, can we? Now, do we need assistance to the conference room?"

"Don't bother. We'll just follow you in."

After the two of them had seated themselves on opposite ends of a very long table, Short asked, "What is it that is so urgent for you to find out that is not already known?"

"How did you know Ivan Lensky was filling in for Kortovsky?" Jacobus asked.

"What does it matter to you?"

"Because with an empty seat in the quartet, who more than you would want to fill it? You might not be too pleased someone else's ass is warming it."

"Look, Mr. Jacobus," Short said, "the last thing I'd want is for Kortovsky not to be there. His absence has delayed my long-overdue satisfaction. Aaron Kortovsky is a fanatic, Mr. Jacobus, in everything, with an ego to match."

"Everything? That's a pretty broad generalization, don't you think?"

"For anyone but him, yes. But with Aaron, everything had to be his way. It didn't matter what."

"Had?" asked Jacobus. "Didn't? Why all the past tense? Has Aaron changed, or are you suggesting there's no more Aaron?"

"Aren't we suspicious now?" said Short. "Who the bloody hell knows where he is or whether he's still alive? Just like him to keep everyone on tenterhooks. Always the boss, whether it's music, his ridiculous rock-climbing, his..."

"Women?"

"Whatever."

"It drove you nuts, huh?"

"What are you insinuating?"

Jacobus avoided a direct answer. "I was told to ask you the story about the broken bow."

"Why? By whom?"

"Let's just say it's an Up Close and Personal."

"I've got nothing to hide, Mr. Jacobus. And you're a violinist so you'll understand." Receiving no response other than a grunt from Jacobus, Short continued.

"Aaron insisted…insists that we always play on the string."

"That doesn't sound too fanatical to me," said Jacobus. "That's the old mantra: You play chamber music *on* the string, you play orchestra music *off* the string; the former for the big, juicy sound you need from a small ensemble; the latter for the articulation and clarity you need from a big group."

"As a general rule, that's absolutely fine and I have no complaint. But *every* fast passage, and *always* at the tip of the bow? *Never* spiccato in the middle of the bow, which is so much more natural and, when it needs to be, so much more incisive."

"Never?"

"Well, hardly ever. Usually if you just experimented with playing off the string he'd stop immediately and make some derisively humiliating insult that either you had no bow control, or… Once, for example, he told me that my tone was like a rodent repeller."

"You poor guy. He hurt your feelings. So you broke his bow."

"You may mock me, Mr. Jacobus, but after a while, after years of being belittled…"

Jacobus heard Short take a deep breath. Preamble over.

"One day we were rehearsing the finale of Beethoven Fifty-nine number three. You must agree that, of any piece in the literature, it is simply too fast to play on the string *and* at the point on the violin, let alone on the cello." Short stopped, apparently awaiting a response.

"I take your point," said Jacobus.

"Well, poor Pravda was doing her best, but Aaron browbeat her mercilessly. I mean, after all, her bow was only obeying the laws of nature. That's why bows are made of wood, isn't it, after all, for their flexibility? Aaron told her

160

that her playing matched her looks. Like a cow chewing her cud. And you know what she did, Mr. Jacobus?"

"I'm sure you'll tell me."

"She just sat there. Impassive. I decided something needed to be said, so I noted that every other string quartet in history has played this fugue in the middle of the bow, and no amount of insulting would change that fact. I knew when I said it there would be retaliation."

"So you waited, knowing it was your turn, and came up with a plan?"

"With an idea, shall we say? As you may have heard, Mr. Jacobus, I am rather corpulent. This is an issue of some sensitivity, as in my opinion, it was one reason the fair Annika, the strumpet, left my embrace for Mr. Fit. I do not deny that I am almost as enamored of food as Aaron is of his sculpted torso, but that only exacerbated the issue, and Aaron knew it when he poked me in the stomach repeatedly with the point of his bow and said, 'With blubber like that no wonder you're obsessed with the middle.' I took offense."

"That's putting it mildly, from what I gather."

"Yes, I suppose. I grabbed Aaron's cattle prod and, as he was not anticipating such a maneuver, it wasn't difficult to disengage it from his hand. I said, 'Now when you're playing at the point you'll be in the middle like the rest of us,' whereupon I broke it in half on my knee and handed it back to him."

"I hope it wasn't a French bow," said Jacobus, trying to maintain a straight face.

"A Dominique Peccatte," said Short.

"*Oy vey!*" said Jacobus. "So then what?"

"I walked out."

"And you were fired."

"Yes."

"You should've expected it, after that."

"Yes, I did. But that's not why I sued. I sued because they besmirched my name throughout the profession and media, labeling me an incompetent troublemaker. And then I found out about their marketing study and it all started to fit together. Adam and Eve were trying to make me into a serpent to get me out of the Garden. And Pravda will be the next victim, I can tell you. By the way, would you like me to ask Miss Dibble to bring you some water?"

"Who's Miss Dibble, and why do you ask?"

"Miss Dibble's the vacuous receptionist you're so fond of, and I ask not only to give her something to do, but because the sounds your stomach is making are threatening to overtake our conversation."

"Thanks, but no thanks."

"Very well. Is there anything else we need to discuss?"

"Yes. Considering what you were just saying, what I don't get is why sue Pravda, too? And why Yumi? She wasn't even there."

"That is not my call, Mr. Jacobus. The Magini String Quartet, or whatever they choose to change their name to, is a nonprofit organization. Legally they are all responsible regardless of their level of complicity. If Pravda or Ms. Shinagawa so decide, they can convince their colleagues to agree to the terms Mr. Carino has proposed—"

"Even if it will cost Ms. Shinagawa her job?"

"There is no one in this entire saga, Mr. Jacobus, who will emerge unscathed. That is the inconvenient truth of the wheel Aaron Kortovsky set spinning. I am sorry for that, but let me be perfectly clear. This is not the first time I have been involved in litigation and most probably not the last. If you so desire I will have Mr. Carino give you the roll call of cases in which I have been the plaintiff. Some have called me 'a litigious fiend,' because of my proper willingness to derive justice from the decree of the courts, but lucre is not my goal. I have never sued unless I believed myself to be morally and legally in the right and, I may add, I have never lost a suit."

"A man on a mission, eh?" said Jacobus.

"If you choose to call it that."

"The way I see it, Short, is that your passion for justice and your hatred of Aaron Kortovsky is blinding you to something very obvious, and for you, very sad."

"Coming from an expert source such as yourself I am particularly interested to hear about my own personal blindness. I shall be mum as well."

Smug son of a bitch.

"Good, because that makes three," said Jacobus.

"I don't understand."

"Blind, mum, and you're also deaf. Deaf to the fact that regardless of Kortovsky's egotism, regardless of his insults, regardless of him stealing and then marrying Annika, your Nordic fantasy, regardless of his market study, and most significantly, regardless of his insistence on a certain somewhat eccentric style of playing, the New Magini String Quartet is arguably the greatest quartet in the world. You were just too busy getting pissed off at his attitude to hear it."

"Perhaps, Mr. Jacobus, you have a fondness for the superficial. Ivan Lensky, a pale reflection of his musical parentage, is, for all his brutishness, the only nonphony of the lot. His brother, Peter, is a true musician and will have nothing to do with the current incarnation of what was once a gem. Is it possible you do not recall the original Magini Quartet, the passion with which they played, their utter devotion to their—"

"Spare me, Short. I don't need Music Appreciation 101 from you. Next you'll be telling me about their extraordinary journey through Beethoven's quartets, 'the Mount Everest of the musical literature.' I've heard the spiel. Yes, they were great, and to tell you the truth I did favor their style compared to the new group's. But you know what? The Russians didn't play quite as well in tune and they didn't play quite as well together as you guys, and even though that didn't bother me—in fact, I prefer the rough edges to these sterile CDs they're cranking out these days—playing in tune and playing together count for something, and no one does it better than the New Magini. Plus, they play with good taste and the best sound around—maybe because they always play on the string.

"I think you had a good thing going, Short. You just didn't know it, and you blew it. But you felt you had to take it out on someone. Maybe you'll win your suit, maybe you won't. Maybe it's a coincidence you threatened Annika Haagen an hour before a severed finger was found in her case. Maybe the

163

finger belongs to—"

"Mr. Jacobus, if you could see me I would ask you, 'Do I look like someone who could kill anyone?' I ask that rhetorically, of course."

Chapter Twenty-One

A gain they waited for Kortovsky, this time for the Carnegie Hall dress rehearsal and—despite Sheila Rathman's frantic phone calls and emails—again they were disappointed, except this time "they" wasn't just the remainder of the New Magini String Quartet. "They" included Power Ramsey and his entourage, The Movement dancers, the video technicians, the sound crew, the dressing-room attendants, the stage hands. Not a good policy to keep so many unionized New York City workers waiting. It makes them unhappy, and Rathman was bearing the brunt of their irritation. Seeking refuge, she called Ivan Lensky out of desperation and reached him on his cellphone at the Circle of Fifths. "Yes, I come," he said, somewhat blearily, "but I am already at A Major." Rathman had no idea what that meant but told him to hurry.

Lieutenant Malachi was also waiting, but he was in no hurry as he questioned Yumi.

"Why should I not think you gave Annika Haagen the finger?" he asked.

"Ha! Another Henny Youngman!" Jacobus said, barging in. "Why would she do that? You've checked out that Yumi was telling the truth that Stevenson did in fact rehair her bow, so she had good reason to borrow Haagen's rosin."

"Here's another one-liner, Jacobus. Miss Shinagawa was having an affair with Haagen's husband. And you're both very well aware of that."

"So what?" Yumi replied. "And why? Why would I do something like that? How could I? It's too grotesque."

"I take it you're referring to the finger and not your sordid affair," said

165

Malachi. "Were you not the last identifiable person to have been with Kortovsky before he disappeared? Were you not the first person found with a finger we now presume to be Kortovsky's, in Haagen's case?"

"Malachi," said Jacobus, knowing he didn't believe what he was telling Malachi. "you're one syllable short of a haiku. Did Rathman not receive an email from Kortovsky saying he would be here tonight?"

"Well, I don't see him," said Malachi. "Do you?"

As Jacobus considered taking what he knew would be an ill-advised swipe in the direction of Malachi's jaw, the sound of Ivan Lensky's arrival and the attendant upturn in the noise level of resumed activity intervened, so he refrained from getting himself into any more trouble.

"I have to go rehearse now," Yumi said. "Will you excuse me, please?"

"Go ahead," said Malachi. "But be warned. At the moment, you're a person of interest. Don't push it."

There were many more people in the hall for this, the dress rehearsal. In addition to all those involved in the actual production, there were friends, family, and Carnegie Hall financial supporters who were invited to be a test audience. The last group was scattered around the hall. They would be the guinea pigs, chosen by the dancers for the climactic dance of death in the last movement of the quartet. This rehearsal would be two non-stop run-throughs, with an intermission in between.

For the professionals involved, even in a unique project of this sort, it was just another day at work. They all had their assigned tasks, and if the format was a little different than what they were used to, it was part of the job, so let's get on with it. For the invited guests, though, who felt they were an indispensable part of some epic history-making artistic enterprise—and with famous people no less!—this was a once-in-a-lifetime event, something they would tell their grandchildren about. Many times.

As a result, there was a great deal of unnecessary and unwanted commotion in the hall. Too much talking. Too much carousing. Too much distraction. Despite repeated but pleas from Mehmet, perhaps excessively polite in deference to the fickle largesse of wealthy donors, committed and potential, the invitees were simply too excited to stay quiet. This made it difficult for the professionals to concentrate, creating even more tension than usual among these normally intense personalities.

So mistakes were made. Lighting was out of synch. Stage monitors weren't properly calibrated. The movie screen would not uncouple in a cooperative manner. The dancers, when they weren't out on Fifty-sixth Street smoking, were confused as to their instructions.

Jacobus heard Power Ramsey bark increasingly harsh commands to whoever was in or out of earshot. It surprised Jacobus, and pleased him, that the only thing going smoothly was the quartet, seemingly unfazed by the disturbances and by Kortovsky's absence. Having had one rehearsal under their belt with Lensky, they already were melding as a group, the animosities of yesterday's brouhaha at Rose Grimes notwithstanding. Yumi, Haagen, and Lenskaya were playing with a bit more verve and incision then before, and Lensky sounded as if he were making an effort to blend, to tone things down a notch. Maybe that was his way of expressing reconciliation, if not remorse. Lenskaya, in particular, seemed to have rediscovered some of her former swagger. Such is the nature of good musicians, thought Jacobus, whether they love or hate each other. Not a word needed to be said. Just listening to each other, and a deadline.

"Well, wasn't that a disaster?" Yumi said laughingly to Jacobus at intermission. "You couldn't tell, but Imogene Livenstock slipped off the edge of the stage at the end when the dancers did their collapse thing. Annika started laughing and I had to kick her. You'd think that after her fall down the stairs she'd be a little more sympathetic, but I'm glad she seems happy."

"Who's Imogene Livenstock?"

"She's the major sponsor of the whole production and had won a raffle to do the death dance with the troupe. I think the only worse thing that could have gone wrong would have been for the whole stage to collapse."

"Ramsey would love that," said Jacobus. " 'A metaphor for the cataclysm of genocide.' But at least you got the most important part right, and that's the music. It's sounding better than I expected."

"Thank you. Here are two tickets for the show tonight. For you and Nathaniel."

"Thanks," said Jacobus, pocketing them. "Just try to stay out of trouble till then."

"What do you mean?"

Jacobus hadn't meant anything. He really hadn't, and should have kept his mouth shut. But couldn't.

"Well, y'know, Kortovsky. Who the hell knows where he is now, with Malachi sniffing around? And, y'know, your fling with him?"

"What about it? What does that have to do with anything?"

"Nothing." He knew he should stop there. "Except he and Haagen, being married. And you and Haagen…"

"Jake, I don't know what the hell you're talking about, except there's nothing for me to be ashamed of, and it's none of your business, or Malachi's, or anyone else's!"

"I know that, Yumi. I certainly do. It's just that now…it just looks a little fishy, that's all."

"Fishy! It looks fishy! Jake, my grandmother has loved you since the day you met, when I first became your student, but for all these years you've treated her with the warmth of a gravestone! Oh, you acknowledge what a fine teacher she is and how smart she is, but where's the feeling? It's no wonder that when I reciprocate someone's affection you think it's 'fishy'! I've got to go. Enjoy the rest of the rehearsal."

As they receded, Jacobus heard Yumi's high heels tap quickly and emphatically, like nails hammered into a coffin. His coffin, maybe. Simultaneously came the sound of a man's gait, approaching more cautiously.

"Well, you did a great job convincing her," Nathaniel said.

"What did I say?" Jacobus asked in exasperation. "I just wanted to give her some good advice."

"You know what they say, Jake. Good advice is the same as bad advice. You just got to know when someone needs it."

"Is that good advice or bad advice?" Jacobus asked.

"We'll find out at the end of the day," said Nathaniel.

"Where the hell have you been?"

"Running around getting all the information you asked me to get. For some reason it didn't work when I tried just snapping my fingers and making it appear out of the blue."

Jacobus heard Nathaniel snapping his fingers.

"Jesus Christ. Why are you doing that?"

"It didn't work to make anything appear so I'm hoping it'll make you disappear."

"You should only be so lucky. What've you got?"

"I found out from Sheila that Pravda Lenskaya stayed at the Bolívar Hotel in Lima."

"That's what you've got? Maybe you should keep snapping your fingers."

"The Bolívar Hotel is only about a half mile from the Maury. An easy walk."

"So?"

"You remember how hard it was for me to find out if the kid, Prince Rupert, had a plane ticket, and I had to find out which hotel Annika Haagen stayed at? Well, just out of curiosity, I called the Bolívar to find out if Lenskaya might've brought someone, too."

"And?"

"And her son."

"Ivan?"

"Peter. Last minute. Separate room."

A couple little things began to click for Jacobus. Peter had told Jacobus that Lenskaya treated him like an invalid and didn't think he could do anything on his own, so it figured she wouldn't want him to be all by his lonesome in Flushing while she was off on tour. Now, he tried to recall, had Peter Lensky walked with a limp when they had their *tête-à-tête*? He had heard Lensky approach the door when he arrived. He heard him get up and go to the bathroom to "ablute." He heard him return with the caviar. He did not recall a limp, though, admittedly, he hadn't been listening for one and his cold was still clogging his hearing. Nevertheless, he would have noticed something aberrant like that. Wouldn't he?

"Maybe we'll have to have another chat with Peter," he said. "What else?"

"I called up a few of my contacts in the instrument world who might have had dealings with Otkar Vasalin. Private dealers who have no shop, no business card, no public reputation. Only a phone number."

"And?"

"No one knew much about him. But I did find out that he's living in his own private little fortress in Quito, Ecuador. It would be harder to get into his estate than for Fidel Castro to get a green card in the U.S."

Jacobus recalled what Oro had said about security in Peru, so was not surprised to hear this.

"The violins," he said.

"No doubt. They're worth millions. But there's more, maybe. I was tracing Vasalin's history back through the archives, going the violin route. A hard name to confuse. I didn't get very far with that, but I did find an old clipping about the purchase he made of an old Rogeri violin which referred to him as a former 'energy czar.' So I went back to his Eastern Europe days and checked out newspapers, magazines, studies, government documents—"

"Government documents?"

"That's what I'm getting to. It seems he was a behind-the-scenes mover and shaker for the energy industry in the eighties. Came up out of nowhere. At first he was just a middleman in oil and natural gas pipelines, buying and selling energy contracts to the highest bidders. Did okay with that. But he made the bulk of his billions only after he got into nuclear energy."

"Nuclear energy?"

"What's with you, Jake? You getting echolalia in your old age?"

"Old age?"

"Very funny. Yes, nuclear energy. He was involved in the design, construction, and oversight of the Chernobyl reactors. And when it blew, he packed his bags and hightailed it to South America."

"This is getting interesting. Good work, Nathaniel, if I say so myself. Maybe you could get hold of Vasalin and find out if there's a Lensky connection. Or at least a quartet connection." The wheels were turning for Jacobus now. Violins and nuclear reactors, an explosive pairing. "Or," he said, "if you can't get through personally, may Oro can use his South American back channels to get hold of him."

"That's a good plan, except for one thing."

"What now?"

" Vasalin's dead."

"Dead!"

"There you go again. I found it in a little obituary in the *International Herald Tribune*. Of all the things, he slipped in the shower and cracked his skull open. A freak accident."

"You think so?"

"How else? With all that security? There's one interesting coincidence, though."

"Let me guess. He was missing a finger."

"No. No such luck."

"What then?"

"The day he died was the day the New Magini String Quartet performed in Quito."

Jacobus and Nathaniel listened to the second go-round of the rehearsal with half an ear. There were fewer unpleasant surprises, both logistically and musically. It's often said that a disastrous dress rehearsal means a great concert, but Jacobus didn't believe that. He believed a good dress rehearsal enabled the performers to be confident and relaxed just enough to take the edge off the flood of adrenaline that was bound to flow when the curtain went up.

When the rehearsal was finally over, Jacobus was anxious to make a quiet but hasty exit so as to avoid another knock-down-drag-out with Yumi. He and Nathaniel had retreated as far as the doors to the lobby, when a voice chimed out, "Not so fast, Jacobus."

"What now, Malachi," he responded.

"Backstage. Now."

A large group had congregated, discussing the discovery of three more fingers. One in Ivan Lesnky's case. One in Pravda Lenskaya's. One in Yumi's.

171

"All from the same hand?" Jacobus asked.

"One would hope so," Malachi said.

Power Ramsey didn't know what to do.

The union technicians protested that the whole production was jinxed and demanded overtime for having to stay to answer questions from the police. Mehmet volunteered that the dance troupe was "freaked by the bad karma" and wanted the concert canceled.

"But we've spent almost all the money already and the tickets have already been paid for," Ramsey said. "All of this has cost a fortune and how am I going to pay everyone back?"

"What's wrong, Ramsey?" asked Jacobus. "Getting disenchanted with your enchantments?"

"Mr. Jacobus," said Ramsey, "you're getting so, so tiring. If you think I have not understood every one of your juvenile barbs, you are mistaken. You are absolutely incorrigible."

"Absolutely?"

The recipients of the fingers, the quartet, argued among themselves. They didn't understand what the appearance of the fingers meant, but it was hard not to believe it was a threat. Even Yumi now conceded that Jacobus might have been right to want the concert stopped. On the other hand, without this concert, what future did the quartet have? But if everyone else decided to cancel it, it would be difficult for them not to go along.

In the end, it was Imogene Livenstock who prevailed, proclaiming she "would not be spooked and intimidated by some childish Halloween stunt." As the major sponsor not only of the Schubert production but of many of the city's higher-profile arts projects, she held the political trump card, and with a mixture of cajolery of the dance troupe, not-so-veiled threats to the union workers, and financial reassurances to Power Ramsey, the decision was made that the show would go on.

Malachi seconded the decision. He concurred the reason for the fingers in the cases was to frighten the musicians into canceling the performance. Since that strategy had not been successful, he suspected that the perpetrator would return to the concert, so for Malachi's purposes the most effective way to find out who that perpetrator was and then to trap him was to proceed with the concert. A strategy fraught with peril, perhaps, but since there was already a determination to proceed, he was not asking anyone to take risks they hadn't already agreed to. Malachi permitted the musicians to take their instruments and cases with them to prepare for the concert, the fingers having been collected and bagged by the forensics team.

On his way out, Ivan Lensky said to Jacobus, "I hear you meet baby brother Peter."

"An interesting character."

Lensky laughed and Jacobus cringed in anticipation of the pounding on his back. Lensky thankfully refrained.

"Yes. Peter. He sing, then he ablute, then he sing again and ablute. Always same. Right?"

"Stress relief?"

"No. Smell relief. Peter is like silent fart. You didn't notice?"

"Maybe he'd just abluted when I got there. And I have a cold."

"Lucky you. See you tonight. Then we drink."

"*Budyem.*"

"Ha!" said Lensky, but his voice was already farther away.

As the rest of the group dispersed, Jacobus heard another voice emerge to address him.

"Enjoy the show," said Malachi.

"Yeah. Well, at least you have no reason to suspect Yumi anymore," Jacobus said to Malachi, as the group dispersed.

"And why is that?"

"There's a finger in her case, too. They've each gotten one."

"So that makes them all innocent? We don't even know what the crime is yet, so no one's off the hook. Plus, who other than Yumi is having something on the side with both Kortovsky and Haagen?"

"Malachi, I don't know what the hell you're talking about, except there's nothing for her to be ashamed of, and it's none of your business, or mine, or anyone else's! And who did you hear that rumor from, anyway?"

"Jacobus, I'm the police here. Not you. But as you may know, musicians can never keep secrets. I'll be in touch."

On the way back to Nathaniel's apartment, Jacobus, in his raspy, guttural voice, hummed what he could remember of the tune that Peter Lensky had been singing when he had arrived at Lensky's residence in Queens, hoping that Nathaniel could identify it.

"I'm not sure," said Nathaniel, "but I think it could be Louis Armstrong. After a long night."

"Jealous."

"But I'll check it out."

"Thanks. You do that."

Nathaniel dropped Jacobus off at the apartment, grabbed his cello, and then left to go uptown to teach at the Rose Grimes School in Harlem. Jacobus walked Trotsky who, unused to being cooped up for the day in an apartment, had converted the living room Castro Convertible into a chew toy and was eager for a diverting change of pace.

Jacobus had compiled a mental list of questions for Oro, including whether the limping man had body odor, and dialed the phone number.

"*Buenas tardes,*" said a voice.

"You speak English?"

"*Buenas tardes.*"

"English? Speak English?"

"*¿Qué? ¿Por favor? ¿Repita?*"

"Oro? There?"

"*¡Ah, sí! Oro no está aca. Está afuera. Afuera. No estoy seguro de cuando regrese. ¿Desea dejarle un mensaje?*"

"Oro! Oro! Godammit!"

"*Lo siento, señor. Por favor, llame más tarde. Gracias. Adiós.*"

Jacobus opened his mouth, ready to continue combat, but when the call was disconnected, he decided it wasn't worth arguing with the dial tone.

174

Chapter Twenty-Two

Because of Con Ed construction, the cab had to stop a half block from Carnegie Hall. Jacobus counted out seven single bills—always singles, in order to know how much money he had in his tattered wallet—and, after an extensive manual exploration of the Plexiglas shield in front of him, found the opening and handed the driver his money. He got out of the cab and with his cane lodged in the crook of his elbow, covered his ears with his hands, lured by the dulcet tones of the Con Ed jackhammer to the entrance of the hall. By the time he got there, his gray windbreaker–which had been green when he bought it, but what did he care?—was already cold and wet from the dark, heavy drizzle.

Jacobus made his way to the box office where he and Nathaniel had agreed to meet. That was his first mistake. From the moment Lilburn's article about the missing Kortovsky and the missing finger hit the newsstands, business at the box office was brisk, and he was jostled uncomfortably by the "will call" crowd. While he waited, he thought about how concertgoers understood so little of the behind-the-scenes activity required to produce a concert, and how naïve he had been in the same regard when he was younger. He had figured that all he had to do was practice his ass off and the rest would take care of itself. They should teach a course in college, he mused, about preparing for auditions, renting concert halls, selling tickets, PR, videochoreography, lawsuits, missing violinists, and errant fingers, and then see how many budding prodigies still wanted to try to be one of the one-tenth of one percent that actually made a career.

"Good evening, Jake" came a voice he recognized.

"Boris."

"It should be a wonderful concert tonight, don't you think?"

"No doubt. If you like a three-ring circus."

"Yes." Dedubian laughed. "I know what you mean. And how are you tonight?"

"Boris. I have to tell you. I don't expect a lot from violin dealers, but I have to say you outdid your profession the other day with Haagen. You were an exceptional prick and now you've come to hear her play? Don't see how that all fits together as a successful business model."

"You know, Jake, I think I got caught up in all the bad publicity the quartet had gotten and had taken sides with Mr. Short. But you're right, business is business, and maybe after the concert I'll have a chance to apologize to her.

"In the meantime I'm supposed to meet a pretty, young lady who just got a job with the Philharmonic. I've got that Guadagnini with me that you liked so much; she wanted to try it out for a few days. You haven't bumped into her by any chance? She was supposed to be right here."

"Tell me what she smells like."

"Jake, you are so funny."

"Okay then, tell me what she feels like. You'd probably know that."

"You make me blush, but I think I see her over on the other side." Jacobus heard Dedubian's quick footsteps. "If she doesn't buy the fiddle, I'll give you a call," Dedubian said, his voice already at some distance.

"Don't bother."

Jacobus heard the crowd begin to funnel through the doors into the auditorium and still no Nathaniel. One thing about professional musicians, when they have to perform they're always on time (otherwise they'd be fired), but when they're on the listening end, who knows when they'll show up? Except Kortovsky, who liked to keep people waiting just for the sheer joyful manipulation of it.

What to do about Yumi? He didn't hold it against her that she had an affair with Kortovsky. He knew it really was none of his damn business. But because she clandestinely saw Kortovsky right before he disappeared and maybe was killed, and was already in Malachi's line of sight because of the damn finger, she was getting herself into serious hot water. How she could concentrate tonight was beyond him. He was just glad he was not in her shoes.

"Sorry I'm late, Jake," said Nathaniel, breaking into his thoughts. "I was coming from uptown and the subway got stuck on Seventy-second and I had to walk the rest of the way."

"Uptown where? Montreal?"

"The music school. Didn't even have time to drop my cello off at the apartment."

"Well, you can sit on it during the concert. Will give you a better view."

"My, we're in a bit of a swivet this evening, aren't we? Would it help that BTower told me to say hello to you for him? He couldn't come tonight because he has too much paperwork, but wanted me to thank you again for turning his life—"

"Yeah, yeah, yeah," said Jacobus. "Just tell him to stick to Bach and not bee-bop. I gotta go to the bathroom."

"There's only a few minutes. You need a hand?"

"What do you mean by that?"

"Never mind. I'll meet you at our seats."

Jacobus made his way against traffic and entered the men's room off the lobby. With the concert about to start, he didn't hear any other patrons as his footsteps echoed in the resonant, marbled room. Rather than having to worry about his aim in public, he chose to sit in a stall rather than stand at a urinal. As he was completing his task he heard the men's room door open—momentarily allowing the flurry of preconcert noise to enter—then close. He got up, remembered to zip up his fly, and was washing his hands when suddenly the tap was turned on full blast, soaking his shirt up to his elbows.

"What the—"

"Ah, Mr. Jacobus," said a familiar voice. "What a chance coincidence to meet you here. We seem to have wet our self a wee bit, I see."

"You always like to drop in unexpected, Short? Come to pout, have we?"

" 'Pout' is not the word. 'Collect' is more like it."

"Give them a break. What were they supposed to do? Kortovsky's still missing."

"Yes, but they chose Lensky, didn't they? Well, you may tell them they will regret their choice. And so will you. Good evening to you, Mr. Jacobus. Enjoy the concert."

Jacobus heard Short's footsteps echo away, dried himself as best he could, and as quickly as possible made his way to his aisle seat, AA 101 in the Dress Circle, next to Nathaniel.

"Looks like you got yourself all wet, Jake," said Nathaniel. "I told you you needed help."

"Fuck you," said Jacobus and explained his encounter with Short.

"I can see Short from here," said Nathaniel. "He's sitting down there on the main floor with Carino. They're not the only interested parties here, either. Lipinsky and Greunig are there too. One big happy family."

"Did they bring their vodka?"

Jacobus felt a pair of legs brush by his.

"Evening, Jacobus. Hey! Looks like I've got the seat right next to Nathaniel."

"Malachi!" said Jacobus. "How did you manage that? I thought they were sold out."

"Easy. I just kept an eye on Nathaniel and kicked out the kid sitting next to him. He'd snuck in anyway—some flea-bitten music student."

"Shouldn't you be backstage where the action is?"

"I figure if there's going to be trouble, you'll be in the middle of it somehow. Besides, just for your information we've got a bird's-eye view—no offense—so I can keep an eye on all our friends from here."

Jacobus began to tell Malachi to also keep an eye out for Kortovsky when Nathaniel interrupted.

"Shh. The lights are going down." Through a spattering of applause, Nathaniel continued. "Power Ramsey's coming out. Guess he's going to tell everyone what a genius he is."

"Ladies and gentlemen," said Ramsey, his voice, to Jacobus's ear, not as haughty as it had been earlier, "welcome to this historic evening in which

178

we celebrate the life and music of Franz Schubert with perhaps his greatest masterpiece, 'Death and the Maiden.' We are experiencing a brief delay, but assure you the performance will begin shortly." When he continued with, "I would like to acknowledge this evening's generous sponsors," Jacobus, aware of the stall tactic, went into daydream mode until he finally heard, "And please turn off all cellular phones. Thank you and enjoy the performance."

Listening to the impatient New York audience murmur its discontent at being unexpectedly discommoded, like the crowd at Yankee Stadium during a rain delay, Jacobus felt a hand grip his shoulder, not all that gently, either.

"That you again, Short? Going to throw me over the balcony? Think twice. I've got protection."

"No, Mr. Jacobus," said a different familiar voice. "It's me, Sheila. Sheila Rathman. You're wanted backstage. Urgently. Lieutenant, Mr. Williams, please come too."

"Sorry, I can't leave my cello here," said Nathaniel.

"Then bring it," said Rathman with unexpected force.

"What's up?" asked Jacobus.

"We have a problem."

"What happened? Kortovsky show up?"

"I wish."

Power Ramsey was having a conniption amidst the entire assemblage.

Yumi and Annika Haagen found Jacobus.

"Jake, you won't believe this," Yumi said. "Ivan and Pravda aren't here."

"So, they're late. The subway from Queens got stuck. It's not unheard of."

"For Pravda it is," said Haagen. "She's always the first one to show up. Sheila called both of their home phones and cellphones. Pravda would always answer one of them."

"Unless," said Malachi, "they're the ones who placed the fingers in the cases. I heard all about the prank mother and son pulled on Haagen at the school yesterday."

"Maybe you should dispatch some officers to check out Lensky's place and the mother's in Flushing," said Jacobus.

"I'm the police here," said Malachi. "Not you...But I'll consider it."

"Those cowards," muttered Haagen.

"Jake, I don't know," said Yumi. "I'm worried about them."

"Them?" Ramsey wailed. What about my performance! Oh, my God! My performance!"

"Get Short to play," said Jacobus. "He's here. He's good. He's a schmuck, but he's good. You don't have much choice."

"I will not play with that blackmailing toad!" said Haagen.

"That would only solve half the problem, anyway," said Yumi. "We'd still need a cellist."

"Then cancel," said Jacobus. "Give them their money back so they can go downtown to Barnum and Bailey for a different circus."

"Never!" said Ramsey. "That would be a fiasco! It will be the end of me."

"And the end of the quartet." said Yumi.

"I have an idea," said Ramsey. "Yes. I think this will work."

"What do you have in mind?" asked Haagen.

"A recording! That's what we'll do! Not to worry, Annika dear. There's a great old recording of the Budapest Quartet playing 'Death and the Maiden,' or maybe the old Kolisch Quartet. Yes, they both recorded it about the same time Marian Anderson recorded the song. We've got the hookups all set up. I'm sure we could find a record in minutes. Yes, that will be even better than—"

"You must be kidding!" Jacobus heard Yumi say, beating him to the punch.

"Why would I be kidding?" Ramsey asked. "At a time like this."

"Two reasons," Yumi said. "Number one, we've signed a contract to perform, so we're going to perform, and if we don't you're still obligated to pay us."

"And number two?" Jacobus prompted, liking what he was hearing.

"Number two is, there's simply no substitute for a live performance. I don't care if it's Jesus Christ and the Guardian Angels Quartet playing, if it's a recording, you're cheating the public. People don't pay good money to watch a wheel of black plastic spinning around, or lights flashing, or a bunch of smoke and mirrors. They pay to hear live musicians creating something before their very eyes and ears that will change their lives, and that's what we're going to do."

Jacobus had never wanted to hug his protégée more.

"We are?" asked Ramsey. "Pray tell me. How?"

"*They'll* play," said Yumi.

"Who's 'they'?" asked Jacobus.

"You," said Yumi. "You and Nathaniel. You're going to play."

"That's ridiculous!" said Jacobus, putting a temporary hold on the hug. "Even if I could, I don't even have a violin."

"Didn't you say," asked Nathaniel, "that Dedubian had been here with that Guadagnini?"

"Yes, but..." Jacobus sputtered. "I haven't played in public since...I can't remember the last time. Nathaniel, when's the last time we performed together?"

"May, 1959. Beethoven. 'Archduke' Trio."

"See?" said Jacobus. "Ages ago. I'm out of shape. We haven't rehearsed. I'm not—"

"What's the matter, Jake?" asked Haagen. "No balls?"

Five minutes later Dedubian was backstage, beckoned there by Sheila Rathman.

"Of course, it would give me great pleasure to have Jake play on this violin," said Dedubian. "It is one of Guadagnini's finest. Owned at one time by the great virtuoso, Eugène Ysaÿe. Made in Turin in seventeen—"

"Enough sales pitch, Bo," said Jacobus. "I imagine a performance on it here might even enhance its value?"

"Yes," mulled Dedubian. "No doubt. Good thinking, Jake."

"In that case, if you want me to play on it, you agree to give Annika here an appraisal on her Gasparo for what it's really worth. No bullshit this time."

Power Ramsey made the announcement, spinning the disaster as positively as possible. While he rambled glowingly about Jacobus's greatness and how honored they were to have him and Nathaniel Williams collaborate with the world's foremost string quartet, Jacobus frantically reacquainted himself with a violin he had played on only briefly, and that was years ago. It was a beautiful-sounding instrument, with a powerfully rich resonance that would make it the equal of Haagen's Gasparo and Yumi's Vuillaume, but every violin is different, and compared to his own Neapolitan instrument, all the dimensions were a fraction of a millimeter off, making it a challenge to play with accurate intonation.

The greater stress by far, though, was not physical; it was psychological. Even though he couldn't see Carnegie Hall, he could feel its vastness compared to the cozy ten-by-fifteen space that was his own and in which had been playing exclusively for the past thirty-plus years. Though he couldn't see the two thousand people sitting out there, he could feel their judgmental, almost predatory presence compared to the single obedient student for whom Jacobus would occasionally demonstrate a phrase or fingering.

What petrified him the most, though, was that he would be performing with Yumi, his former student, and the thought that he might embarrass himself in front of her, that he might fail when she was so reliant upon his ability to rescue her in her moment of greatest need, made him almost unable to walk, let alone play the violin. What if, after all the things he had told her about music, about the violin, with such great confidence and certainty, he were now to fall on his face, ruining Yumi's career, not to mention his own reputation? Would it make a mockery of all that he had taught? Would the world consider him a fraud? Worse, would Yumi consider him a fraud?

He wished he were still in his high balcony seat with the rest of the audience, comfortable and eager and relatively carefree. Better yet, he wished he were still in his hovel of a home, away from this unreality, where he could grouse endlessly and unimpeded about the sorry state of the world.

When the quartet walked onstage—Yumi's arm entwined in Jacobus's to lead him to his seat—the audience stirred with a combination of unease and interest and indecisive applause. To Jacobus it felt like a hanging jury and he was on trial. It would definitely be a noteworthy performance in the storied annals of Carnegie Hall. But it also might be the worst.

Jacobus pictured the disposition of the quartet in his mind's eye—Yumi to his left, then Annika Haagen to hers, and finally Nathaniel opposite Jacobus to complete the semicircle—and contrasted his and Nathaniel's appearance with Haagen and Yumi, dressed, no doubt, in sleek black concert dresses. At Ramsey's suggestion Jacobus had removed his still damp jacket only to reveal equally inappropriate concert attire—frayed flannel shirt and brown corduroy pants. Even the white shirt and tie Ramsey had scrounged up from somewhere backstage would do little to boost their rankings in the marketing study. Jacobus couldn't remember whether he had shaved that morning—probably not. Of course, he had no need for a music stand in front of the chair in which he was now sitting. He assumed Nathaniel was wearing his trademark African dashiki—the day Nathaniel had quit his desk job with the insurance company to become a freelance consultant was the last he had worn a jacket and tie. Gauging the edgy silence from the audience, Jacobus thought it must have been on a night like this that the word "disconcerted" was invented.

He tried to block out his anxiety. He would just pretend he was at home. After all, wasn't he playing with his best friend and his former student? What could be easier than that? "Death and the Maiden" had been so easy at Yumi's lesson—after all, he knew the music intimately—but to perform one of the most challenging quartets in the repertoire? And at Carnegie Hall in front of a paying audience, with no rehearsal? Ludicrous! He was not a performer. Hadn't been for decades. He was tempted to get up and walk out. His hands were ice cold and sweating. For a moment he couldn't even remember the first note! The hell with blocking out his fear; it was impossible.

He heard Nathaniel dig his endpin into the stage floor, then give the A. It was too late; he'd have to go through with it. How could he possibly remember every nuance of every note of a piece of music almost an hour long? He couldn't. It was impossible, he repeated. He played his A, tuning it to Nathaniel's, as did Yumi and Haagen, which helped disguise the fact that his hand shook and his bow slid all over the fingerboard.

Once they finished tuning, there was nothing left to do but start. Jacobus knew that the eyes of the quartet and the entire audience were upon him. It was his responsibility, as first violinist, to lead the entrance. He froze in his seat. What was he supposed to do? End the charade, is what I'll do. Just get up and walk off the stage.

"Jake," Nathaniel whispered almost inaudibly to him.

"What?" he replied.

"Just one thing."

"What?"

"Don't fuck up."

"Thanks a lot," Jacobus said, hearing Yumi and Haagen stifle a laugh.

He knew his violin technique was no longer a match for Kortovsky's, Lensky's, Short's, or Yumi's, and he knew he could not maintain the fast tempos he had heard at the rehearsal. He had to find something else in the music, not just to avoid disaster or disguise his own weakness, but to give it meaning in a different way.

Inevitability. The inevitability of death is what this quartet is about, he thought. Mine, his, hers, everyone's. It doesn't have to be fast. It only has to be relentless. Inexorable. In the manner of a conductor holding a baton, Jacobus raised his bow arm, creating a gesture in the silent upbeat to mirror the violently defiant character and tempo of the first phrase they would play in rhythmic unison—a five-note brasslike fanfare in which he and Nathaniel repeated the same note, D, while the inner voices, Yumi and Annika, started on D, then descended scalewise to G, like dark stairs down to hell. A unique opening to an inimitable piece of music.

Jacobus took a final deep breath, and came crashing down on the first note, the long unison D, fortissimo. Miraculously, the other three had followed him. It was together! Then Jacobus showed them the next group of notes—not with blinding rapier-like speed as Lensky had done, but each note separate, more like individual saber thrusts. The other three followed him perfectly. No, they weren't following—they were joining. They sensed his intent and understood where he would be going.

The next phrase repeated the rhythm and intensity, but the inner voices in the second violin and viola went in a different harmonic direction, so

Jacobus took a microsecond of extra time landing on the downbeat of the fourth bar. Then came the echo of the phrase, pianissimo; questioning, expressing doubt of the resolve of the previous four bars. Unlike Lensky and Short, Jacobus played these notes *on* the string, a bit longer, more likely the way Kortovsky played them. Since only Jacobus had the quick notes here, the others would immediately understand what bow stroke he wanted for the rest of the movement. By the time they reached a pause in measure fourteen a few seconds later, the final moment of rest before the music begins with unremitting energy and motion, Jacobus was beginning to feel a sense of liberation and joy he had not experienced since before he lost his sight. How ironic, he thought as he played, to feel this way in the expression of death, at which point he told himself he had better concentrate on the music or else he would indeed fuck up.

When they finished the first movement—in better shape than he had imagined possible—Jacobus was already mentally and physically exhausted. Not having had enough time to warm up—a few weeks might have done the trick—his left pinkie wasn't working properly; it was hurting and sluggish. His right arm, from the constant energetic playing, was sore and heavy. How he would manage to survive the remaining three movements was a mystery.

They began the Andante con moto, the variation movement based upon Schubert's song that gave the quartet its title, with deathly calm and simplicity. Jacobus played the pianissimo elegiac chorale with no vibrato except where Schubert indicated a subtle swell in the sound. The others responded as if they had played together for years. Of course, Yumi and Annika had, and they were at the top of their game as quartet players, trained to understand and react immediately to musical ideas with technical proficiency. And Nathaniel—he must have been keeping a secret from Jacobus because his playing was as good as it had been when they had their trio together.

The calm beginning to the movement allowed Jacobus to regain some of his energy and to relax his hands, and he was able to play the first variation, in which his part was essentially that of a breathless maiden pleading for life, supported by the other three in a quietly throbbing accompaniment.

During the variation, though, he heard some restlessness from the audience, and remembered that this was where the video images of genocide on the big screen were being shown. He remembered that tonight he was part musician, part backup in a production number, and silently cursed Ramsey for taking the audience's attention away from the music as it gained dark momentum in the second and third variations.

The fourth variation was the only one in a major key, but was nevertheless frail and pallid, the last breaths of a dying maiden recounting fleeting moments of joy. Jacobus tried to ignore the unrest in the audience that had turned into audible outbursts—he made his best effort to concentrate fully on his playing—but finally recognized that people in the audience were sobbing in response to the music they were hearing and the horrific images they were seeing. He thought of his parents, who had died in the greatest genocide of the twentieth century—who's to say which genocide is the "greatest"?—and his brother Eli, missing for so many years. Tears welled up in his blind eyes—fortunately he had his dark glasses on so no one could see—but his nose started to run and there was nothing he could do about it while he was playing.

They second movement faded peacefully into eternity, and Jacobus had a moment to collect himself and blow his nose.

Yumi whispered, "Jake, are you okay?"

"Hell, yeah. Let's go."

They dove into the third-movement Scherzo that recalls the dark energy of the first movement, and then the finale, the driving D-minor Presto, a tarantella that gallops to doom on a black horse. Now Jacobus gathered all the remaining energy in his being because he knew that even when he was in his best form he would be exhausted by the end. This was also the movement that Ramsey's dancers were to select audience participants and dance themselves to death, but he didn't give a shit about that now, because if he diverted his concentration for a split second it would be catastrophic. The movement went on and on, never relenting, never accommodating. He was mounted on that black horse. It was killing him to stay on it. It would kill him to fall off. Then, just when the piece should end and all has been said melodically, harmonically, and psychologically, Schubert does the unthinkable, turning up the heat one last notch from presto to prestissimo! Jacobus had nothing left. He couldn't go on. Yet he had to. His hands were numb, his mind was a blank, yet he played on, tears streaming down his eyes. Death surrounded him and he was hurtling into the abyss.

The last three chords crashed down. He was in hell.

As per instructions, the quartet remained seated and the audience remained silent. Since there was a mound of humanity heaped in front of them—and Jacobus could hear their heavy panting and smell the fruit of their exertions—standing for a bow would have been meaningless anyway. Though too exhausted and shaken to stand, Jacobus felt a sense of exhilaration—he would not call it triumph—that seemed to liberate him from a pent-up internal bondage whose very existence he had never realized. This performance about death had validated his life. It was his redemption—Kortovsky's tacit participation in it moved fleetingly through his consciousness—yet the absence of applause made him feel cheated in this, his great achievement. Peter Lensky, whose invisible presence he felt in the silence, could talk all he wanted about the primitiveness of the act of clapping one's hands, and Jacobus could not disagree with him conceptually, but the silent void now made him realize that he had the blood of a performer, and his musical red corpuscles needed to be oxygenated by a visceral response, barbaric or not. At the very least, applause would acknowledge the effort; at best, it would be a spontaneous combustion of a primal fire that his performance had ignited.

So the silence disturbed him, and he was grateful to hear the big screen slide down from above, and then the nostalgic popping noise of old film enter the ambiance of the hall. The film was about to start. It annoyed him, though, how much vestigial noise there was—people in the audience were still fussing, people onstage moving about, whispering, trying to get comfortable enough in their awkward "death" positions to endure their physical discomfort for the three minutes of Marian Anderson's rendition of "Death and the Maiden."

He imagined Jonel and Fern, with their lithe dancers' bodies, capable of effortlessly contorting themselves into spandexed pretzels, entangled with heaving, sweating bellies in gray suits, and almost laughed out loud. He knew that the urge to laugh was no more than a tension release, but the difficulty in stifling it was compounded when an earlier prediction he had made to Ramsey of rampant body odor, reminiscent of the fecund earth, was being borne out. So Jacobus bit his tongue as hard as he could, held his breath, and thought depressing thoughts, hoping that the vocal performance of "Death and the Maiden" would help him regain the solemnity appropriate for the occasion.

The pianist played the brief choralelike introduction and Marian Anderson began to sing. Jacobus, not surprisingly, had always considered the violin to be the king of orchestral instruments, but whenever he heard Anderson sing, it reaffirmed his opinion that the human voice at its greatest trumped even the violin. In the first stanza, that of the maiden pleading for life, the fragility of fear in Anderson's soprano register was palpable. Then, only moments later, when Anderson's voice changed and became the voice of Death, he could feel the hall turn cold, as the becalmed power of the inevitable emanated not just from her mouth or her vocal chords or her diaphragm, but from her being.

The register of Anderson's voice descended into the abyss, finishing a full two and a half octaves below her highest soprano note, well into the range of a male basso. Jacobus, no longer giddy, felt himself trembling on that last note, not just for Schubert's and Anderson's incredible technical three-minute achievement, but for how deeply it had reached inside him, opening awareness of eternity as a vast space that now surrounded him and that he felt he would soon enter.

When that last note died away, the faintly frightened murmur from the audience signaled to Jacobus that the house had momentarily gone black.

"Afraid of the dark, huh?" Jacobus whispered to Nathaniel, indicating by his inflection he meant the audience and not his friend.

"They're not used to it like you are," whispered Nathaniel back. Jacobus heard the dancers and audience members onstage rise to get ready for their

188

bows, apparently still in the dark, as there was still quite a bit of jostling going on. "As soon as the lights go on I'll bet they give a standing ovation. Ah ha. Lights are coming up."

Now he and the quartet would receive the momentarily delayed accolades from the audience. Truly a historic performance. Lilburn would write the review in the *Times*: "Death and the Maiden: New Life for the New Magini." Or something like that. If nothing else, Yumi would be proud he gave it the old college try. But it was the last time he'd let her rope him into something so ridiculous. Before their bows, he wanted to reach out to her and hold her hand. He wanted to make it clear he did it for her and not for Power Ramsey. Power Ramsey! Jacobus was ready for a return trip to Circle of Fifths.

The applause began. Jacobus could hear the mass of humanity, dancers, and selected audience members alike, that had, according to Ramsey's instructions, piled up in seemingly random fashion onstage in front of the quartet, now organize itself, separating like a human curtain to display the quartet seated behind it, waiting to take its bow.

The volume of the applause increased for a moment, ready to erupt. But rather than gaining momentum, suddenly it began to disintegrate, with unintelligible vocal emanations emerging from the hall. Something was not right. There was yelling, calling for help, then a scream. Not pain or revulsion this time. Just fear.

"Nathaniel, Yumi!" said Jacobus, "Where are you? Tell me what's going on."

"She's not moving!" said Nathaniel. Jacobus felt Nathaniel's hand gripping his shoulder, squeezing it painfully. "I think her neck's broken. I think she's dead."

"Who's dead, Nathaniel? Who?"

"Annika. Annika's dead."

"Yumi!" Jacobus yelled, in a panic. "Yumi. Are you all right? Where are you, godammit!"

"Jake," said Nathaniel. "Yumi's gone."

Jacobus wasn't the only one in a panic. Chaos swirled around him—shouting, crying, feet moving in every direction. The crescendo of tumult portended a riot. Jacobus, frozen in his seat, heard a familiar voice next to him on the stage.

"Ladies and gentlemen, I am Lieutenant Albert Malachi of the New York City Police Department," he said into a microphone. "Take your seats immediately. This is an order."

Jacobus wasn't sure by what authority Malachi could order two thousand people to sit down at a concert, but he wasn't about to begrudge him the point because, surprisingly, the command seemed to be working.

Malachi continued. "Ladies and gentlemen, astounding as it may seem, Carnegie Hall is now a crime scene, and I need your cooperation. Within a few minutes, the ushers will escort you out the front of the building, one row at a time. All those onstage and backstage will be escorted out the stage door. At the doors, you will give the officers your name, address, and phone number and show them your ID, after which you will be excused and be allowed to leave. This will take a little time, but knowing how famous we New Yorkers are for pulling together in times like this, I know I can count on you. So please remain seated and relax until it's your turn. Thank you."

Not so easy to relax when there's a corpse sitting in front of you, Jacobus thought, but to Malachi he said, "Good job, Malachi. Never figured you to have the gift of gab. Now I got to get out of here."

"You'll wait your turn, like everyone else."

Malachi ordered his troops to make sure no one approached Haagen's corpse.

Jacobus was not displeased to hear a lot of cops—he didn't know how they had managed to get there so quickly—funneling everyone onstage in the right direction. Several of the dancers, only a few feet from Haagen, sobbed convulsively. He heard one voice—Imogene Livenstock's, he was pretty sure—say, "Buck up, girls. Do as the officers say." Others were talking with unnatural rapidity of what they professed to have heard and seen. There were footsteps all around, which on the stage sounded like a herd of cattle, but gradually there evolved a semblance of order and process, the talking quieter and calmer. Jacobus waited impatiently for his turn to leave.

190

"Jake," said Nathaniel. "Malachi wants to talk to you. He sounds pretty hot under the collar."

"What'd I do now? I'm just sitting here."

"I don't know. Here he comes."

"Jacobus!" said Malachi, harshly.

I guess I'm not one of the famous New Yorkers, thought Jacobus.

"Were you with Yumi between the dress rehearsal and the concert?"

"No."

"Do you know where she went between the rehearsal and the concert?"

"I'm not her goddam *oba-san*. No. Why?"

"Ortiz, put an APB out for Yumi Shinagawa. Stake out her apartment. If you find her, arrest her."

"What the hell's going on?" Jacobus demanded.

"What's going on is I was just informed that Ivan Lensky and his mother, Pravda Lenskaya, were found murdered in Lenskaya's home. Slashed. Time of death, about three or four hours ago."

"You think Yumi did that?"

"And then there was one, Jacobus. She's the only one left, and now she's hiding."

"Don't be so damn melodramatic, Malachi. Use your brain. What about Crispin Short?"

"I had a plainclothesman sitting next to him the entire concert. Now get out of here so I can do my job." He called to Ortiz. "You're in charge here. I'm heading out to Flushing."

Jacobus had his own destination in mind, and if he was right, it would be dangerous. He made his way backstage, found Yumi's case, and under the guise of caring for her violin, deftly expropriated the cellphone that was still there. He received a thirty-second tutorial from Nathaniel on how to use it—no, it did not have a rotary dial—so they could stay in communication, and sent Nathaniel off to tail Short. He picked up Yumi's case with feigned nonchalance, as if it were his own, and on his way out he instructed Power Ramsey to return the violin he had just performed on, the Guadagnini, to Dedubian. Ramsey, vaguely responsive, must have been a daze. Jacobus had a hard time getting him to say anything other than some babbling, "My enchantments! My enchantments!"

Moments later, Jacobus pushed his way to the front of the line at the stage door.

"Call me a cab," he hollered at the security guard.

"You're a cab!" said the guard. It was the same voice that had tried to kick him out of Carnegie Hall, the belittling voice, he recalled, from which he had been protected so recently by Annika Haagen.

"Damn you," said Jacobus, meaning it.

He exited onto Fifty-sixth Street into the rain, but knowing how few cabs drove by there at this time of night, circled around the building to the front of the hall and made his way to the curb. To avoid the construction he stepped out onto Fifty-seventh Street, heedless of being run over, and extended his arm to signal for a cab.

A taxi skidded to a halt on the wet pavement.

"Hop in, buddy," said the cabbie, "before you get killed."

Jacobus gave him the address.

"That a violin?" asked the driver. "Or a machine gun?"

"Violin," muttered Jacobus, hoping a truthful answer would forestall further conversation, and wondering if everyone in New York had done a stint in the borsht belt.

"Hey, listen to this," said the driver. "Just the other day, this tourist gets in my cab and says, 'Mister, how do I get to Carnegie Hall?' You know what I told 'im?"

"Fuck you, buddy," said Jacobus. "I'm not interested."

"Exactly! That's exactly what I told 'im!" said the cabbie. "How'd ya know? Hey, for guessing right, you want me to introduce you to a nice girl I know? She likes meeting interesting people."

"That leaves me out," said Jacobus. "Just get me where we're going as fast as you can."

"Whatever you say," said the cabbie. The taxi lurched forward, throwing Jacobus back in his seat.

Chapter Twenty-Three

Yumi opened her eyes. Or at least it felt as if she had. She wasn't sure because it was just as dark when she opened her eyes as when they were closed. She blinked a few times to test them, but the result was the same. Her consciousness seemed to ebb, then return. Where was she? How long had she been unconscious? She was fairly certain she was indoors because the intense, unnatural blackness matched the darkness of the Carnegie Hall stage. Undoubtedly, if she were outside in New York City—assuming she still was in the city—there would be a light coming from somewhere.

She wished she had Jake's ability to perceive sounds and smells in darkness. She tried emulating Jake, analyzing all nonvisual stimuli, but so far she was coming up blanks.

She tried to trace events back to the last moment she could recall. She was sitting onstage. Marian Anderson's video performance of "Death and the Maiden" had begun. The human mound of dancers and their selected audience members, panting but trying to maintain their frozen positions in the darkness, separated the quartet from the audience. They wouldn't have long to wait. Soon the stage lights would be turned on and everyone would stand for bows. Yumi had been thinking what an amazing, if unanticipated, achievement it had been for Jake and Nathaniel, but Jake especially, to have performed "Death and the Maiden" without any rehearsal, from memory, and with such stunning conviction.

And then, at the end of Anderson's first stanza, the voice had whispered in her ear, "Pravda needs you. She needs you now. There is a cab waiting for you at the stage entrance."

There had been soothing urgency in the voice, though in its hushed tone she couldn't tell whether it had been male or female. It was a voice she felt drawn to trust, though she had no idea whose it had been. Unseen by the audience, still riveted to the singing on the big film screen and on the other side of the dancers piled on the stage, it was not difficult for Yumi to scurry undetected into the wings. Not knowing her destination, she left her violin in its case next to Jacobus's. She thought it odd that the voice hadn't waited for her but chalked that up to the urgency it conveyed. Conflicted by a sense of haste yet determined to avoid a disturbance as the concert continued without her, she trotted on her tiptoes, like a foal, to the stage door.

Exiting, she looked for the cab, but there was none, so she waited. None of the traffic and bustle on Fifty-seventh Street at the front of the building was to be found here at the back. The audience inside was still transfixed to the film, so she was alone on the street. The weather had turned chilly again; it was dark and it had started to rain. She became impatient. Was this a hoax? She looked to the right since Fifty-sixth Street is one way from the west, to see if her cab was coming...

That was the last thing she could remember. Had the voice led her into a trap? Or had something else gone wrong? And now she was here, wherever here was. How long she had been here, she had no idea. She strained with her eyes, ears, and nose to ascertain something—anything—but was unsuccessful in all her efforts. Unexpectedly, her head began to nod. Was she still drugged? Perhaps it was the total absence of stimuli. Perhaps it was the utter futility. Perhaps it—

A terrifying thought jumped, unbidden, into her mind. Had she become blind, like Jake? The silence, too, was profound. Was she deaf as well?

She tried to reject the notion, but in sudden vertiginous panic she attempted to stand up, only to find her hands and feet tied to the chair in which she was sitting. She struggled unsuccessfully against the bonds holding her down.

"So you're finally awake."

She recognized the voice.

194

"Aaron! Aaron, is that you?" Yumi asked, peering into the blackness.

"Who did you expect?"

"Where have you been? What's going on?"

"I'm afraid we have a bit of a problem."

"Well, just untie me and let's get out of here."

"I'm afraid that it's not that simple. You see, you're the problem."

"Me? What are you talking about?"

"Well, the little *liaison* we had—you know, in Lima—and everything that led up to it. It didn't go over very well with Annika. She felt betrayed. Very betrayed, by both of us. Now it's necessary to make things right."

"What do you mean, 'make things right'?"

"We're going to have to forget about that marketing study and bring back Crispin."

"You mean you want me to resign? Because you seduced me and now you're feeling guilty? Okay, we seduced each other. But is this the way you negotiate? Drug me, kidnap me, and tie me up? Do you think you can intimidate me like that? You've really outdone yourself this time."

"I'm afraid it's gone even beyond that," said another voice, chuckling, "if you can believe it."

"Crispin!" said Yumi. "You're in on this, too?"

"From the beginning, love," he said. "I'm afraid we've committed a no-no, and now we've got to make amends."

"What are you talking about?"

"Just that we've all come to the conclusion that we need to get back to basics. No marketing studies, no behind-the-scenes hanky-panky. Just some solid, all-for-one, one-for-all music making. Sorry to say, you're the odd girl out. Permanently."

"What do you mean, permanently?"

"Haven't you figured that out yet, dear Yumi? We're going to have to do you in. We've no other choice."

"You're going to kill me? This makes no sense. It's ridiculous!"

"Why you say redeekooloos? "

"Pravda! What's happening? I don't understand what's happening!"

"Look," said yet another voice.

"Ivan!"

"Let me tell you what was. Aaron is first violin, right? He leads quartet. He is like big boss and make decision. It's his job. His decision: He want Crispin back; he want you dead. So what can we do? We say bye-bye and then we drink you toast. Ha!"

Yumi's head was swimming.

"Yumi, dear, it will be all right. It's just something we had to do."

"Annika?"

"Yes. It wasn't an easy decision. It's been wonderful having you in the quartet, and, *pfff*, I'm just sorry things haven't worked out better, but…"

"Annika, please. Don't let them."

"Hey, honey, enough with the tears."

"Jake!" said Yumi. "Thank God you're here! I don't know what's going on. Maybe it's the drugs they gave me. Tell them that they're all crazy!"

"So maybe they're a little meshuga, but who isn't? This kind of stuff comes with the territory."

"Jake, what are you saying? Why is this happening to me?"

"I'm saying deal with it. Death comes to all of us sooner or later. No one can help it if yours just happens to be sooner. Look, no one forced you to be part of the quartet, right? You've talked the talk, honey. Now you've gotta walk the walk."

"No, Jake. Please. You can't mean this."

"But he is right, Yumi. After all, I'm only the first violinist, but he was your teacher. You need to listen to him."

"No, Aaron. It's not right," she pleaded.

"That's what everyone says. But it *is* right. And it *is* time."

"Yes, love. Time to pay the piper, isn't it? Ta-ta, then."

Yumi felt a pair of hands around her neck. Aaron's? Crispin's? Pravda's? Ivan's? Annika's? Jake's? There was nothing she could do, and, since she understood nothing, there was nothing she could even think of doing. Her breathing became constricted, but why struggle?

She heard a thumping. Was it her heart, beating its last? A hand was placed

196

over her mouth, and a voice said, "Be quiet or I'll kill you." Someone was knocking at a door.

Chapter Twenty-Four

"Well, if it isn't Comrade Kutcherpekirov!"

"Jake?" Yumi gasped. Light from outside the room flooded in. Dim though it was, it blinded her.

"Mr. Jacobus, this is a surprise," said the one voice she didn't recognize. "This was meant to be, I see now. Please come in. Ah! You have brought your violin. Will you give us another concert? Please come in."

Yumi, still adjusting to the light, found herself seated against the back wall of the quartet's rehearsal room. She could see Jacobus standing in the doorway on the other side of the piano.

"Jake, what's happening? Why are we in my studio? Where is everyone?"

"As my *compadre* Oro likes to say, all in good time, Yumi dear," Jacobus said.

"You don't want me to die?"

"Are you kidding? Of course not. You haven't paid me for your last lesson yet. We'll just be packing our bags and leaving Lensky here to clean up your rehearsal studio," Jacobus said.

"Lensky?" said Yumi, addressing the only other individual in the room. "You? You're not Ivan Lensky!"

"Not Ivan," said Jacobus. "Baby brother Peter, with a little secret. Peter, would you care to join us for a visit to the police station and tell them all about it? That's probably your best option."

Suddenly Jacobus felt his arm being grabbed. He held the violin case tightly as Lensky hustled him into a chair so forcibly it almost tipped over, nearly spilling him onto Yumi's lap. Jacobus placed the case and his cane next to the chair. Too bad Trotsky's not here, Jacobus thought. The wittle woozie would lick Lensky to death.

"I am sorry this must happen, Mr. Jacobus," Lensky said, locking the door. "You are one of the few people who understands that what they called a concert at Carnegie Hall tonight was a, a…"

"A travesty?" Jacobus offered.

"A blasphemy! And if not for you, it would never have happened. This video! This light show! This dancing! It was painting the rouge of the whore on the face of the Virgin Mary. When the purity of music is defiled—"

"Hey, I'm with you on that score, Rasputin!" said Jacobus. "Those were almost my very words and you will get no argument from me. I think Power Ramsey can dance off into the sunset to the steps of his videochoreography and never come back. It's just when you go around murdering people that we go our separate paths."

"Murder?"

"Isn't that what you call it when you chop people into little pieces? Or, have you forgotten about Lima, for starters?"

"This is all very interesting, Mr. Jacobus," said Lensky, "but if I were to have committed murder, why would I go all the way to Lima?"

"Two reasons: convenience and coincidence. You went there because shortly before the tour Crispin Short told you—emailed you, to be more precise—that Kortovsky and Haagen were going to fire your mother. Since your mother always felt that special maternal need to take care of you, and you're a pro at playing that game, aren't you—you've been acting the poor invalid for years—you figured, 'Hey, now's my opportunity. Five zillion miles away from home, and I'll make it look like a drug killing and who'll ever know?' Right?

"Ironically, though, that whole marketing study *mishigas* wasn't true. Dear Crispin was just trying to get you all fired up so you'd convince Mama to go for his deal. He just wanted to be part of the gang. He didn't realize heads would roll. Literally. Your mother was not going to be fired, according to Annika."

"Obviously, you can never prove that, now that Haagen's dead," said

Lensky.

"Oh, my God, no!" said Yumi.

"And just how is it we know that she's dead, Peter, m'boy?" asked Jacobus. "Telepathy?"

Lensky had no response.

Jacobus hoped his plan to contact Nathaniel was working, because if Lensky's need to "ablute" was related to his anxiety level, his body odor was already in the danger zone, as ripe as the aged gorgonzola he had eaten at Lensky's lair.

Jacobus had dialed Nathaniel's number on Yumi's cellphone and put it in the violin case, leaving it on, before he had knocked on the door. Nathaniel should have been able to hear both Yumi and him mention that they were in the rehearsal studio. Nathaniel should be here any moment now.

"You speak in a frivolous tone, Mr. Jacobus," Lensky finally replied. "But I sense you speak out of fear. There is no need to fear death. You should view it as a comfort, especially someone like yourself: infirmed, old, your skills wasting away. You should welcome death. You should welcome *me*—"

"The singing Kevorkian?"

"For I am someone with whom everyone on earth will someday be familiar," said Lensky.

"You're from the IRS, then," asked Jacobus. "Jehovah's Witness, perhaps."

"Ah, you try to mock me, but your jest will not help, because I am Death. I am despised and acquainted with grief, and I am here for you."

"Well, that's very kind," said Yumi, "but as you probably can tell, I'm still quite young. And fit!"

"Young or old, who among us knows when the end will come? When you will step off a curb and be killed by a speeding cab whose driver is racing to a fare, listening to some rock-and-roll monstrosity on his MP3 player? Or when you are in your apartment, practicing a Mozart quartet, and an errant bullet from a drug transaction a block away shatters your window and pierces your brain? Or when a harmless, microscopic cell receives a command to multiply inside your body until it becomes the living force and you the parasite?

"Death begins from the moment of birth. We are each a cell-manufacturing factory, and though at first we churn them out, sooner or later production becomes sluggish; our cells deteriorate faster than our bodies can replace them and the living ones are overwhelmed. Sooner or later I take you with me."

"To tell you the truth," said Yumi, "I'm feeling pretty good about my cells at this time—"

"You think it is not yet the right time for you," said Lensky. "I ask, when is there a wrong time? Is it not better to go when you are still young, vibrant, alive, then to suffer as your body and mind decay through old age? Which would you putrefy first, Yumi Shinagawa? Would you rather have an active mind while a prisoner in your moldering body? Or live until you are ninety or a hundred but with a mind that can only recall the applesauce someone just spooned in your flaccid mouth and is now drooling down your chin?

"Wouldn't you prefer to spare your loved ones the anguish of watching you waste away little by little as your mind and body gradually disintegrates, like Daniel Jacobus? Wouldn't it be better to spare them the heartbreak of deciding when to pull the plug?

"Come, when I unbind you, take my hand and your end will be painless."

"And if I decline your gracious offer?"

"Then it will be painful."

"Why didn't you just do it painlessly when I was unconscious and get it over with?"

"Your free will will give me great joy."

"That makes me feel much better. That way it won't seem so much like murder."

"Murder! Manslaughter! Friendly fire! Abortion! Euthanasia! Suicide! It is all death. I am Death! I come to all of you, Yumi Shinagawa. I now give you the choice. Do not fear me. Will you take my hand?"

"No."

"No? I am disappointed. Yes, you will meet death, but on my terms, not on the whore Haagen's, not on Kortovsky's, not in a farce like Ramsey's, but in purity and honesty. Listen!"

Jacobus and Yumi heard the familiar simple piano chords introducing "Death and the Maiden." Lensky sang the first stanza in a fragile, heartbreaking soprano expressing anguish and despair over the prospect of imminent death. In the second, in which Death reaches out with its icy hand, offering eternal comfort, Lensky's voice turned deathly cold. Neither male nor female, it was no longer human.

"Gib deine Hand, du schön und zart Gebild!

Simply put, Jacobus had never heard a sound like this. Not even the great Marian Anderson's performance sent the chill through his body that Lensky's voice now did. He felt the fear of death; he smelled the grave opening up for him. Lensky's smell. He was pulled by the voice to follow its course. Lensky had unleashed a power in music that Jacobus had never thought possible. In disbelief, but hypnotized by the music, Jacobus felt himself giving up. He had always wondered why his parents, and millions of others, had not resisted. Now he began to understand what Schubert understood. What Smetana understood. When the inevitable is about to occur, why struggle? Why not embrace the end? He knew now that the "beautiful and tender image" that Schubert was talking about was only a metaphor; in reality, it was life. His parents' life; his brother Eli's. His.

"Bin Freund, und komme nicht, zu strafen."

Lensky was right. He, Lensky, or Death—whatever, it didn't matter—was a friend. What more did he have to live for? Arthritis? He had just given his own greatest performance and now he was listening to something far, far greater. What better way to end? Painless! And even if it wasn't, it would only take a moment.

"Sei gutes Muts! ich bin nicht wild."

Yes, be in good spirits! Nathaniel—good old Nathaniel—will take care of

Trotsky. Dumb dog. Ah, he's not so bad. Poor Yumi, though. Still so young. She hasn't said a word. But clearly, at her lesson she said she had no fear facing death. Good girl. And now they would go together. Jacobus waited with liberating joy for *"Sollst sanft in meinen Armen schlafen!"* "You should sleep gently in my arms." And then his suffering would be over. Silently, he mouthed the lyrics from Schubert's *Winterreise*, *"Ich kann zu meiner Reisen nicht wählen mit der Zeit."* I cannot choose the time of my journey; I must find my own way in this darkness.

"Oh, I went into a baker shop to get a bite to eat—"

What the hell is that? Jacobus thought. Yumi's voice? But now, at the very moment that he finally comprehended Lensky's insight, why did she have to interrupt? How annoying. How disrespectful.

"'Cause I was so hungry from my head to my feet."

It was the childhood song Jacobus had taught Yumi on the train, to the tune of "Turkey In The Straw." But why?

"*Sollst sanft in—*" came Lensky's voice, a bit louder to subdue Yumi's.

"*So I picked up a doughnut and wiped off the grease,*" Yumi sang louder. "*And I handed the baker girl a five-cent piece.*"

"*Sollst sanft in meinen Armen—*" Lensky, sang, harshly this time, trying to overwhelm Yumi's voice into submission, but the spell was broken. Jacobus, reawakened, shook its residue from his head. Like "Death and the Maiden," there was only one more stanza. He now understood, and joined in.

"She looked at the nickel and she looked at me,
And she said 'Kind sir, you can plainly see—'"

They were in full voice now.

"*...in meinen Armen schlafen!*" screamed Lensky. "You should sleep gently in my arms!"

" 'There's a hole in the nickel and it goes right through'.
"Said I, 'There's a hole in the doughnut, too.' "

Maybe I won't be sleeping in anyone's arms, at least not just yet, thought Jacobus. Maybe there's still hope. No Nathaniel, but a little hope. He squeezed Yumi's hand.

"Shave and a haircut, two bits!" Yumi added for punctuation, but the sinister silence that followed was perhaps even more emphatic.

"You think," Lensky said, very quietly, "that your infantile humor will somehow change your fate. The only difference is now it will be painful. It is time."

"No," Jacobus said in a moment of revelation and in a last-ditch effort to stall. "It is not the time."

"I cannot stop," said Lensky, his voice rising. "Schubert directs me."

"You're wrong there, pal! You've been operating under a false premise. No one dies in that song."

Lensky did not respond.

"They're just bargaining!" Jacobus shouted.

"Idiot."

"Who's the idiot? There are two stanzas. First the girl states her position and then Death propositions her. Right? But nothing actually *happens* to her in the song. No one knows what the hell is going to happen to her."

"But death is inevitable."

"That's not exactly a new idea, Einstein. But we don't know...we don't really know...whether our damsel in the song is going to die the next minute or whether she's going to live to be a wrinkly old hausfrau *mit grosse* bosoms, do we? And that's part of the greatness of Schubert's song, in my humble opinion. It leaves what is going to happen outside the frame reference of the music and inside the mind of the listener. You've been operating under a false premise, *meine Freund.*"

"Mr. Jacobus, you tire me with your academic pedantry. It is now time—"

"Well, between you and me, pardner, you're not Death. You're just an extraordinarily talented young fellow who's gone off the deep end and killed a bunch of people."

"A bunch?" asked Yumi.

"Have I?" said Lensky, ignoring her. "I think not. I prefer to think I am sane and the world has gone mad. It's a matter of perspective, is it not? Give me one reason you think I am sick."

"Try this one on for size: *'Evviva il cotellino!'* Eh, Peter?"

Jacobus heard an indescribably animal sound boil up from inside Lensky. Then his voice rang out, again Schubert, now a strident baritone: *"Will kein Gott auf Erden sein, sind wir selber Götter!"*

Jacobus understood the German: If there is no God on earth, then we ourselves are gods!

Then came the onrush, accompanied by an inhuman roar that was the opposite of music. Lensky was upon him almost immediately, his hand around Jacobus's throat. He heard Yumi, still bound, shouting behind Lensky, "Stop!"

"Murderer!" she screamed in desperation. "I'll kill you!"

Maybe someone will hear us, Jacobus hoped, then recalled that the room was soundproofed and that all the businesses on their floor had long ceased operations for the day. The hands around his throat tightened like a vise. He tried to pry them off with his own but Lensky was far too powerful. He felt the pressure building inside his head as his circulation was cut off and he could no longer inhale. He opened his mouth, but air could neither enter nor exit.

Suddenly, he felt yet another pair of hands on his own, pulling them away. He was unable to resist. Then he felt the fingers of those hands wedge themselves between Lensky's hands and his neck. They were strong hands, these new ones, and determined. Floating on the edge of consciousness, he felt the pressure on his throat gradually ease until Lensky's hands were off of him. Woozy and unfocused, Jacobus vaguely thanked Nathaniel for saving him yet again, grateful for the strong hands that a lifetime of cello playing had given him.

The crash roused him. Nathaniel, who had not uttered a word, was grappling with the growling Lensky. As big as he was, Nathaniel would be no match for the powerful man more than thirty years his junior. It wouldn't last more than a moment.

"Jake!" shouted Yumi. "Get off your butt! Untie me!"

Jacobus shook his head violently, forcing himself into alertness. He felt for Yumi's hands, tied behind the chair, as Nathaniel and Lensky continued to struggle, the thudding of their grunting bodies absorbed by the room's soundproofing. Jacobus used whatever strength was left in his aged hands to loosen Yumi's bonds, and when those didn't work, he used his teeth. Little by little, Yumi was able to assist in her liberation, first freeing her hands, then untying her feet.

Jacobus heard her leap up and without a word fling herself into the maelstrom.

The three combatants crashed onto the piano keyboard, igniting a cacophonous havoc of dissonant, clashing chords and cascading glissandi that would have made John Cage blush. Jacobus rushed toward the fray, shouting incoherently at the top of his lungs, diving toward the noise, pulling blindly at who he supposed was Lensky, but he had little strength left. For the briefest of moments he grasped the overwhelming despair of impotence and almost felt sympathy.

Someone was tossed into Jacobus, and they both tumbled to the floor. Jacobus fell against his violin case, and making a fist, pounded it in frustration. Yumi groaned next to him.

"Yumi, are you okay?" asked Jacobus.

"I'll live," said Yumi, pain etched in her voice. Jacobus was alarmed with her flat tone. He felt her hand clasp, then squeeze, his. He had no idea what to do next. Their only hope was Nathaniel, and Jacobus held his breath when he heard someone fall heavily to the ground. Who was the last to remain standing?

"Fools!" roared Lensky. "All of you! Fools!" He began singing in a vindictively piercing soprano coloratura, swooping down with cascading, lightning-fast scales. It was a voice under the most extreme mental and physical control, but wild. Insane.

CHAPTER TWENTY-FOUR

"Chi temea Giove regnante
Pria che Giove fulminante
Cominciasse a lampeggiar?

"Who feared Jove the ruler
Before Jove the thunderer
Began to fire his lightning bolts?"

Lensky finished abruptly, and Jacobus heard him plodding, snarling toward them. Jacobus, lying on the ground, gauged their relative positions. He tracked Lensky's odor, which now stunk like the skunk cabbage that graced the banks of the Williams River near his house in the Berkshires. Jacobus had a cane, a rope, and a violin case at his disposal, and seconds to decide how he would defend himself. Clutching the bottom end of his cane, he sensed his adversary's position, feigned swinging it, then extended the curled end of it until it caught on the back of Lensky's ankle. He jerked with both hands with all of his strength.

Lensky came crashing down with a howl. Jacobus heard his head crack against the floor, where he lay, stunned and moaning.

"I think the recital may be over," Jacobus said to Yumi. "You'll be okay from now on.

"Nathaniel, what took you so long?"

"*Discúlpeme*, Maestro Yacovis, I am not the person who you ascertain me to be, but first perhaps you can hand me the rope next to you."

"Oro! You're not Nathaniel!"

"God bless you for your perception, Maestro."

"What the hell are you doing here? How did you unlock the door?"

"All in good time, Maestro. But first, the rope, *por favor*, before Señor Lensky makes the renaissance. He is a very strong man. Then we may catch our breaths."

Jacobus reached out with the rope that Lensky had used to tie up Yumi.

"Ah, the justice of the poetic," said Oro.

While Oro was engaged in making sure Lensky was securely bound,

Jacobus said to Yumi, "Hey, I've got another song for you," circling his right arm behind her shoulders to support her.

"Schubert?" she asked, her voice thin.

"Better. Do you know 'Around the Corner'?"

"No. Teach it to me."

Jacobus cleared his choked-up voice.

"Around the corner, and under a tree,
A pretty maiden once said to me:
'Who would marry you, I would like to know,
'Cause every time I look at your face it makes me want to go
Around the corner, and under a—' "

"Jake," said Yumi, coughing, "don't, you're making me laugh."

"Make you laugh?" he asked, "but I was planning on singing that at Carnegie Hall...next time."

"I think we are now safe," said Oro. "I have tied his hands together and his legs to the piano. But before I take the opportunity to congratulate the two of you on your fine performance of 'Death and the Maiden' tonight I must call my colleague, Lieutenant Malachi, to take the possession of Señor Lensky. Is there a phone I may use?"

"If you knew to come here, why didn't Malachi?"

"The good Lieutenant is at the residence of the unfortunate Señora Lenskaya. It appears Señor Peter killed her and Señor Ivan between the final rehearsal and the concert. Señor Ivan and Señora Lenskaya were wearing clothing for concert. They apparently intended to play tonight. I think Señor Peter didn't permit them. But more of that later. A phone, *por favor?*"

"There's one in my violin case," said Jacobus. "It's Yumi's but it doesn't work. I had it on for Nathaniel. He was supposed to come here once he knew where we were. I dialed his number and left it on the whole time."

"Are you sure you pressed Talk, Maestro?"

"Ah, shit."

Sergeant Ortiz arrived shortly thereafter. He and Oro conversed in rapid Spanish. Ortiz handcuffed Lensky, still dazed, and before escorting him from the studio called for an ambulance.

"And now I think we must all go to the hospital, especially Señorita Shinagawa. The injuries and the shock must be treated for this brave young lady, who played so beautifully and fought so courageously."

"Don't worry about me," said Yumi. "I'll live."

As the ambulance headed for Mount Sinai Hospital less than two miles away, Jacobus asked Oro, "So, tell me. Why the hell did you come here in the first place?"

"Well, let us just say that I am here in the unofficial incógnito, which is why I wished not make me known to you. Number one, I desired to confirm if the large, limping man I saw at the concert in Lima was indeed Señor Peter. Number two, I desired to hear the New Magini String Quartet perform 'Death and the Maiden.' It was such an occasion of history not to be missed. But it turns out that so much more has been accomplished in one visit to your magnificent city. How could I have guessed that you would be the first violinist of this great ensemble? It is my honor to know you, Maestro Yacovis. And to not only identify Señor Limper, but to assist in the apprehension of such!"

"But how did you find Yumi and me at the rehearsal studio?"

"This is the easy question to answer. After the tragic demisement of Señora Haagen, I was standing next to you in the backstage of the Carnegie Hall. What a magnificent auditorium! If only Lima had such a—"

"Oro! Tonight, please!"

"Discúlpeme, Maestro. Since no one knew who I was, I simply pretended to be one of the workers. I have learned it is always easy to fit in when you just look busy. When I heard the Lieutenant Malachi was going to the home of Señora Lenskaya, I decided to follow you in one of your famous New York taxis. I assure you they are so much more *cómodo* than our *ticos*."

"Why follow me and not Malachi?"

"The lieutenant had many armed officers with him. I decided to follow you in the unlikely eventuation you might need my small assistance."

"Then, if may be so bold as to ask," said Jacobus, "what took you so goddam long to get to us?"

"Ah, Maestro, again you have discovered the heart of the matter! I told my taxi driver, 'Follow that car!' with the best sound of Humphrey Bogart in my voice."

"And?"

"And he followed my instructions perfectly. There was only one difficulty."

"Yeah?"

"You see, the taxis in Lima are very cheap. You can go almost anywhere for one or two of your American dollars. But here, I didn't prepare so well. I offered the driver all of my solares, but he was not entirely felicitous with that arrangement, so we spent some time finding a machine where I could use my credit card to obtain the necessary dollars to pay him. *Discúlpeme.*"

"And how did you get in? Lensky had locked the door."

"That was much easier. I used the same credit card. Policemen are almost as good as the thieves in opening the doors."

When the ambulance arrived at the hospital, Yumi, refusing to be wheeled in on a gurney, was the first to be escorted in. Before he entered the building, Jacobus felt a moist, refreshing breeze, funneled by the crosstown streets, blowing from the west. He turned to face it directly, hoping it would purge the misery of the previous hours out of him.

"Just out of curiosity, Oro," Jacobus said, "the first time I talked to you, you mentioned that the New Magini had performed your favorite Mozart quartet in Lima, but you hung up before I could ask you which one it is. So tell me, which is it? The 'Dissonant,' maybe?"

"I am surprised you would not guess correctly right away, Maestro," said Oro. "It is the 'Hunt.' Of course."

Chapter Twenty-Five

FRIDAY

"*Evviva il cotellino?*" asked Malachi.

"Long live the little knife!" said Jacobus, massaging his sore throat. The three of them had been treated and released from the ER. Yumi hadn't gotten off as easy as he had, but was not complaining about her broken rib, sprained ankle, and mild concussion when it could have been much worse. Oro, bruised and battered by the much larger Peter Lensky, nevertheless managed to have had his suit cleaned, pressed, and deodorized at an all-night dry cleaner. No one had gotten much sleep.

Jacobus felt perversely at ease sitting in Malachi's office at the police station; being surrounded by cops going about their business on this gray Friday morning provided a sense of security and normalcy that he hadn't felt for some time. Once in a while a cop would come by and quietly say, "How ya doin'?" but he sensed those comments were directed more toward Yumi. One cop tapped him on his shoulder and handed him a paper cup of instant coffee, with non-dairy creamer and too much sugar. Jacobus accepted it in his left hand, as Yumi had been holding his right hand the entire time and seemed disinclined to let go for the foreseeable future. He appreciated what he was holding in each hand.

Oro had also been offered a cup and after taking one cautious sip asked politely what it was. When told it was coffee, he explained in great detail the traditional Peruvian way of serving coffee, with separate hot pitchers

211

of thick, syrupy coffee, water, and milk, all combined in proportions determined by the drinker's personal taste. One of the cop's had said, "You're just missin' one thing." When Oro asked what that might be, the cop said, "the doughnut!" and all the other cops started laughing, with Oro joining in.

"And what exactly is the doughnut?" he had asked.

After that was explained, it was Malachi's turn.

"*Evviva il cotellino?*"

"That's what they used to shout at concerts in Italy in the eighteenth century," Jacobus said, "after a castrato finished a particularly virtuoso performance of an opera aria. Kind of like *bravo* except a little more specialized."

"That's gross," said Yumi.

"Sorry."

"Not what you said. The horrible things they did to those young boys. Just to get them to sing like girls."

"Not that I'm condoning it, but some of those boys were offered up by poverty-stricken parents who thought their best chance for family survival was to have their sons undergo the operation. Some of those castrati were the rock stars of the seventeenth and eighteenth centuries and lived the lives of the rich and famous."

"It's still disgusting."

"And you say that triggered Lensky? '*Evviva il cotellino*'?" asked Malachi. "Why?"

"I guess I touched a sensitive spot, so to speak," said Jacobus. "Peter Lensky had testicular cancer. He contracted it as a result of the Chernobyl catastrophe, the disaster that his father was blamed for, and imprisoned and died for, that his mother went into exile as a result of, and that Otkar Vasalin made his millions off of. In short, so to speak, Lensky was castrated as part of his cancer treatment. It was all kept quiet by the family. Peter recovered enough physically, and he acquired a remarkable voice—an amazing, an uncanny voice—to go along with the musical talent everyone in his family had. Maybe it was even his illness and isolation that turned his talent into musical genius. Who knows? It can happen. But mentally and emotionally, he was ruined."

"I still can't believe those voices in the dark were all his," Yumi said.

"Believe it. It can happen when you combine that kind of gift and that kind of insanity. Plus you were half drugged, in the darkness—"

"And scared out of my mind? What was that song he sang, Jake, when you provoked him? About the thunderbolts?" Yumi asked.

"I didn't know at the time, but I asked Nathaniel when he met us at the ER. It's a supposedly famous aria from the opera *Berenice*, which Leonardo Vinci composed for the great—the greatest—castrato, Farinelli."

"You did a cruel thing there, Jacobus, taunting a sick person that way," Malachi said.

"Sick? Hey, we've all got our *tsores*. Illness, accidents, deaths. Who the hell knows what's going to happen to us in the next minute, huh? It doesn't mean we have to be killers just because we catch a bad break. Because of poor little Peter's peter, Kortovsky, Haagen, Ivan, Pravda—they're all dead. And I'm cruel?

"It's Pravda you've got to feel for for taking overzealous care of him. After all, she lost her husband to Chernobyl, and almost lost Peter. She felt a maternal need to protect him from all the potential disasters of the external world, and in so doing created an internal disaster. So when I found out from Nathaniel that he had accompanied Mama on the South America tour, it began to all fit together.

"I got the distinct feeling that Peter didn't care for his mother traipsing through his fortress of solitude in Flushing. Plus, he was a big boy and she was making enough dough, so for these three reasons of course they had separate rooms in Lima. This enabled Peter to come and go as he pleased, and she had no idea that Peter was off carving up Kortovsky. Why should she have? On one hand, he loved it that Mama was taking care of all his creature comforts. He could sit in his little world all day, day after day, performing his Schubert and Porpora to his heart's content and not have to worry about where his next meal would come from. On the other hand, he resented the shit out of her for treating him like a cripple, though mentally he was, or at least became one after playing the part for so many years—"

"If I may say so," Oro interjected, "from what you have told about Señor Peter, he never went to the concerts. Therefore, when he went to the concert in Lima, it must have been not because of his love affair with Mozart and Beethoven, but only to stalk and kill Señor Kortovsky. You tell me no one in the quartet knew where any of the others were staying, so the only way he could follow Señor Kortovsky was from the concert hall. When the quartet was taking its well-deserved bows, Señor Peter went backstage, hid there in the darkness, and when the opportunity presented itself, removed the endpin from his mother's cello, which he then hid with ingenious down the leg of his trouser. This was the cause of his limp, though I did not realize the significance of this at the time.

"Señor Peter then followed Señor Kortovsky, and dare I say, Señorita Shinagawa, to his hotel in a cab. The Hotel Maury."

"I'm so sorry, Jake," said Yumi. "It was only a fling, really."

"Hey, no need to apologize, my dear. I hope Kortovsky is thankful, wherever he is, but he didn't deserve you. It did manage to get you onto Malachi's shit list. He had half the NYPD circle your apartment last night ready to arrest you for Annika's murder."

Malachi grunted. "Go on," he said.

"So Peter followed Kortovsky and Yumi to the Maury Hotel," Jacobus continued. "From what Oro here told me, according to Angelita the receptionist, Lensky waited until Yumi departed and then invited Kortovsky to the historic hotel bar, where, according to the bartender, Peter plied him with a bevy of their famous shaken pisco sours and engaged in polite conversation. Yumi had told me about Kortovsky's telltale alcoholic breath, so it's not unlikely Mama also had regaled Peter with stories of Kortovsky penchant for overindulging.

"When Kortovsky was in a sufficiently pliable state, Lensky led him to a nearby tenement, where he tied him to a chair, maybe giving him the spiel about him being Death, and he then skewered him using Mama's endpin as a harpoon, which he considerately wiped off and replaced in her cello soon after, before it was loaded onto the plane."

"We'll be checking on that endpin," said Malachi, "to see if there is any residue."

"A very resourceful of you," said Oro.

"Poking someone through the gut, though," Jacobus continued, "was not as easy as Lensky thought, and like his mind, the endpin ended up bent, so when Mama tried to extract it from the cello in the very room where I attended their first rehearsal after the tour, it got stuck."

"This is all very melodramatic," said Malachi. "And you're connecting the dots with a lot of speculation."

"Perhaps," said Oro, "but Maestro Yacovis has the gift of perception and I believe he is correct. When Señor Peter killed Señor Kortovsky, he took several steps to conceal the identity, with the hope that I, Espartaco Asunción Ochoa Romero, would interpret the mutilation as torture. First, he found a discarded piece of broken glass and attempted to disconnect Señor Kortovsky's left hand. I thought this was interesting, because *uno*, from the evidence forensic I was able to determine that Señor Kortovsky was already dead when it was attempted, and *dos*, it is more the custom to amputate the *right* hand when the victim is still alive as it installs more of the fear. However, Maestro Yacovis had the perspective of the violin expert; he found it interesting because it was the *left* hand, and if the body was indeed Señor Kortovsky, there were those toldtale grooves on his fingertips from pressing so hard on the strings. Señor Peter would have known that about him—Maestro tells me it was Señor Kortovsky's claim to his fame. Has it been possible, Lieutenant, with your art-of-the-stage forensic science, to determine if the fingers you have gathered had the toldtale grooves?"

"Given the condition of the fingers, it would be easier to find Neil Armstrong's footprints on the moon with a pair of binoculars," said Malachi. "This groove business also seems a little too far-fetched to me."

"Don't worry," said Jacobus. "I'm getting closer-fetched, because next Lensky started hacking away at Kortovsky's neck from the left side and then stopped."

"This is significant?"

"Yes, sirree. Again, Oro had his theory. He thought Lensky had given up because it was just too difficult to get through all that tissue and bone to cut off his whole head with a little bitty piece of glass. My take is that he just wanted to cut out the prominent callus Kortovsky had on his neck from holding the violin the way he did. Poor guy, he had such sensitive skin. It was just lucky for Lensky they didn't find the body for a month or else they might have ID'd Kortovsky, but by the time they got there his face was pretty much gone. So everything pointed to two conclusions: one, that the body was Kortovsky and not some cartel groupie; and two, that the killer knew about violinists' unique physiognomy."

"Tell us about the missing parts."

"After Lensky cut off Kortovsky's fingers he probably first intended to just throw them away to hide the clue that would lead to Kortovsky's identification. But then he had an idea. He decided to keep them and stored them in his piano bench for safekeeping because he now had a new plan. Phase one, putting a finger in Annika's case as a warning to scare off the quartet. 'Look what happened to Aaron! And you're next!' Except that no one else understood that that's what it meant."

"Not so fast!" said Malachi. "How do you know Lensky stored the fingers in the piano bench?"

"I don't know for sure, but when I was visiting Peter, Trotsky did his Iditarod imitation and dragged me to Peter's piano bench for a sniff-fest. You might think in my dotage my imagination has run amok, but just go and check inside the bench for any traces of dead finger residue. I think that's where he kept his souvenirs, and who would've known otherwise? He wouldn't let his mother in, and visitors were few and far between. By the way, you might also want to check his place for Kortovsky's computer."

"What about...the other appendage?" asked Malachi.

"You mean the you know what?"

"Whatever."

"Aren't we adults here?" asked Yumi. "I'm not a little girl anymore."

"Okay. His *peckerino*. There, I've said it."

"Jake! You're disgusting," said Yumi.

"So sue me. No, never mind. It was that particular amputation, along with everything else, that convinced me it had to be Peter and no one else. It all fit together. But this was not a warning. This was rage. Sheer rage over Kortovsky's sexuality and Peter's lack of it."

"Let me get this straight," Malachi said. "You're proposing four different reasons for what you say Lensky did to Kortovsky. One, he killed him because he believed Kortovsky was a threat to music and to his mother; two, he mutilated Kortovsky's fingers and neck to obscure ID; three, he further used the fingers to provide a warning to the quartet members; and four, he emasculated Kortovsky out of uncontrolled rage. Is that what you're telling me?"

"I couldn't have said it better."

"Sí," said Oro. "This was a crime of the greatest complexity from the highly complex individuality."

"But aren't you forgetting the email from Kortovsky to Sheila Rathman, saying he would be returning for the dress rehearsal?" asked Yumi.

"Yes." Malachi chuckled. "What about the email? If Kortovsky had no fingers, how could he have typed that email?"

"Very witty, Malachi," Jacobus said. "Poe would be proud of your juxtaposition, if not your logic. I know very little about technology, and as far as I'm concerned the less the better, but it occurred to me that, unlike a real letter that you put a stamp on and an address and lick the envelope and put in a mail box, an email can be sent from any computer from anywhere, and since handwriting is not involved, it can be signed by any one. All you'd need is Kortovsky's email address, a password, and the user something, and you're in business. But that was privileged information for the quartet. Not even Sheila Rathman had it. Peter, though, had it because after he killed Kortovsky, the ever-resourceful young lad removed Kortovsky's clothing, found his room key in a pocket, went back to the hotel room, and stole his computer. He wanted to create the impression that Kortovsky was still alive, so the next day he sent an email to Sheila Rathman saying he would be at the first rehearsal. This served two purposes: one, since the quartet was on vacation for a month, no one would ever suspect there was a problem, let alone that Kortovsky was dead; and two, when he failed to show up it would inevitably disrupt the plans for the Power Ramsey extravaganza that Peter abhorred.

"But Peter didn't know that Kortovsky had sent an email containing similar information the night before, which made the second one strangely redundant. And considering the difference in the tone of the message, it wasn't a stretch to think that it was written by a different person.

"And then I remembered something he said when we first met, just after Trotsky almost discovered the fingers he was hiding in the piano bench. He said, 'But in the large scheme of things, Kortovsky was small potatoes.' 'Was,' Malachi, not 'is.' His linguistic skills are too good to have made that grammatical mistake. He knew Kortovsky was already dead. Then, when the third email, supposedly from Kortovsky, arrived on the eve of the dress rehearsal, I remembered that I had mentioned to Peter that Ivan was going to be replacing Kortovsky for that as well. So Peter tried to pull the same stunt again, getting poor Sheila Rathman to believe lover boy was still planning on showing, in order to create what he hoped would be a fatal impediment for the concert to proceed."

"But how was he able to put the fingers in the cases?" Yumi asked. "How did he get backstage to kill Annika and lure me out? It's hard to believe no one at Carnegie Hall saw him."

"I don't know. Ask Oro. He managed to pull it off with aplomb, too. Maybe because it was dark. Or there were lots of people there who aren't ordinarily there. Or the security guards are idiots. Or he knows his way around stages. Or he has his different voices. People think they see him but can't be sure. The man is a chameleon. He's known how to make himself invisible. Like Death."

"How do you know that it was Short who told Lensky that his mother was going to be fired by Kortovsky and Haagen?" Malachi asked.

"Who else could have made him think that? Kortovsky and Haagen were keeping their plans hush-hush. They would be the last people to divulge that to anyone, let alone Pravda's sons, if that was their plan. They knew that would only add fuel to Short's fire with his lawsuit. So who was left that would have anything to gain by suggesting to Peter that Pravda's job was on the line? Someone who was one of the only musicians Peter explicitly declared respect for—Crispin Short. It seems the influence Short had over Peter grew and grew over time. I started thinking that when Short referred to Annika as a strumpet, when only a day earlier Peter had referred to his mother using the same term of endearment. Who uses the word 'strumpet' since Charles Dickens, except for the English? I think Peter's innate gift of mimicry inadvertently blew his cover. The two of them must have been in conversation, and in Peter's mind Short was the only counterbalance to the power of Kortovsky, which Peter viewed as corrupting both the music and his mother's integrity. It must've been Peter, in fact, who told Short that Ivan had been invited to fill in for Kortovsky at the first Carnegie rehearsal, which infuriated Short, almost to the point of attacking Haagen on the street. Peter must've heard it first from Ivan or Pravda, and channeled it right through to Crispin."

"What tipped you off about Lensky in the first place?" Malachi asked.

"Trotsky," he said.

"Why's he called Trotsky, anyway?"

"Because he can't...never mind. Trotsky, the brain-addled bulldog, took a real shine to Lensky, and with good reason. They have a lot in common."

"However, is it not true, Maestro," said Oro, "that the canine has the ability to perceive evil in the people? Do you not find some strangeness that Trotsky could not do so in this case?"

"Why is it," said an exasperated Jacobus, "that nobody can appreciate my dog's exceptional lack of intelligence?"

"If he's so stupid and Lensky's so brilliant," asked Malachi, "what do you mean when you say they've got a lot in common?"

"Lensky noticed immediately that Trotsky had been neutered, but Lensky called it 'castrated.' That seemed odd to me considering his linguistic skills, unless he had heard the term in some other context. Then I considered his vocal prowess, his remarkable range, the beauty of his upper tessitura, his fondness for music about loss, and music composed especially for castrati. So I asked myself, what does this all mean? And then I remembered. Chernobyl, 1986. Nathaniel did a little research for me. Did you know that when the power plant blew, it soaked the atmosphere with a hundred times more radiation than the atomic bombs dropped on Hiroshima and Nagasaki in August 1945? Peter was a young boy at the time, when his father was made a scapegoat and died. And Peter was there to suffer all the consequences. Chernobyl produced the biggest outbreak of cancers ever from a single incident, mostly thyroid and lung cancer, but also cases of lymphoma and, in Peter's case, testicular cancer."

"And that's where Vasalin comes in?" asked Malachi.

"It just so happens that Otkar Vasalin was able to buy all his seventeenth-century Cremonese toys after making his fortune in the energy business. Nathaniel found that Vasalin had a rather large investment in the Chernobyl plant that he managed to deposit in Swiss banks just before hightailing it out of the USSR. He ended up living the quiet life in Quito, at least until the day he died, which just so happened to be the day Peter was there on tour with the New Magini String Quartet. Peter blamed Vasalin for everything that happened from the day Chernobyl blew, and I can't say that I blame him."

"Lensky denies killing Vasalin," said Malachi.

"You surprised?"

"He says that name isn't familiar to him."

"I guess it just slipped his mind, the same way Vasalin slipped in his shower and accidentally stove his head in."

"Let's get to Haagen," said Malachi. "You were there, as I recall."

Jacobus felt Yumi tighten her grip on his hand.

"He killed her right after Yumi left the stage," he said. "He did it quietly and quickly—he's a strong boy, Peter is—not because he was humane, but because he had to, to avoid detection and knowing Yumi would be at the stage door waiting for the cab. He even made sure that Haagen's viola didn't drop on the floor and make noise. He put it on her lap."

The only response Jacobus heard were Yumi's quiet sobs.

"I am sorry, Yumi. Very sorry.

"To finish up, Malachi, it was Kortovsky's libido compared to Lensky's own impotence that gnawed at him. That's why Kortovsky went first. But then there was also Haagen. It also gnawed at Peter that she swung both ways and he swung neither.

"I have to admit that for a while I really thought Haagen was complicit in Kortovsky's disappearance, but I didn't know whether she was a culprit or a co-conspirator. On one hand, she bore him a grudge as heavy as a sledge hammer: He didn't give a shit about their kid, who she loved. He was a philanderer, which she claimed didn't bother her until it got too close for comfort. On the other hand, they apparently worked together to beautify the image of the quartet, getting rid of Short in the process, and then both, of course, had to defend themselves against him. The idea that Kortovsky was going to sell his Amati violin to Vasalin wasn't all that far-fetched, especially after that scene at Dedubian's with Haagen trying to up the appraisal on her Gasparo viola.

"But then, when Nathaniel confirmed that Prince Rupert had accompanied his mother to South America and they had gone on vacation together, it just didn't seem to me that Haagen could be that cold-blooded. The clincher, of course, is that Annika couldn't have broken her own neck."

"How did you figure out where Lensky took Yumi?" Malachi asked.

"I wasn't sure. That's why I sent Nathaniel to follow Short. I knew you had the other places covered. But I figured, what better place than a soundproof room in a vacant building, so I went there."

"Why do you suppose he didn't try to kill Yumi onstage, like Haagen, during the Anderson film?"

"Dammit, Malachi! You expect me to know everything. The damn film is only five minutes long! How many people can you kill in five minutes with your bare hands? Maybe he got nervous. How the hell do I know?"

"Sorry. What do you know about the deaths of Ivan Lensky and his mother?" asked Malachi.

"Nothing. Only heard about it from Oro last night. Why?"

"The two of you. You and Yumi. If not for Oro...You're lucky. Very lucky."

"Some luck."

"What creates your understanding that Señor Peter murdered his brother and mother?" Oro asked Malachi.

"They were killed in Pravda's living room. No forced entry. Nothing stolen. They had their concert dress on, presumably on their way to Carnegie Hall. So Jacobus's theory and all the facts make a fit. Someone as strong as Ivan Lensky would've put up a struggle if it had been a stranger. Peter had flipped out. He had done everything he could to prevent the performance from happening, but it hadn't worked. Maybe he tried one last time to talk them out of playing. When that didn't work either, the knife did."

"I can't believe he could kill his brother and his mother," Yumi said. "Even after last night."

Malachi responded. "Two months ago we had a mother drop her three little kids out of a twentieth-floor hotel room window. She said she had a headache and the air-conditioning wasn't working. Don't underestimate the human capacity to be inhuman."

"That is the way of the world, is it not?" said Oro.

"What's Peter saying about everything?" Jacobus asked.

"Cy Rosenthal's representing him. Once he arrived, Lensky's denying everything."

"Figures."

"But before that, he told me to give you a message. He wrote it down. Maybe you can tell me what it's all about."

"Read it."

"Oh dear Art, during how many gray hours,
When life's savage cycle traps me,
Have you lit my heart to warm love,
And placed me in a better world!"

Chapter Twenty-Six

One by one, Jacobus shook the bottles of bourbon to hear which ones had anything left in them. He pulled the cork on the bottle with the distinctively almost flat contour—that would be the Woodford Reserve—encouraged by its level of sloshing.

It had been a long and somber day. Oro's departure had been an anticlimax. For some reason he had been in a hurry to get to the airport and take the earliest flight possible back to Lima. He offered polite, if somewhat curt apologies and then was gone.

Nathaniel had picked up Yumi and Jacobus after Malachi released them, and they went somewhere for a breakfast that they didn't eat. Yumi was torn between staying in the city or going with Nathaniel and Jacobus. In the end she decided to stay and help Lipinsky and Greunig with the funeral arrangements.

"Hey, now that there's no quartet left, I've got plenty of free time, don't I?" Yumi joked with an absence of mirth. "Poor Crispin, though. After he gets my violin and apartment, he'll still come up a few million short." She escorted Jacobus and Nathaniel to the curb, gave them a cursory hug, and thanked them for their performance the night before.

"And Jake," she said.

"Yeah?"

Yumi paused. "Have a good drive," she said, and walked away.

Jacobus already had one leg in Nathaniel's VW Rabbit when he heard Yumi call him.

"Jake!" she said, running up to the car.

"Yeah?" he asked again.

"I just want to tell you," she said. "I heard what Power Ramsey said to you yesterday. I think he was wrong. I don't think you're absolutely incorrigible. Sometimes I actually think you're corrigible."

Jacobus reached his hand out the car door and found Yumi's cheek. He let his hand linger on it for a moment, feeling its warmth and vitality.

"Don't bet on it," he said, smiling.

When Jacobus and Nathaniel left the city, after having stopped at Dedubian's, the sun was trying to come out, as New Yorkers like to say when they're sick of the rain, but by the time they stopped at the Collective Reference Academy near Mt. Kisco on the way back to the Berkshires, it had turned blustery. They had met with the school psychologist, a Ms. Fogent, who had previously been informed by the police that Prince Rupert's mother was dead, and his father missing and presumed dead.

"Has the boy been told?" Jacobus asked.

"He has been told that he'll be visiting his maternal grandparents in Finland soon. For a holiday. They agreed to pay for his ticket. The paternal side expressed their wish to discontinue further contact with the child, and we are going to honor that."

"Where's the boy now?"

"He's out playing with his friend, Epifany," said Ms. Fogent. "Would you like to speak with him?"

"Nah, no need," said Jacobus. "I'd just scare the kid."

Jacobus explained to Ms. Fogent that he had taken the liberty of giving Annika Haagen's beloved Gasparo viola, which the police had decided was not needed as evidence, to Dedubian for temporary safekeeping and eventual sale, subject to the instructions in Haagen's will, as yet undisclosed. He had Dedubian put their agreement in writing, along with an updated appraisal for $400,000, which, though no guarantee, would help it fetch a higher price. He also had pressed Dedubian to pay the substantial insurance premium on the instrument for as long as it was in his shop. Regarding Kortovsky's Amati violin, Cy Rosenthal conjectured that until Kortovsky's death was legally verified, the instrument trunk would remain unopened. If in fact the violin ultimately was found in the trunk, then it would in all likelihood transfer to Prince Rupert, assuming those were the instructions in Kortovsky's will, which of course would not be disclosed until it was confirmed he was dead. Lawyers, thought Jacobus, as he handed the letter to Fogent.

"Thank you, Mr. Jacobus," she said. "Have a good Labor Day weekend. I'm sure the family will appreciate this."

"Well, whatever," he said.

Jacobus opened the flimsy cupboard doors above the shelf of bourbon bottles—one of these days those damn hinges were going to fall off—and extracted two large glasses.

"Want one?" he asked Nathaniel.

"I guess you've decided for me. Just one, though. Then I've got to hit the road. It's already dark, and who knows what's with this weather. They say if you don't like the weather in New England, just wait five minutes."

"They say if you don't like the weather in Seattle, just wait five minutes, then commit suicide. Say when."

Jacobus poured. Nathaniel added a little water into Jacobus's glass, the way he knew Jacobus liked it. Trotsky shifted his bulk under the table and exhaled. Jacobus and Nathaniel drank in silence, and though the alcohol relaxed and warmed him on this chill, rainy evening, Jacobus was still troubled by the unsatisfying conclusion to his efforts and the three—actually four—phone calls he had received earlier in the day.

As if reading his thoughts, Nathaniel said, "Malachi will find him. Then they'll figure out what charges will stick. He can't hide forever."

"Thanks for your false confidence," said Jacobus.

The first call had come before they had even entered his house. Trotsky almost knocked the door down in order to attack the ringing phone. There was no preamble.

"Lew Carino. Cy Rosenthal asked me to call you." There was tension in Carino's voice.

225

"Carino," repeated Jacobus. "Crispin looking for someone new to sue, now that there's no more quartet?"

"Crispin Short won't be suing anyone."

"And that's bad news?"

"He's killed himself. Hanging. He left a very precise note, not the typical rambling manifesto. He blamed the quartet for ruining his life, and the dissolution of the quartet by their deaths for ending it."

Jacobus laughed bitterly. Carino continued through it.

"He felt that in the public eye he would forever be tied to the deaths of the members of the quartet, however wrongly. That he would henceforth always be an outcast and never again be able to ply his trade. In other words, his life was, for all intents and purposes, over."

"For once I agree with him," said Jacobus.

"But if I can confide in you, Mr. Jacobus, between you and me, I think it had more to do with guilt over his inordinate influence over Peter Lensky, which catalyzed Lensky to do what he allegedly did. Crispin didn't want anyone dead. He just wanted his fair due. Though not much good has come of this entire episode, with my client's death at least your former student, Ms. Shinagawa, is now off the hook, there no longer being any impetus to continue the lawsuit."

"You mean no one to pay your fee."

Carino didn't take the bait, so Jacobus, seething, continued.

"Off the hook, huh? I hadn't thought of it quite that way. But yes, other than her colleagues being dead, and she being hospitalized, traumatized, and unemployed, in part because of your former client's alleged 'inordinate influence,' she's off the hook. That's great news."

"That's not how I meant it, Jacobus. You've taken my words and—"

Jacobus put the receiver on the table, and though Carino continued talking, Jacobus didn't listen to a word. Finally the talking stopped and Jacobus hung up the phone.

He was brought back to the present by the sound of Nathaniel placing his empty glass on the table with just the right amount of extra emphasis for Jacobus to know that he was finished, but not so loud as to insult his sensitivity to being blind. A thoughtful one, that Nathaniel.

"Sorry about Short," Nathaniel said. "I feel like maybe I spooked him."

"Yeah? How so?"

"Well, when I followed him and Carino out of Carnegie after Annika was killed, they were getting into a taxi. I didn't want to lose them and since we still thought Short might be a suspect, I went up to them and asked if they had been together the whole time during the concert. Short was pale as a ghost and didn't say a word—I think he was in shock. Carino said 'Yes, explicitly so,' and I believed he was telling the truth, but then later on I thought, How could he be sure during the blackout and all that dancing and goings-on? They got into the taxi, and that's the last I saw of them."

"Well, not your fault. You can't be held accountable for someone's bad conscience. According to Dedubian, Short also made a deal with him to buy Haagen's viola at a low cost, and he offered Dedubian a higher commission, which is why he gave Haagen such a low appraisal. He wanted to get her coming and going. So Short was a scumbag no matter how you look at it."

The second call, from Cy Rosenthal, had come at two o'clock. Trotsky was outside, chasing leaves in the gathering wind, so Jacobus didn't have to worry about damage to the phone when it rang.

Having been retained to represent Peter Lensky, Rosenthal notified Jacobus that Lensky had undergone a thorough psychiatric evaluation and had been released on bail in the alleged attempted assault on Yumi.

"Alleged! Attemped!" Jacobus sputtered. "He kidnapped her and tried to kill her!"

"My client, admittedly, had been under a great deal of stress, what with his late mother's and brother's situation in the quartet, and is quite remorseful over the means by which he obtained Ms. Shinagawa's presence at the studio—he openly expressed to the judge his willingness to pay the price for that misunderstanding—but he only wanted to perform 'Death and the Maiden' for Yumi the way he thinks it should be performed. He's quite the purist when it comes to music and does not like to see great music devolve into mere entertainment by the application of tangential media. I gather that sentiment is one that the two of you share."

Jacobus ignored the implication.

"But he threatened her," Jacobus said. "If I'm not mistaken, he proclaimed he was Death incarnate."

"Did you not also tell Ms. Shinagawa at a recent lesson that she too was Death?"

"How do you know that?"

"I just had a long talk with her. She tries to protect you—why, I can't fathom—but in her honesty and openness she is very revealing."

"That bit about Death was just a metaphor, dammit."

"Well, there you have it."

"But Lensky attacked her. And me and Oro. He would've killed her, if not for—"

"If not for the three of you—three of you!—subjecting my client to physical and emotional harm, and involuntarily restraining him after you baited him into a frenzy by falsely accusing him of a whole assortment of deaths and disappearances in which he played no part, and furthermore by preying upon his personal physical tragedy as his motivation, and insulting his masculinity in the process. You should stay away from playing doctor, Mr. Jacobus. It could get you in trouble. Even though someone suffers from testicular cancer, rendering him sterile, it does not necessarily render him impotent. Far greater can be the emotional damage from that illness—not ever being able to have a family, or feelings of inferiority, for example—to all of which you exhibited not one iota of sensitivity or compassion when you confronted my client."

"But what about Haagen's murder? Picture that for a minute, Rosenthal, before you give me your sob story about Lensky. Someone—someone strong—someone who knows how the staging works—goes up to her from behind, breaks her neck while we're sitting there in the dark listening to Anderson singing 'Death and the Maiden,' and knows enough to prevent her viola from falling and making noise, leaving it on her lap. And at the same time, Yumi gets abducted, which you admit was by Lensky, and you've got the gall to tell me that's a coincidence?"

"As you just said, Mr. Jacobus, 'at the same time.' How could those things have happened at the same time? Are you suggesting my client broke Ms. Haagen's neck, then immediately sashayed over to Ms. Shinagawa and whispered in her ear? Is that what you're saying? I would say it's more likely someone else killed Ms. Haagen. Your friend, Mr. Williams, was sitting right next to her. He's a strong—"

"Fuck you, Rosenthal!"

"I'm sorry. I take that back. I shouldn't involve myself in mere speculation, as you have. After all, I'm an attorney. As I say, there has been a series of tragic events, all of which need to be thoroughly investigated. In your confused state you see my client as a perpetrator, but according to the law, he is, if anything, an unfortunate victim."

"So what are you telling me about the murders of Kortovsky and Vasalin and Haagen and Ivan and Pravda? That they're *all* coincidences?"

"That's for the police to figure out, not me. Don't you find it a bit strange, Mr. Jacobus, that there has not been one verifiable eyewitness who could place my client at any of the crime scenes? My client is a big man, which perhaps you are not able to notice, and would be hard to miss."

"But Oro saw him at the concert in Lima!"

"At a concert! This makes my client a serial killer? Kortovsky was alive and well long after the concert. It would be my fondest dream, Mr. Jacobus, if I walked into the courtroom and the DA's case against my client amounted to someone possibly having seen him…at a concert! In summary, there is no evidence tying my client, who has no prior criminal record, to the deaths of Haagen and Peter's family. Regarding the others, as far as I know, Kortovsky's disappearance has not been classified as a death, let alone a murder, and Vasalin's death has been classified as an accident. In any event, their cases are out of our jurisdiction."

"Ah, yes. Jurisdiction! Aren't you forgetting the small detail that Malachi doesn't seem to agree with your bullshit? That he arrested Lensky for—"

"For alleged attempted assault on Ms. Shinagawa, as I said. That is the one and only charge. The murder investigations are ongoing. No one has been arrested for those yet. And if my client is implicated, Jacobus, as you and I know all too well, Malachi has been known to err in his judgment."

Jacobus, not being able to disagree on that point, had no response. He himself had been suspected by Malachi in the murder of Victoria Jablonski years before, and Malachi had arrested BTower in the death of René Allard, only to be exonerated by Jacobus mere moments before his scheduled execution.

"In conclusion, Mr. Jacobus, I would strongly recommend that not only should you refrain from medical diagnoses, you should stop kidding yourself about your self-styled police work. You've concocted dangerous fairy tales that leak like a sieve, and though you may be a fine musician, as a detective all you've done is endanger people, and if you aren't careful you may well find yourself at the wrong end of a lawsuit of your own. Have a nice day."

After that call, so he wouldn't have to think about anything, Jacobus took a nap, awakened by the smell and sound of Nathaniel frying bacon and eggs for dinner. They had just begun to eat when the third call came. Jacobus quickly handed Trotsky a piece of burned toast—the way they both liked it—to keep him quiet while Nathaniel answered. It was Rosenthal again.

"So what did you call for this time, to gloat?" asked Jacobus.

"No, Mr. Jacobus," said Rosenthal, unusually subdued. "I'm calling to tell you that my client never showed up for his appointment with me today, and he doesn't answer at his home. I'm calling to tell you...well, to take care of yourself."

"You mean you don't believe any of the bullshit you told me before?"

"Just...be careful. Okay?"

"Yeah. Thanks for your concern," Jacobus said, and hung up. He took one bite of his egg, then gave the rest of his dinner to the dog. By the time he said, "Don't choke on it," Trotsky was already nuzzling his leg for more. That's when he had decided to slosh bourbon bottles.

"Well, I better be heading out," Nathaniel said. "It's almost three hours back to the city," he added unnecessarily.

"Just watch out for the deer on the Taconic. And the cops."

He heard Nathaniel lumbering on the creaky wide pine floor toward the door.

"Oh, I almost forgot to tell you," Nathaniel said, "I found out what that aria was that you first heard Peter Lensky singing. Not that it's important now."

"Yeah? 'Sentimental Journey' in Italian?"

"Actually, something like it. From an opera, *Sedecia*, by Antonio Caldara. It was written for Farinelli. I don't remember the Italian, but the translation was…hold on, I've written it down."

Jacobus heard Nathaniel retrieve a piece of paper from his pocket and unfold it.

"Here goes: 'Prophecies, of me you proclaimed that in peace I would perish. Tell me in this hour, how can I have peace in such bitter destiny? What did I say? Death might as well come. Let it bring peace evermore, that moment that guides my days.' It's actually quite beautiful. What a wasted talent, Peter Lensky. Well, see you later. Sure you're okay?"

"Yeah, yeah, yeah."

The front door opened and closed, and Jacobus was alone. He poured himself another bourbon. When some of it spilled over the top of the glass onto his hand, he stopped pouring.

The final call came when the glass was still in hands but long empty.

"*Mi amigo Yake*," began Oro.

"Knock it off, Oro," said Jacobus. "What's the problem?"

"Ah, señor, you have missed your calling. You should have been a detective."

Unlike his usual ebullient self, Oro too somehow seemed to have been affected by the funereal drizzle that now chafed against Jacobus's windows.

"As I said, knock it off. What's the problem?"

"At one time you asked me to review the autopsy report. To see if there was something interesting about the victim's right hand."

"Yes. So?"

"They did find something curious, but we do not know if it is interesting. Can you predict me what that would be?"

"The right index finger bent to the right, especially above the middle knuckle."

"You are absolutely correct! Absolutely. But please tell me, how did you know this, and what does it mean?"

"It's nothing any violinist doesn't know. Over time, the pressure one puts on the bow with the right hand will tend to slightly realign the index finger. In someone who played with Kortovsky's strength and intensity, that realignment might become pronounced. Especially considering he always wanted everyone to play at the point of the bow, which takes even more pressure from the index finger to produce a big sound, it only figures."

"Well, Yake, that would seem to confirm that our victim was Señor Kortovsky..."

"Well, that doesn't sound like a problem. It sounds like a solution. So I repeat, what's the problem?"

"There seem to have been two recent sightings of Señor Kortovsky."

"What do you mean, two sightings?"

"One near Puno by the Bolivian border, in the mountains not far from Lago Titicaca. A local craftsman who makes the ocarina for tourists reported a climber bearing the resemblance in the photo of Señor Kortovsky. Perhaps he only wanted the reward.

"Also, the agents of my counterpart in Quito have heard that there might have been a sighting. There was a man, a stranger, with a violin case, of Kortovsky's general description, though with darker hair and a short beard which, of course, could have been grown in this last month."

Jacobus took a few moments to let that information and its implications sink in. Oro let him take all the time he wanted.

"It's not definite?"

"No. Neither one. It has not received the corroboration."

Jacobus filled Oro in about his earlier discussions with Rosenthal, finishing with the uncomfortable fact that Lensky had vanished.

"Ah, yes, that is a reason I left so suddenly this morning."

"You knew Lensky was going to escape?"

"No, no. Not that. Only that I watch your informative Perry Mason on television every night—actually very early in the morning—so I understand your legal system is sometimes unpredictable. I know that Lieutenant

232

Malachi, as a fellow policeman, would have some sympathy for my actions last night, but I also know that if Señor Lensky had a good lawyer, and now I see that he has, I could also easily be arrested for assault and many other infractions, such as entering your country with a false visa. This would not be very good for my reputation as the director of law enforcement for my city, would you not say? With this consideration in mind I departed quickly from John F. Kennedy airport on the first flight to any country in South America, and I now call you while I wait for my connection.

"So I am safe once again, but it does give me deep trouble that Señor Lensky is now in large," Oro continued. "I have a friend with whom I went to the public school," he said contemplatively, "who teaches the violin at the Conservatorio Nacional."

"You've got a conservatory in Peru?"

"I am proud to say my country had a *conservatorio* long before your pilgrims first set foot on the Plymouth Rock. The one in Lima is only one block from the Maury, so it was very convenient for me to visit my friend while I investigated the missing of Kortovsky. I had not seen him for a long time, so we talked about many things. One thing my friend told me is that there is a little piece of wood, a little stick, inside the violin that connects its top to the bottom. I never knew this! A little stick, and he says it is important."

"Yes, it transmits the vibrations throughout the instrument. Without it, there would be no sound."

"So it is glued in, then?"

"Are you kidding? It's wedged in, but if it's too tight or too loose, or a half a millimeter in the wrong place, or the grain of the wood was lined up in the wrong direction, the violin would sound totally different."

"And if you removed this stick?"

"Number one, the violin would have no sound at all, and number two, when you played, the top would cave in because you wouldn't have any support for all the tension on the strings. Without the sound post you could easily destroy the instrument."

"What did you just call this stick, Yake, in English?"

"The sound post."

"Ah, yes! The sound post! In Spanish, we call it *la alma*. Do you know what *la alma* means?"

"Yeah. The sound post."

"Ah, you are a fast learner, but in Spanish it means something else also. *La alma* means 'the soul.' What I am saying is that Señor Peter may have had all the attributions of a fine violin, but I am troubled that he may have no sound post.

"So you must take the precaution, please," Oro said somberly after another extended silence. "It is hard to know which is more dangerous, a deranged killer seeking the revenge or a deranged innocent seeking the vindication."

"When he's found, would he be extradited?" Jacobus asked. "To Peru?"

"I am sorry to shatter your bubble, my friend," said Oro, "but there would be several impediments to that conclusion."

"Such as?"

"*Uno*, though you and I still believe in our hearts that the body in Lima is Señor Kortovsky, this is not proved. *Dos*, though we believe the culprit to be Señor Lensky, we have no solid evidence. *Tres*, extradition is less a police matter than a political matter, so..."

There was silence on the line that neither party bothered to interrupt.

"So it seems our mate is stale, *mi amigo*," Oro continued.

"I'd say our mate is check."

Again the silence.

"Oro, I've got a question."

"*Sí*, Maestro."

"Is it true they eat guinea pigs in Peru?"

"*Cuy!*"

"No, I'm serious."

"No, you misunderstand. *Cuy* is the word for guinea pig. It is one of our traditional delicacies, served mostly in the Andes. It is usually roasted, but sometimes fried. I find it very delicious."

"Do you think it might taste like squirrel?"

"I think there is a very fine opportunity that it does. Is there anything else I can help you with?"

CHAPTER TWENTY-SIX

"No, that'll do it."

"Then it has been a pleasure working with you, Maestro," said Oro, finally.

"Yeah, it's been dandy."

"*Abrazos*, then. *Cuidado*. Take care."

"Yeah. *Hasta la vista*," said Jacobus, hanging up.

Jacobus began to pour another bourbon, but the bottle was empty, so he lit a cigarette instead. He listened to the rain, now close to inaudible, but the cold and damp had not diminished with it. It was too late to start a fire in the woodstove, and until the weather got colder this would probably only create a back draft, filling the house with smoke.

With nothing better to do, Jacobus decided to go to bed. The stairs creaked under his tired tread as he held onto the banister and struggled to pull himself up, Trotsky loping patiently behind him. Nine, ten, the eleventh and top step not as high as the others. People with sight had tripped on that one. He had never stumbled, he thought smugly.

The air was dank and musty upstairs in his bedroom, as he had left the windows closed when they went to New York. If Indian summer ever arrived, he'd pry open the window to let some fresh air in. That is, if it were possible to reopen windows that decades of repainting and warping had made almost immovable. Jacobus stripped down to his underwear and eased himself onto the mildewed single mattress, unsteadily supported by a rusted Harvard frame. Comfort. He lay on his back, winded from his ascent up the stairs. He heard Trotsky slowly circle seven or eight times like a large recalcitrant turd being flushed down a clogged toilet, finally plopping himself down with a thud on the fraying braided rug next to Jacobus's bed, in the identical spot he did every night. The dog smacked his jowls a few times and soon was snoring.

Fatigued as he was, Jacobus was unable to sleep, feeling somehow captive in his own home, captive of his thoughts. Shadows of death had followed him since his youth, but now he was engulfed by them, making existence even darker than his blindness. He pressed hard on his useless eyes to stanch his inner pain but could not extinguish the mental image of his brother Eli. His chest heaved and Jacobus regurgitated, not vomit, but a single word.

Why?

Stifling, he kicked off the sheet, but his efforts brought him no respite. He thought about going downstairs and opening the living room windows, but remembered that Nathaniel had barred them before they had left for New York, and he didn't have the energy to get out of bed, let alone remove the wedged-in pine boards.

"Fuck it," he said aloud and turned to his redeemer, Beethoven, for solace. He decided to listen to Beethoven's "Pastoral" Symphony in his head—specifically George Szell's interpretation with the Cleveland Orchestra—from beginning to end. Jacobus hoped that the music, which had been a poetic oasis in the composer's turbulent life, would soothe his own torn soul. By the time the peasants had celebrated autumn in the first movement, meditated by the brook in the second, and enjoyed the fruits of their harvest in the Scherzo, Jacobus was asleep, well before the storm movement.

There was no way for him to know the time, but he was sure it was still in the middle of the night when he awoke, cold and shivering, infected by a sense of dread. He heard a downstairs window rattle. Trotsky uttered an uncharacteristically low, lingering growl. Jacobus reached for the sheet and pulled it over him. *One* window?

Was it the wind? He strained his ears to hear any fluttering of the browned and dried English ivy that enveloped the walls of his house. Certainly, if it were windy the sound of the leaves should precede a rattling window, but he detected nothing. Yet, one by one, each of the windows rattled.

It could be Lensky. It could be his own brother. It could be a blind beggar. Or it could just be the wind.

"Go to hell!" shouted Jacobus. There was no response, but after continuing for another few moments the rattling ceased, and with that Trotsky's growl. Jacobus listened for footsteps in the autumn leaves—had they not been damp and decaying, it would have been easier—but there were none.

Acknowledgements

One great thing about writing within your own field of expertise is that you don't have to do a lot of research. Other than doublechecking some dates and spellings, all you need are a pretty decent memory and some interesting colleagues. Though I can't claim that my powers of recollection are anything above average— to verify this, ask all those people whose names I can't recall after ten minutes—I can state with confidence that you will find no greater wealth of bizarre, poignant, hysterical, ridiculous, and profound stories than in the world of classical music, with equally engaging personalities to tell them. So if I can remember just ten percent of those stories, I have enough material for a dozen books, more or less.

For *Death and the Maiden*, I have to specifically acknowledge my dear Russian colleagues for providing both the stories *and* the personalities, because it is clear to me that Russia—or more accurately, the former Soviet Union—has produced not only great violinists for the past hundred plus years, but also great storytellers. If I have dressed their tales up a bit differently from the way they were related to me, it wasn't to make them any better (because they can't be); it's only so they'll fit into the bigger story line. So thank you Slava, Aza, Victor, Manny, Manny, Mischa, Mischa, Ashot, Valerie, and Pavel.

For the spicy Russian toasts, and their translations, I would like to thank my well-traveled friend, Todd Fogelsong for his linguistic expertise. And for helping me with my remedial Spanish syntax, I would like to thank my talented former violin student, Shadai Gociman, from Arequipa, Peru. My frequent travels to Peru have left me with a deep appreciation of that country's rich culture and heritage, which I have attempted to convey in a small way in *Death and the Maiden*. For the translations of the Schubert lieder in the book, my thanks go to my multilingual friend, colleague, and cooking companion Sergio Pallottelli, and for the Italian arias, my darling daughter, Kate.

Heartfelt gratitude goes to my former colleagues in the Abramyan String Quartet–Lynnette Stewart, violin; Scott Lewis, viola; and John Eckstein, cello–for years of inspiring musicianship and friendship, and for making our time together much more congenial than that of the New Magini String Quartet.

An overdue thanks to my former Boston Symphony colleague, Harvey Seigel, the true creator of the crafty, though totally fictional, Dr. Krovney, who has had cameo references in all my books. Few BSO rehearsals passed when the peerless Dr. Krovney, aka Harvey, would not be able to provide heretofore unimagined remedies for the most confounding violinistic challenges, many of which left us in tears, to the chagrin of the conductors.

The more books I write, the more I appreciate the team effort involved in getting them into a form suitable for public consumption. So my hat is off to my editor, Shawn Simmons, and the rest of the Level Best Books staff. Major thanks, as always, goes to my agent, Josh Getzler at HG Literary for making it all happen.

Finally, my loving appreciation to various members of my family: to my father, Irving, who passed down to me when I was a mere tyke the "Doughnut Song" and "Around the Corner" from earlier generations of Eliases (you can be certain my own children have memorized them); to my brother, Arthur, and sister, Estelle, for traumatizing me in my childhood with the dead finger trick; to my daughter, Kate, an exceptional modern dancer and human being, who opened my eyes to the potential of dance as an art form; and of course to my wife, Cecily, and my kids, Kate and Jacob, for their candid critiques and their ongoing encouragement and support.

About the Author

Gerald Elias leads a double life as a world-class musician and critically acclaimed author.

Devil's Trill, the debut novel of his award-winning Daniel Jacobus mystery series that takes place in the dark corners of the classical music world, was a Barnes & Noble *Discover: Great New Writers* selection. In 2020 he penned *The Beethoven Sequence*, a chilling psycho-political thriller. Elias's prize-winning essay, "War & Peace. And Music," excerpted from his memoir, *Symphonies & Scorpions*, was the subject of his TEDxSaltLakeCity2019 presentation. His short stories and essays have appeared in prestigious journals ranging from *Ellery Queen Mystery Magazine* to *The Strad*.

A former violinist with the Boston Symphony and associate concertmaster of the Utah Symphony, Elias has performed on five continents and has been the conductor of Salt Lake City's popular Vivaldi by Candlelight chamber orchestra series since 2004. He maintains a vibrant concert career while continuing to expand his literary horizons.

Also by Gerald Elias

The Daniel Jacobus Mysteries, New Editions and New Releases from Level
Best Books
  Devil's Trill
  Danse Macabre
  Death and the Maiden
  Death and Transfiguration
  Cloudy With a Chance of Murder
  Murder at The Royal Albert